Chris swallowed hard, the sound echoing in her ears, so loud, she was sure it was bouncing off the canyon walls for all to hear. But there was only Jessie, eyes locked with her own. Chris silenced the voice in her head that urged her to turn and go, leaving Jessie to follow if she chose. Instead, she stepped closer to the eyes that beckoned, unable to resist any longer. Their eyes locked again, then Jessie moved into her arms, her mouth searching for Chris's waiting lips. The flashlight fell unnoticed between them as Chris pulled her closer, her hands on Jessie's hips holding her flush against her. Their mouths moved together, tongues meeting as they let their desire rage unchecked.

"Oh, God, yes," Jessie breathed, pressing her hips more firmly against Chris. She let her desire overtake her, felt her knees grow weak as Chris's hands moved up her sides, stopping just beneath her breasts. Jessie tried to remember a time she'd wanted another's touch this desperately. There was none. The countless, nameless list of strangers paraded through her mind in seconds and then there was only Chris, whose hands stoked the fire within her.

Visit

Bella Books

at

BellaBooks.com

or call our toll-free number

1-800-729-4992

SIERRA CITY

GERRI HILL

Bella
BOOKS
2007

Bella Books, Inc.
P.O. Box 10543
Tallahassee, FL 32302

First Edition, 3rd Printing July 2007

Editor: Anna Chinappi
Cover designer: Sandy Knowles

ISBN-10: 1-931513-98-8
ISBN-13: 978-1-931513-98-2

Dedicated to:

Diane, my favorite camping buddy . . . among other things.

Chapter One

"How the hell should I know?"

Frustration was creeping into her voice and she pulled to the side of the dirt road, tossing her sunglasses on the now dusty dash of her open Jeep. She had half a mind to toss her cell phone there, as well. If there was one thing Chris McKenna hated, it was being lost.

"Goddamn, McKenna, how hard can it be? You're supposed to be an expert at this."

"Don't start with me, Roger. If you'd let me take the main road out of Reno, I would be there by now." She glanced around, her frustration preventing her from enjoying the beauty of the backroads Roger had suggested.

"If you could follow directions, you'd be here by now."

"If you could *give* directions," she shot back.

"Listen, I think you're on Forest Road seven-thirteen."

"You *think*?"

"If you continue on, you'll find Forest Road seven-forty. Take it to the left. That'll hook you up with the road you were supposed to be on in the first place, seven-oh-nine."

"You know, Roger," she started, her voice now low and threatening. "It will be very embarrassing if you have to send someone out to look for your new SAR. You're sure of your directions this time?"

"McKenna, one more thing. I think the sign for seven-forty is missing. You'll just have to keep your eye . . ."

"If you tell me to turn at the big pine on the corner one more time, I'm turning around and going back to fucking Yosemite!" she yelled before disconnecting. This time she did toss the phone on the dash.

She was hot, tired, and dusty. The pleasant drive through the mountains had turned into a fiasco. She should have been there two hours ago. Instead, Roger had her traipsing through the mountains on forest roads without a map.

"A cold beer," she said out loud. She turned off the engine and got out, stretching her arms overhead and popping her sore back. A loud meow brought her around and she stared into Dillon's cage. Her normally passive cat glared at her.

"I know, I know. I promised it would be a short trip." Then she grinned. "Probably gotta pee, huh?" She rummaged into the cooler for a beer, pulling the bottle from under the ice. "Well, you'll have to hold it a little longer."

Taking a long swallow, she sighed, finally allowing the beauty around her to register. By the time she had left the spectacular grandeur of Lake Tahoe behind and traveled into the foothills of the Gold Country, she had been too intent on remembering Roger's directions to pay attention to the scenery. But she had climbed out of the river valley and back into the high country, again surrounded by tall pines and spruce, but not tall enough to block the rugged mountains springing up around her. The Sierra Nevada Range.

She had worked in Yosemite for so long, she thought she had become immune to sights such as this. She realized that her indifference sprung from the constant crowds of people and the increasing crime in the park. There had been little time to enjoy the scenery. Search and Rescue had become a full-time job. That's why she jumped at the opportunity to come to Sierra City. That, and it offered her another chance to work with Roger. He had taken her under his wing in Yellowstone when she had been fresh out of college and had shown her the ins and outs of the Forest Service. She, like most first-timers, knew little about the politics of the Service. She soon grew tired of being a tourist guide and weary of the manual labor expected of the younger rangers. But no matter how hard they all struggled, in the end it all came down to politics and money. It hadn't taken but a few years for her to lose her enthusiasm for the job. That's about the time Search and Rescue was just coming into its own, with the local law enforcement agencies no longer able to handle the demand caused by the explosion of tourists in the parks and National Forests. Volunteer SAR teams had begun to organize, all with good intentions but little money and training. When the Park Service finally began training their own, Chris was one of the first to volunteer. Her training took her from the classroom deep into the backcountry and she finally found what she had been looking for when she joined the Forest Service.

Now, nearly all of the National Parks had full-time Search and Rescue teams, but National Forest Land was still mostly volunteers. Roger had finally persuaded his managers at Lake Tahoe that the Sierra ranger district warranted its own SAR and he had called Chris away from Yosemite, luring her with a promise of uncrowded trails and little or no crime. He didn't have to ask twice.

She finished her beer and tucked the empty bottle back inside the cooler. As she passed Dillon's cage, she stuck a finger inside to scratch his head, then withdrew quickly as he threatened to bite.

"Okay, let's see if we can find the elusive seven-forty so we can get this tiger out of his cage."

She brushed her fingers through her hair and shoved the sunglasses back on before heading along the bumpy road, her frustration over Roger's earlier directions fading.

Forty-five minutes later she pulled in front of the ranger station, a charming log building tucked neatly into the forest. She looked back over her shoulder, the dust just settling back on the dirt road and she watched a large white dog run along the edge toward town. She noticed only a handful of cabins along the road and she supposed the main part of Sierra City was at the other end of town, toward Sacramento.

Chris tried to straighten her wind-blown hair with her fingers, then gave up. She must look a sight and she bent down to look into the side mirror.

"Jesus," she murmured, but there was little she could do about her appearance at this point. She gave Dillon's cage a gentle shake. "Just a little longer, Tiger."

She walked into the ranger station and watched the different groups of tourists milling about. Only a few gave her curious glances and she went to the counter, impatiently tapping her fingers while she waited for the receptionist to finish restocking the brochures.

"May I help you?"

Chris offered her a quick smile then glanced around again, hoping Roger would show his face. Maps and pictures of the local wildlife lined the walls, and both were for sale on a rack in the corner. A topographical map was taped on the counter. It was faded from too many fingers running across its surface, looking for hiking trails and cross-country ski routes. Before Chris could answer, the radio scanner broke with static before a voice came on, calling the county sheriff to a minor traffic accident on Highway 89.

"I'm looking for Roger Hamilton," Chris finally replied.

"I'm sorry, he's out on the trails. Can I help you with something?"

"I'm McKenna . . . Chris," she said, sticking out her hand. "He's expecting me."

"Oh? The new Search and Rescue? You're the one that got lost," she stated, but gave Chris a firm handshake.

Chris smiled briefly. "His directions left a lot to be desired."

"Well, I'm glad you finally made it. We were all pretty excited to learn we were getting our own SAR. I'm Kay, by the way. I tend to the paperwork around here."

Chris nodded. "Any idea when Roger will be back?"

"No. A group of scouts came out on Monday and we're short-handed, what with Matt being sick. Mr. Hamilton went around to check on them."

"Great. He gets me lost for two hours then bails on me." But she softened her words with a quick smile. "Listen. I'd about kill for a shower. Any idea where I'll be staying?"

"Oh yes. Mr. Hamilton has a cabin rented for you. Pine Ridge Cabins, only about a mile out of town. I'll call for you and let them know you're on the way."

"Thanks. I'd appreciate it."

Kay went to her desk to call and Chris walked to the wall, studying the map tacked there. She had been in Yosemite the last five years and knew the trails like the back of her hand. She hated the thought of starting over, but at least she knew Roger. He would make it okay. She listened to Kay on the phone, thinking it would be different living in such a small town. She had only worked in National Parks before, where the only full-time residents were Forest Service and the summer concessionaires. Everyone generally went about their own business, all too busy to worry about their neighbors. But here, in this small town, everyone knew everyone else and no doubt they all kept tabs on each other.

"You're all set, Chris. Ruth has your cabin all cleaned and ready. Keep going towards town and turn right on Spruce. It's well before you get into town. The office is about a mile down that road. Ruth will give you directions from there."

"Thanks so much. I'll be back later to check in with Roger."

Following Kay's directions, Chris found Spruce Street easily, thinking it was aptly named as the boughs of the trees covered the road, blocking out the sun in places. She pulled in at the first road, a sign painted red telling her it was the office. Before she could get out, a tiny gray-haired woman opened the door and came out to meet her.

"You must be the new ranger," she stated, offering her hand.

"Search and Rescue, actually," Chris corrected. She was surprised at the firmness of the woman's handshake.

"Oh, well, same thing," the woman said in a singsong voice. "I'm Mary Ruth Henninger. Some call me just Ruth, though." She turned and headed back inside as fast as she had come out. "Come along," she added, motioning for Chris to follow as she glided up the steps.

Chris followed the old woman inside and found herself in the middle of a large kitchen. The smell of cookies baking hit her and there were already two dozen or so cooling on the table.

"Just be a second, honey. Let me get this batch out."

Chris watched as the woman, in one fluid motion, opened the oven, snatched the pan and closed the oven door with one quick kick of her foot. Chris's grin turned into a laugh as the woman took all of ten seconds to add the fresh cookies to the pile already cooling. Chris admired this woman's energy, especially as she suspected her to be in her seventies.

"Mr. Hamilton says you'll be here for awhile and that you would probably like your privacy, so I've given you cabin number eight. It's stuck off by itself with no neighbors in sight. Of course, when the wind blows right, you can hear what's going on at number seven and vice versa," she said, her singsong voice making Chris smile.

"Number eight, huh? Right now, I just want a shower."

"Well, I wasn't going to say anything . . . nowadays, women are traipsing all over the mountains not giving a hoot about their appearance," she said, hands placed firmly on her tiny hips. "Why, in my day . . . well, never mind. I know you're in a hurry dear. Linens and towels are collected once a week, Saturday mornings. You're responsible for bringing your own trash to the dumpster. Don't leave it out at the cabin, bears will get it. Mr. Hamilton had your refrigerator stocked with essentials, he said, but I haven't checked on his meaning of that. You know men," she said with a wave. "He also had some firewood delivered for you, but it won't get you anywhere near to winter. Now sign here," she finished, pointing to the form she had been writing on.

Keys dangled before her and Chris took them from weather-worn fingers.

"Thanks."

"It's a lovely cabin, Chris. I can call you Chris?"

"Of course."

"Good. I'm sure you'll feel right at home in no time at all."

Ruth Henninger whisked Chris out the door as quickly as she had pulled her inside, shoving a bag of cookies into her hand as she hurriedly rattled off directions to her cabin.

"Rent's due at the first of each month," she called as Chris started her Jeep.

Chris sat there for a moment, realizing that she had said all of two sentences and yet she felt exhausted. Mary Ruth was nowhere to be seen and for a moment, Chris wondered if she had imagined the whole thing. But the smell of freshly baked cookies said otherwise, so she shrugged and headed on down Spruce a little farther, taking the second left on Pine, then a right on Fir. The winding road simply disappeared into the forest and ended at the driveway of the cabin.

"Private and secluded. Thanks, Roger."

With Dillon's cage in one hand and her cooler in the other, Chris walked to her new home, pleased to find a couple of incense cedars close by. She stopped, stuck her nose into the bark, inhaling deeply, savoring their aromatic scent. She walked around the back, surprised at how cozy it was. A covered deck followed the length of the small cabin and there were two wooden chairs sitting side by side, just waiting for company.

"Okay, Tiger, let's get you out."

Dillon nearly burst from his cage, finding the nearest bare spot to dig and relieve himself.

Chris opened a beer and relaxed for a moment on the steps, watching Dillon as he sniffed his new surroundings. It only took a second for him to shimmy up the small spruce at the corner of the deck. He gingerly climbed from limb to limb, occasionally looking back to make sure Chris hadn't left him.

"You're such a baby," she said. She called him down after a few minutes, though. She needed to unload the Jeep and she desperately wanted a shower. One trip to the Jeep brought in a duffel bag and the box from her bathroom.

The cabin was furnished comfortably, with a table and four chairs separating the kitchen from the living room. A quick inspection of the refrigerator found that Roger had left beer, a bag of chips and a half-full jar of salsa, nothing else.

"Essentials, Roger?"

There was an old sofa and one oversized chair, both facing the windows looking back towards the driveway. The large, functional fireplace was tucked neatly in the corner and two good-sized windows covered the other wall, offering a view of the deck and the forest beyond. Tilting her head, she mentally rearranged the room. She wanted the sofa facing the fireplace.

She was pleased to find a propane heater in the small bedroom. Crowded inside were a regular sized bed and an old, scuffed six-drawer dresser with an equally old mirror hanging over it. The only other furniture in the bedroom was a tall, skinny nightstand with two wicker shelves. The closet was larger than she would have expected and it would hold her limited wardrobe without a problem.

The bathroom had two doors, one off the kitchen and the other through her bedroom. She stuck her head inside and nodded with approval. It looked newly remodeled and where a tub once took up space, a shower was installed and extra shelves for storage lined the wall. Clean linens and towels were folded neatly on one shelf. The sink and mirror were nearly brand new and she glanced at herself, her reflection again indicating her immediate need for a shower.

She stripped where she stood, sweaty T-shirt following dirty shorts and socks. Dillon sat patiently on the toilet seat while she let the warm water wash away nearly four hours of dust. Washing her hair reminded her that she was well past time for a cut. Maybe Roger could recommend someone in tiny Sierra City.

She didn't bother unpacking the few boxes she had squeezed into her Jeep. They lay scattered on the living room floor and she would tend to them this evening. There wasn't a lot anyway, a few personal items, her small portable CD player and some books. She had never been one to collect things, anyway. She had lived in Forest Service housing for so long, moving frequently, it didn't make sense to acquire household items of her own. She brought her summer clothes with her. The winter items were being stored at a friend's place in Yosemite. Chris would either have them shipped or make the drive back to pick them up later on.

She put on clean hiking shorts and a T-shirt and went out on the deck, letting the breeze dry her hair. She leaned on the railing, listening to the bird sounds and the wind moving through the trees and she heard the faint sound of running water. With fluid grace, she hopped over the railing and landed neatly on the ground, long legs carrying her quickly into the forest, searching for the sound of water. She found a small stream, three or four feet across in most places, flowing past her on its way to meet the larger Gold Creek in town, then eventually dumping into one of the many rivers in the area. Probably the Bear River, she thought. A sound to her right brought her around and two chipmunks scurried past, disregarding her as they chased around a large spruce. She grinned. That will keep Dillon busy. He was the only cat she knew that had absolutely no hunting skills. The closest he had come to catching anything was when a hummingbird had flown into a window and lay stunned on the ground. She had scooped the bird up just as Dillon was in mid-pounce, his look of disappointment enough to make her laugh out loud.

She smiled at the memory, not thinking it odd at all that Dillon remained her closest friend after eight years. She looked up at the trees and sighed. No sense getting all sentimental and emotional now. Still wouldn't change the outcome.

She turned and made the return trip to the cabin, pausing beside the deck for a second. It was charming. Nothing like the cabins in Yosemite, built right on top of each other in little clusters. This would be almost like a home, something she hadn't had in years.

Chapter Two

Roger had his back to the door pointing to the large trail map tacked to the wall, two hikers listening intently. Chris nodded at Kay, then walked to the counter to listen.

"Once you come to the first fork, Ridge Trail veers to the left. It's very steep and I wouldn't recommend it this late in the day. Take the Lake Trail cutoff. It's only about two miles round trip, easy walking and you'll end up right back at the trailhead, provided you don't miss the turn."

Chris smiled. She hadn't seen Roger in nearly ten years and they had spoken only a handful of times over those years, but it was as if no time had passed at all. His hair was still sandy blond, kept a little too long. His moustache still blended with a few days' stubble and he was still shorter than she was.

As if sensing her presence, he turned, surprise evident in his eyes. "McKenna?"

"Hello, Roger," she drawled, offering him her hand. He took it, then grabbed her in a bear hug.

"My God, McKenna, you look great!"

"Well, finally lost my baby fat," she said, patting her flat stomach. When she had known Roger, she had been at least fifteen pounds heavier. He, too, looked to be in great shape.

"What happened to your beer gut?"

"Took up jogging, if you can believe that," he said and they laughed. "Damn good to see you, McKenna. Glad I didn't have to call out the volunteer SAR team to find you."

"Your directions sucked, Roger."

"Just testing your tracking skills, McKenna." He wrapped a strong arm around her shoulder and led her behind the counter. "Come on back. Let's catch up a bit. Kay told me you came by and she sent you to the cabin."

"I needed a shower. And Roger, the cabin is great. Thanks." She took the seat he motioned her to in front of his desk.

"Small, but private. I thought you'd like it." He leaned back in his chair and comfortably rested folded hands behind his head and studied her.

"What?"

"Never thought you'd leave Yosemite."

"I never thought I would, either. But it got too crowded and busy for me. Every damn weekend was like Fourth of July in Yellowstone."

Roger leaned forward then, resting his arms on the cluttered desk before him. "Won't have that problem here, although we get more crowded every year. Tahoe is no longer a sleepy little village and folks wanting peace and quiet hear about Sierra City. They tell two friends and so on. I've been here six years, McKenna, and they've only allowed me one more position in that time. Wouldn't be getting SAR now if those three skiers hadn't gotten lost and died this spring. Hell, we had two goddammed volunteers and me looking for them."

"Sorry, Roger."

11

"Yeah. But it happens. What I'm saying is, don't think you're going to be strictly SAR. We all wear a lot of hats here. Although I remember your aversion to being a tour guide."

A comfortable silence followed while they looked each other over, then identical smiles touched their faces.

"I've missed you," she said.

"Hell, me too." Then he leaned forward. "Remember that old bar in Gardiner, just across the Wyoming border?"

"Oh, yeah," she nodded. "That's where you taught me to drink."

"My ass. You could drink me under the table. We've got the Rock House Café here. The Rock, as the locals call it, is the only bar in town. Let me buy you a cold beer. Maybe we'll stay long enough for dinner. They've got great steaks."

"You're on, but . . . I'll have to skip the steaks. I'm a vegetarian," she told him.

"McKenna? A vegetarian? What the hell is wrong with you?"

She laughed. "Some woman turned me on to it awhile back."

"No doubt. And was this woman someone special?" he asked with a grin.

"She was," Chris agreed.

"But not anymore?"

Chris didn't answer for a moment, not really wanting to bring up all that old baggage. It had been so long, anyway. But Roger was Roger and she remembered when he had helped her through her very first breakup, only a few months after she had met him. She looked up and met his eyes, knowing he was remembering that, too.

"It's been eight years," she finally said.

He raised his eyebrows. "Bad breakup?"

Chris laughed. "I made a total ass of myself," she said. "Damn near chased her to San Francisco."

Roger laughed, too. "If I remember, McKenna, you were always the one being chased."

"Yeah, well, I was in love," she said dramatically. She scratched a nonexistent itch on the back of her neck before continuing.

"Actually, she decided she liked men better. Talk about a blow to your ego," she said.

"Sorry, McKenna."

She shrugged. "Well, this particular man was the only child of a millionaire father. Who could blame her?" she said sarcastically.

"Women are fickle," Roger murmured. "Who needs them."

Chris smiled. "That mean you're single?"

Roger grinned. "Hell, no. Got me a woman here in town. I was just trying to make you feel better."

"Thanks a lot. I think I'll take you up on that beer now."

"Sure. And we'll see if Dave can whip something up for you."

Chapter Three

She rushed in, barely pausing at the receptionist's desk on her way past.

"She ready?"

"Yes, Ms. Stone, she's been waiting."

Jessie knocked lightly on the door, then stuck her head inside, smiling apologetically at her therapist.

"Jessie. Come in." Dr. Davies's smile was brief. "You're late. Again," she added.

"Sorry, Doc. I couldn't break away."

Jessie tossed her purse on the opposite chair before sitting. After all these months, she was still nervous whenever she visited Dr. Davies. Whenever she managed to keep her appointment, that is. It was supposed to get easier, she was told, but there was just something about facing her week after week, knowing the good doctor knew all the intimate details of her life. Well, those she would share, anyway.

"You missed last week. Again." Dr. Davies leaned forward, resting her elbows on her desk. "I was worried. After our session the last time, you seemed upset."

"I always seem upset." Jessie sat back in her chair, her ankle resting casually on her knee and she absently twirled the string of her black Reeboks. "I'm just trying to wrap up the book. I get so involved, days just pass by. You know how it is."

"So you haven't given thought to what I suggested?"

Jessie swallowed nervously, her eyes moving quickly around the room, bouncing off the now familiar paintings and prints that adorned the walls, lighting everywhere except on her therapist.

"I can see you have," Dr. Davies said quietly.

"No. I just can't see myself going back to Sierra City after all this time. I might very well end up as a character in one of my books."

Dr. Davies laughed lightly. "You already are a character in one of your books. Several times over, I think." She paused before continuing. "You've been coming to me for nearly two years, Jessie. I hate to admit it, but we've made little progress. Perhaps confronting your mother . . ."

"She's not my mother," Jessie spat.

"I'm sorry. Annie. I think if you would go back, confront her, talk to her, get some sort of closure on that part of your life, then we can go forward from there."

Jessie stared at her, unblinking, then let her eyes slide away. Six therapists in the last five years and all but one had suggested she go back to see . . . her. Then Jessie wryly flicked her eyes to the ceiling. Of course, the lone dissenter had suggested Jessie see a psychiatrist, hinting at hospitalization, shortly after she had read Jessie's latest book and its graphic depiction of murder.

"Let's seriously give it some thought, Jessie. I'm not suggesting you go back to reconcile, I'm only suggesting you go see her and talk about what happened, tell her how you feel about her."

"Oh, believe me, she knows how I feel."

Dr. Davies nodded. Jessie could see frustration in the doctor's eyes for the first time and she suddenly understood why they all suggested the same thing. They made progress only to a certain point, then each session consisted of rehashing the old stuff over and over again. Jessie suspected they got just as tired as she did discussing the same thing until they beat it to death, only to see it find life again the next week.

"It's been two weeks since we talked but I know you're finishing up your book. Have you gone out?"

Jessie nodded. "A couple of times."

"And?" she prodded.

"And what?" Jessie stood quickly, rustling the papers on Dr. Davies's desk as she walked past. "Nothing's changed, Doc. I didn't suddenly find a conscience and a set of morals in the last two weeks."

"Tell me what happened."

Jessie paced back and forth in the large office, remembering the two encounters. She shook her head. She hated this part. So she tried the casual approach.

"Just meeting new friends at the bar, you know. No big deal. One was even quite nice," Jessie added.

"And you took her to your place?"

Jessie stared. "Are you kidding? I didn't like her that much."

Dr. Davies leaned back in her chair and watched Jessie pace. "And why do you think you didn't invite her to your apartment?"

Jessie turned on her. "Why do you ask me that every week? I keep telling you, I don't like them that much. I don't want them at my home. It was just sex."

Dr. Davies pointed at the chair in front of her desk. "Sit down, Jessie, you're making me dizzy."

When Jessie finally settled in the chair, she continued. "Do you even remember their names?"

"I don't recall asking," Jessie replied.

Dr. Davies sighed wearily. "I don't need to tell you how destructive this is, not only to yourself but to these women as well."

"Oh, please. These women go willingly. They're not out looking for love, Doc, just a quick release and then it's right back out there."

"Are you sure? None of these women were actually attracted to you? None of them took a liking to you for what's inside?"

"What's to like? I'm not a nice person," Jessie admitted.

Dr. Davies paused, studying her, and Jessie shifted nervously, only barely talking herself out of bolting from the room.

"Let's go back, Jessie," Dr. Davies suggested. "We've discussed your childhood and your adult life. We always seem to skip over your adolescence."

Jessie shrugged, her brain desperately trying to recall memories.

"Tell me about . . . ninth grade," Dr. Davies suggested.

"I don't remember anything special. Just starting high school."

"Boyfriends?"

"No."

"What about birthday parties?"

"No."

"Were you in any clubs?"

"Not that I recall."

"Well, what did you do in high school?"

"Do? I didn't do anything. I went to school."

"Jessie, you must have had some outside activities. What about at home? What did you do for entertainment?"

Jessie stared hard at her, trying to read behind the questions. "I don't remember doing anything."

"What about your father? You remember him when you were a child. How about later? Did you still go camping with him, fishing?"

Jessie shook her head. "No. He died."

"You were seventeen when he died. What about before?"

Jessie shrugged. "I'm sure he was there," she murmured. "I just don't have any memories of him then."

"What about your mother? Annie?"

"What about her?"

"Was she there when you came home from school?"

"She was there. That was all. She didn't concern herself with me."

"Why do you think she didn't concern herself with you?"

"She didn't care what happened to me," Jessie said loudly. "She just . . . she just didn't care."

"Did she not ask you about your grades?"

"No."

"What about your father? Was he concerned about you?"

Jessie pulled her eyes away, landing on a familiar painting behind the doctor's head.

"I don't remember. I guess."

Dr. Davies sighed and rested her elbows on her desk, slowly pulling her glasses off.

"Jessie, we can go over and over these questions . . . and we have. But your answers are always the same. You don't remember. Why don't you remember, Jessie?"

"Don't you think I ask myself that?"

Dr. Davies nodded. "I know you do. Why else would you be seeking my help? I'll suggest it again, Jessie. Go back. See her. Ask her."

"I don't know what I would say to her," Jessie murmured.

"Jessie, if you ever hope to find peace in your life, to find happiness, to find someone to build a life with, then you've got to deal with your past. And you're not dealing with it. You ran from it all those years ago and you're still running. That's why you must go back and face your fears. Then maybe you can start to have a real life here."

Jessie slumped back, her head hung back as she stared at the ceiling. Shit.

"I haven't spoken to her since I was seventeen. Over sixteen years, nearly seventeen. I don't even know if she's still there," she said weakly.

Chapter Four

"McKenna, how did you get into this line of work, anyway?"

Bobby Daniels was panting and struggling to keep up with Chris as they hiked the steep part of Fire Lookout Trail.

"I started out working summers in Yellowstone during college. That's where I met Roger." She kept walking, smiling a little as Bobby slipped on a rock. "When I first got hired, Search and Rescue was still mostly volunteers or they were county or state people. Yellowstone finally hired a couple full-timers but Yosemite was one of the first to hire a regular SAR team," she said, continuing up the hill.

"Hey, slow down, will you?"

Chris stopped and leaned against a tree, pausing to catch her breath. Three weeks of walking these trails and she already felt like she knew them better than Bobby, who had been living here two years now. He had graduated college in Sacramento and wanted to take a summer off so he'd come here to work at the Pine Creek Lodge. He hadn't left yet. In fact, Bill and Peggy Witt, owners of the lodge, treated Bobby as their own son.

But Chris had a knack for directions, always had. It was almost like she had a compass in her head. The first week she was here, a seventy-two-year-old Alzheimer's patient turned up missing. She, Bobby, and the only other SAR volunteer, Greg Manning, had combed the trails alone that first day, adding volunteers from town by the end of the afternoon. She figured she walked every trail there those first two days. She remembered every step. At noon on the second day, they started searching the forest off the main trails. She finally found him, only two miles off the trail. He had spent the time curled against a tree trunk and by the time she got to him, he was completely incoherent. He had to be sedated before they could walk him back to the lodge. Since then, she'd only had one other search, that involving a ten-year-old boy with epilepsy. She and Bobby found him the same afternoon. He was fine, just lost.

"You know, you spend an awful lot of time out here for a volunteer, Bobby. Why haven't you hooked up with the Forest Service yet?"

"We looked into it last year. Roger is so short-handed, he thought they might authorize another position up here, but they said there wasn't enough money. Not if Roger wanted to get SAR up here, too. And, of course, they had just brought in Hatcher the year before." Bobby shrugged and looked off into the forest. "I mean, I could have gotten hired. When someone who's been in as long as Roger puts in a word for you, it's a lock, but I didn't want to relocate. Could've gone south to Sequoia or someplace up in Oregon, but this has become home. And I really wasn't interested in hiring on as maintenance."

Chris nodded. "So, college educated and working in a lodge. Ain't that the life?"

Bobby grinned. "I make enough to pay my student loans and I've got free rent. And it beats the hell out of working in a high-rise, that's for sure."

"Can you imagine fighting traffic every damn day to get to your job, only to be locked inside some depressing building for eight hours?"

"Yeah. Then traffic all the way home again, too." Bobby playfully tossed a pinecone at her. "We've got it made up here, McKenna. You know it?"

Chris agreed. "Pay's not so great but look at this view."

She turned a complete circle, eyes following the jagged face of Sierra Buttes to the west, outlined perfectly against the blue, blue sky, then back down the trail which they had just hiked. Beautiful.

The radio broke static just seconds before Roger's voice disturbed the silence.

"McKenna?"

"Yeah," she said, taking the radio from its holster at her hip.

"What's your ten-twenty?"

"Fire Lookout Trail."

"How far? Have you passed the lake cutoff?"

"Yes. We're just past the steep part where it levels off," she said. "You need us to go back down?"

"No. Up. I've got a frantic mom here. Her two boys were going to hike to the tower. Were supposed to be back down by now."

Chris and Bobby exchanged glances.

"No one signed in at the trailhead," she told Roger.

"No. They would have started on the Lake Trail and cut across. I've got Matt covering that one." He paused only long enough for Chris to notice his frustration. "Besides, they probably wouldn't know to sign in."

"Meaning?"

"They're young, McKenna."

"How young?"

"Grade school."

"Grade school? Jesus Christ! Who lets children hike up . . ."

Roger cleared his throat. "McKenna, she's already heard it from me."

"Ten-four. I'll radio from the top." She was already striding off while putting the radio back in its holster. "Come on, Bobby," she called over her shoulder.

Fifteen minutes later, they topped the ridge, the old fire tower in sight. They paused to catch their breath while Chris searched with her binoculars.

"They're under the tower," she said. "Shit. One is prone. Goddamned stupid mother letting them go off by themselves," she murmured as she ran towards them.

"They probably convinced her they were old enough," Bobby panted behind her. "You know how kids are nowadays."

"Actually, I think it's how parents are nowadays. They look all of eight years old."

She had her backpack off by the time she reached them, relieved to see both boys conscious.

"Hey guys," she said. The boy lying down had blood on his forehead and the other one had obviously been crying. She touched his arm gently. "What happened to him?"

"He fell," he said, wiping his nose on the sleeve of his T-shirt.

"From the tower?"

"Yes," he whispered, his voice trembling.

She shook her head, but held her tongue. They were eight and ten, she guessed. Jesus Christ! Up here alone. The mother is the one who needed a good ass whipping. She bent to the boy on the ground.

"Can you move your arms? Your legs?"

He could. She took the first aid kit from her backpack and cleaned the small gash on his head. He apparently hit a rock when he fell. Chris guessed he had been knocked out or else they would have attempted to hike back down. She turned back to the older one.

"How long was he out?" she asked quietly.

"A long time," he said before he started crying again. "I thought he was dead."

"And he could be. That was a damn stupid thing to do." She handed the radio to Bobby. "Let Roger know we found them."

She put antiseptic on the boy's gash and nodded when he jumped. At least his reflexes seemed to be normal. She put two butterfly bandages on before speaking.

"What's your name?"

"I'm Kyle. He's Kurt," the older one said, pointing to his brother who was now sitting up.

"Does he talk?"

"Yes."

"Kurt, how high up were you?"

"We crawled over the wire," he whispered

"Jesus Christ! You could have broken your neck. Do you know that? There's a reason for that sign, a reason those steps are closed off." She stared at them, trying to make them understand how lucky they were to be unhurt. "Hike up Ridge Trail. You can stand on a rock and see forever. Just like up there," she said, pointing to the tower. "But don't ever come up here again. You hear me?"

"Yes, ma'am," they said, lips trembling, eyes tearing again.

"McKenna, Matt's here," Bobby said, pointing to the lone figure walking towards them.

If there was one person Chris had taken an instant liking to, it was Matt Henderson. No matter what the circumstance or situation, Matt had a smile on his face. He had been in the Sierra District four years and he was well respected in town and depended on by Roger to handle even the most mundane chores.

He greeted them now with a wave and a smile, his long hair tied in a ponytail and bouncing on his neck as he walked.

"Found the little monsters, huh? Hi boys. How are we feeling?"

Chris smiled and stepped out of the way, bringing Kurt around for Matt to inspect.

"Got a nice gash here," she said. "Probably a headache, too."

"Stitches?"

"Gonna need a few," she said. At Kurt's horrified look, they laughed. "Be thankful it's only stitches, Kurt. We could be hauling you out of here by helicopter."

"Let's take them back down the way you came up," Matt suggested. "It'll be quickest and all downhill."

"You go ahead. Bobby's going to show me the shortcut to Ridge Trail."

She headed down the trail Matt had just come up and left Bobby still talking. He chased after her, catching up just as she disappeared into the trees.

"Hey, wait up, McKenna!"

"Well, come on, it's getting late."

"They're about the fourth ones this summer," he panted beside her.

"Then why in the hell is the thing still standing?"

"It's old, I guess. Built in 1906, Roger says. Some think we should just open it up, so people could just walk up the steps instead of climbing over the wire."

"That's great," she said dryly. "The tower is a hundred feet high. That'll be pretty."

"It was just a thought, McKenna. It's not like we've got the personnel to keep watch, anyway."

"No. And it's not like the wire is doing any damn good."

Bobby stopped her with a tug on her sleeve and pointed into the woods.

"There."

"Where?"

"What did I say to look for?"

"The rock with the face in it," she said, her eyes glancing over the rocks lining the trail. Then she laughed. "A face, my ass."

Bobby shoved her arm playfully. "But you found it."

She picked her way carefully across the rocks, finding the well-concealed trail between two spruce trees.

"Clever," she said.

Bobby shrugged. "Well, I didn't make it," he admitted. "But it's about forty-five minutes shorter than taking Ridge Trail all the way around. If you don't mind climbing over a few boulders on the way down."

"But not coming up?" she asked.

"Oh, God no. It's all uphill. This is strictly a short cut on the way back down."

They reached the Lake Trail in no time and followed it around to the trailhead. Chris tossed her backpack into the Jeep and pulled out a full bottle of water from behind the seat. She took a mouthful, then handed the bottle to Bobby. He handed it back after his turn, then stared at Chris silently.

"What?" she finally asked.

"Matt. He likes you."

"Yeah? So? I like him, too."

"No. I mean, you know, he *likes* you."

Chris laughed. "You mean like boy-girl kind of like? Aren't we a little old for this?"

"It's not like he's said anything to me or asked me to tell you. I can just tell, you know. Besides, I think you'd make a cute couple."

Chris laughed again. "Sorry to disappoint you, kid, but I'm really into the girl-girl kind of relationships."

Bobby stared, his eyes wide. "But, Roger said I should go ahead and tell you, he said you were as straight as they come."

"Get in, will you?" Chris started the Jeep and pulled away, letting the wind cool her hot face. "Roger was just having a little fun, Bobby. Apparently, it doesn't take much to amuse him," she said dryly.

"So, you and Matt, that's out, I guess?"

Chris grinned. "Does he have a sister?"

Chapter Five

She was sitting on the sofa reading that night when Roger knocked on her door.

"Hey? Can I join you?" He held up a six pack of beer.

"Of course, come in." She took the beer and put them in the refrigerator, handing him a cold one of hers.

"Mrs. Patterson wanted me to thank you for finding her boys this afternoon." He sat down beside her. "They tell me you have a little temper and that you yelled at them."

"Me? Hardly. I hope you yelled at the mother, though."

"Oh, yeah. I don't think she'll do anything like that again."

"By the way, thanks for encouraging Bobby to play matchmaker. Straight as they come, huh?"

Roger's laugh shook the windowpanes and Chris joined in.

"Bobby was going on and on about you and Matt but he suspected you might be gay and it was such a shame and so on that I just wanted him to shut up about it. I told him to tell you because you were a little dense when it came to men."

"Thanks a lot. I think I broke his heart."

"He idolizes Matt. If I didn't know better, I'd think he had a crush on him."

"Maybe he does."

"Don't think so, McKenna. Bobby's got him a little gal in Reno." He picked up the book she was reading and smiled. "J. T. Stone. Have you read all six of hers?"

"No, this is just the third. Have you?"

"Yep. She's from around here, you know."

"Really?" Chris flipped over to the back and looked at the picture of the author for the hundredth time, looking briefly into the very dark eyes that stared back at her. "Says here, she's from New York."

"Well, she grew up around here. Her mother still lives here." He took the book from her and looked at the picture of J. T. Stone. "Jessie Stone. Still so beautiful. Tragic story, really."

"The book?"

"No, her life. Her mother's, too. Annie."

"The hermit lady, as Kay calls her?"

"She's not really a hermit, not like what they called them in the old days, anyway. She just prefers her own company and doesn't like to get out. I was friends with her and Jack when I worked here in the seventies, before I went to Tahoe. Jack Stone was the Regional Supervisor for this district."

Chris was intrigued. Ever since she had picked up one of her books and seen the picture on the back, she had been curious about J. T. Stone. Her books were dark, mysterious. Her picture on the back was mysterious, too, and her nearly black eyes revealed little, perhaps adding to the mystique.

"Well, tell me the story," she said, drawing up her legs under her and pulling Dillon into her lap.

"Jessie was a teenager when I met her. Jack was older, already in his mid-fifties, but we became friends. He could party, that one. Very seldom was he seen in public with his wife. That would be Annie. I think that's why people call her a hermit. They assumed she didn't want to go out, when actually, Jack wouldn't allow it. He controlled her totally, right down to taking Jessie away from her."

"What do you mean, taking her away?"

"Well, he was already forty when she was born. That girl could do no wrong in his eyes. If Annie tried to discipline her, Jack was there to take her away with him, out on the trails, out fishing, anything to get away from Annie. So, naturally, Jessie grew up following him everywhere and had little to do with her mother. Jack wouldn't allow Annie to go along with them, you see. He said it was his quality time with his little girl. Now, a lot of this I've learned from Annie over the years. Jack would never have told me all that."

"Abuse?" Chris asked.

"What?"

"Jack. Sexual abuse. With the kid," Chris suggested.

"Jack? Oh, no," Roger said. "He loved Jessie."

Chris raised an eyebrow. With what little Roger had just told her, she would bet a hundred dollars this Jack wasn't just simply fond of his little girl.

"You know what I mean. He wouldn't hurt her. He worshiped her."

"Okay," Chris said, still skeptical. "Then tell me the rest." Chris was enjoying the story. She had a ridiculous teenage crush on the author already, all from just a picture. Perhaps Roger could give her some insight into J. T. Stone's personality.

"Well, needless to say, Jack and Annie didn't exactly have an ideal marriage. Jack had girlfriends all over the place. Everyone knew about them. Even Annie. Of course, Jessie never knew. Well, Annie started going to San Francisco more and more and Jack found out she had a man there. They had a terrible screaming match, he called her a whore, unfit mother, you name it. Annie came right back at him about all the women he had on the side and how their marriage was a farce. Anyway, they thought Jessie was outside, but she heard the whole thing. She would have been sixteen, I think. Maybe older. Annie said Jessie only said one thing to her. She said, "So, this is all your fault." Well, Jack took Jessie away. Took her out hiking or something. Came home like nothing had happened. Next day, went to work like normal and didn't come home. We found him lying at the bottom of Milford Canyon. He had fallen off the ledge up on Ridge Trail."

"Jesus. Did he jump?"

Roger shrugged. "Who's to say? Annie thinks so. So do I."

"Why?" She got up to get them another beer, pouring out the rest of her warm one.

"Annie thinks because he couldn't bear the thought of Jessie finding out about all the woman he had on the side. I think he couldn't stand the thought of his friends finding out that Annie had been cheating on him. That would have made him less a man, you see."

"So you kill yourself?"

"Well, I wouldn't, no. But you'd have to know Jack."

"So what happened to Jessie? She found out he was nothing but a liar?"

"After they found him, Jessie blamed Annie for his death, I guess. When she turned seventeen, she left and hasn't been back since. Sixteen, seventeen years, probably."

"She hasn't seen her mother?"

"Hasn't even spoken to her mother," Roger said.

"No wonder the mother is always the first to get murdered in her books. And not very pleasant deaths, either," Chris added.

"Yeah, I know. But Annie is okay now. I'm not sure how she survived the first few years, but she's one strong woman."

"I'd like to meet her, Roger. Kay says you take her groceries and stuff."

"Yeah. I go see her about once a week or so. Before I came back here, she would only go into town every other month and stock up, then no one would see her again until the next time. That's how the hermit thing stuck. We can go see her tomorrow, if you like. I don't think she'd mind."

29

Annie was sitting on the porch, a thick book lying in her lap, when they drove up. She waved twice, then got up to meet them.

"Why, Roger, what a surprise." She turned to Chris. "Hello. I'm Annie Stone."

Her voice was as strong as her handshake and Chris smiled politely.

"This is Chris McKenna, new Search and Rescue. And a friend," he added.

"Finally got your SAR, Roger? Good. Well, I'm pleased to meet you, Chris McKenna. Come inside. I have fresh brewed tea. It's so hot out, isn't it?"

Chris exchanged a glance with Roger as they followed her inside. What a pleasant woman, Chris thought. Absolutely nothing like she had been envisioning. Chris looked around the well-kept house, pausing in the living room before following Roger and Annie into the kitchen. The walls were cluttered with paintings and numerous others lay scattered about, some leaning against the wall. She looked closer and saw Annie's name scribbled at the bottom.

"Oh, don't look too closely, Chris. That's just my hobby. Some of the better ones I've hung, but the others . . . well, I'm out of room in my studio." She pointed to the stack leaning against the wall. "Those are on the way to the basement. I can't bring myself to paint over them yet."

"Well, they all look very good," Chris said sincerely. She knew little about art, but they at least looked like trees and mountains. "What style would you call this? Abstract?"

"No. More like Impressionism. I tried abstract art, but it wasn't for me. And my talent doesn't quite go far enough for Realism." She shrugged. "But it's just a hobby," she said again.

They took their iced tea to the back deck, shaded this time of day. Chris waited while Roger found another chair for her. She doubted Annie ever had need for three. They were silent for a long moment, all three looking out toward the mountain as the sun reflected off the western facing slopes.

"Well, Roger, it's unlike you to show up unexpectedly. Did you need something or are you just showing me off to the new SAR?"

"Can't I just visit, Annie? Chris just happened to be along."

"Bullshit, Roger. We've been friends too long," she said, bringing a smile to Chris.

"I wanted to meet you," Chris admitted.

"Why? Have you heard the rumors about me and you wanted to see a real live hermit for yourself?" she asked with a laugh. "I'm not really a hermit, dear," she said quietly. "Just don't have a whole lot of use for people, is all."

Chris thought again what a delightful woman she was and she was glad that Roger brought her here.

"I was filling her in on the local history last night, Annie. Your name came up," Roger said.

"Oh, all that again?" She turned to Chris. "Do you know of my daughter, Chris?"

"I've read a couple of her books, yes."

Annie nodded. "Then you know about as much as I do." She looked away, eyes closed for a moment. "How old are you?"

"I'm thirty three," she said, resisting the urge to fall back on her standard reply of twenty-nine.

"Jessie will be thirty-four this fall. She was a tall girl, although I don't think as tall as you are. She always had a dark complexion, like you, but your hair is much lighter. And of course, she didn't have your pretty blue eyes. She had her father's eyes, dark as the night," Annie said quietly. Then she looked up, a smile returning. "Oh, well. Another life. Now, how long have you been here?"

"First of this month," Chris said.

"You probably haven't had a decent meal since you got here, then. Knowing Roger, he has you at the Rock every night."

Chris nodded, her eyes flicking to Roger.

"I'll expect you for dinner tomorrow night at six."

31

"Dinner?"

"Yes. You do eat?"

Chris nodded again. "I'll be here."

That evening, at the Rock House, Chris joined Roger and Ellen for dinner. Ellen Burdett owned the only grocery store in Sierra City. Widowed at a young age, she took her insurance money and bought the store from Mrs. Ramsey, who had wanted to move to Oregon to be closer to her daughter. She and Roger started seeing each other shortly after Ellen moved here. Chris would bet money that they had never spoken of marriage. Roger would run screaming into the night and Chris suspected Ellen knew that.

"Roger tells me you're having dinner with Annie Stone tomorrow," Ellen said.

"Yeah. Surprised the hell out of me." Chris raised her hand and waved at Martha. "Still waiting for that beer," she yelled.

"Keep your pants on, McKenna, I'm the only one here," Martha yelled back.

"Ah, small town politeness. Gotta love it," Chris murmured.

"If you're dying of thirst, have some of mine," Roger offered.

Chris took a sip, then pushed the mug back to him.

"I've been here five years and I have yet to meet her," Ellen said.

"Annie? You're kidding? Why haven't you gone with Roger?"

Ellen shrugged. "I didn't want to impose on her and it would be rude. I mean, I would be going mostly out of curiosity."

Chris turned to Roger. "Why do you allow these rumors to continue? She seemed a perfectly normal, healthy woman to me."

"And she is. I think Annie enjoys the rumors. It keeps people away, that's for sure. And it's not like she never leaves the house. She goes to San Francisco a couple of times a year and she's an avid hiker. She's been all over these mountains and rarely stays on the trails. Most of her paintings come from something she's seen on her hikes."

"Why would she feel comfortable going out in San Francisco and not here?" Chris asked.

"She never went out here, even when Jack was alive. She doesn't

32

have any friends here. Not one." Then he shrugged. "Well, other than me."

"That's a very sad life," Ellen said.

"Of her choosing, let's don't forget," he said.

Martha finally came with Chris's beer, sloshing a little on the table when she set it down.

"Dave's got some pasta concoction he's made up for you, McKenna."

"Thanks. Can't wait." Chris turned to Ellen. "I've really got to start cooking. These nightly surprises of Dave's are getting stranger by the day. The other night, he gave me a bowl of cottage cheese with pinto beans on top."

"I warned you to stick with the baked potato," Ellen said.

Chapter Six

Jessie stood on her balcony staring out at the lights of the city, her wineglass held lightly in her hand. She looked up, like she did nearly every night, trying to spot a star, even make out a constellation that she remembered from her childhood, but the lights of the city were too bright, like they always were. Her shoulders drooped and she let out a heavy sigh. Ever since Dr. Davies mentioned going back to Sierra City, she had thought of little else. She remembered chasing after her father down the hiking trails when she was barely old enough to walk, learning to tie flies on her fishing rod, learning the names of the trees in the forest, the birds, and animals. She remembered camping with him high above timberline, so cold, even in the summer, that she would shiver all night long. She remembered taking horses from the stables at the lodge and riding into the high country, so far back that it would have taken them days on foot. She remembered the waterfalls they had bathed under and the clear streams they had swam in and the many campfires they had sat around, him telling her stories of his camping trips with his father when he was young. How old had she been? Ten at the most?

What was she doing in this city, so far from the mountains of her childhood? She knew she would go back. Just the thought thrilled her. Before coming to New York, she had spent the first eight years in San Francisco but she hadn't dared go to the mountains. She couldn't imagine what it would really be like to step into the forest again, to look up at the giant trees. She wondered if Mary Ruth Henninger still rented cabins or if she had passed on? She wondered if the Rock House was still there. She had been too young back then to visit the bar, but she remembered an occasional dinner there. Then she thought of Annie and her heart grew cold. Her so-called mother, the woman who had never been there for her. The woman her father despised. She wondered if Annie even knew she was a writer now, a successful writer. She wondered if Annie even thought of her anymore.

She would go in late August, she decided. After the summer crowds had thinned. She swirled the last bit of her wine and allowed a small smile. It would be good to go back, she admitted. Just to soak up memories, if nothing else.

Chapter Seven

Chris parked under the small juniper tree at the edge of the front porch and walked up the steps. Before she could knock, Annie's voice broke the silence.

"I'm back here," she called.

Chris walked into the empty living room and glanced around, wondering where Annie was. She hesitated a moment, then went into the kitchen, leaving the bottle of wine she brought with her. She was just about to call out when Annie came from down the hall, drying her hands on the apron she wore, which was stained with paint. She greeted Chris with a smile and ushered her back into the kitchen.

"So glad you could come, Chris." She spotted the bottle of wine on the counter and picked it up. "Nice. But this was not necessary. I have plenty. On my trips to San Francisco, I stock up on wine. I have quite a cache down in the basement."

"Well, I wanted to bring something," Chris said.

"That was thoughtful, but you'll take this back with you so you can enjoy it another time. I should have warned you though, I don't eat meat. However, I think anyone can get by at least one meal without it. Even Roger."

Chris laughed. "I knew there was a reason I liked you. I'm a vegetarian, too."

Annie grinned and clasped her hand. "What a pleasant coincidence. Now, how about a glass of wine? It's been so long since I've had someone over for dinner, I'm afraid I've forgotten my manners."

Chris watched as Annie pulled two bottles from her refrigerator and held them for Chris's inspection.

"I didn't know which you would prefer. This is a lovely sauvignon blanc, one of my favorites. And a chardonnay. Both will go beautifully with pasta, so you choose," she told Chris.

"Let's do the sauvignon blanc then," Chris suggested.

They sat on the porch drinking wine while the casserole finished baking. Mountain chickadees were fighting for the seeds on a bird feeder hanging off the porch. An ear of corn in an adjacent tree kept the squirrels busy and two chipmunks were underneath the feeder, foraging for the dropped kernels. The hummingbird feeder was busy as well and they watched in silence as the tiny birds buzzed by. Chris enjoyed the quiet and took a deep breath, savoring the smell of the cedars and pines.

"You like it here?" Annie asked.

"Very much, yes."

"I could tell. The mountains aren't for everyone. Especially women. It takes a certain type, don't you think? One who's not afraid to be alone? I grew up in the city and only came out here for holidays and such. When I married Jack and moved out here, though, it was like coming home. I've never thought of leaving, Chris. Even in my darkest moments, I would never consider going back to the city."

"Do you have family left?"

"No, I've lost touch. There may be cousins and the like. In fact,

I'm sure of it, but none that I know. I've been up here forty years, Chris."

"I guess this is home, then."

Annie nodded, watching the squirrels fight for the ear of corn. "You must think I'm a strange bird," she said quietly.

"No. Not at all," Chris said.

"Well, I've got my hobbies and my books. I do miss company, though. I usually talk Roger's ear off whenever he comes by." She stood suddenly. "Let's get that meal on the table. You must be starving."

She went back inside and Chris noted the way she almost floated when she walked. She was a small woman, still very graceful, just a hint of what she was in her younger days, Chris thought.

"This is delicious," Chris said after her first bite. "Dave is nearly starving me to death."

"I figured you ate there." She shook her head disapprovingly. "Nothing but grease, Chris. I doubt the Rock has even one meal with pasta."

Chris nodded. "I think he keeps a bag on hand just for me. It's always a surprise to find out what he plans to serve with it."

"Well, I insist you take leftovers home."

"Okay. But only if you let me help with the dishes."

"Deal. And we'll plan to do this again, if you like."

"I look forward to it."

Chapter Eight

Chris and Greg Manning were riding in the backcountry, looking for a hiking club from San Francisco. They were only a day past due and that normally wouldn't cause concern, but this group consisted mostly of kids. They had started up the South Rim Trail, which by itself is twenty-seven miles long. But, inevitably, hikers miss the loop trail and keep on into the backcountry, hiking the Nevada Trail for many miles before they realize it.

"You ride pretty good for a girl, McKenna."

"So do you, Greg."

Chris rolled her eyes to the heavens, cursing Roger for making her take Greg along. Besides Bobby, Greg was the only other trained SAR volunteer in Sierra City, but they clashed and Chris would just as soon only use him in emergencies. Roger, however, thought otherwise. Greg was strong, a body builder, and he didn't hide the fact that he thought SAR was no job for a woman. When things slowed down at the end of summer, Chris planned a training session with Greg and Bobby and she'd show him just how qualified she really was. In the meantime, she had to put up with his sexist comments.

"What was Yosemite like?" he asked, ignoring her comment.

"Crowded. Busy. Lots of lunatics from the city."

"You must have fit right in," he said sarcastically.

"Oh, absolutely, Greg," she said just as sarcastically. "You would not have though. Neanderthals were pretty much extinct there." She gave her horse a nudge, breaking into a trot and away from Greg.

They stopped at dark, setting up camp along side a small stream. She radioed in while Greg collected wood for a fire.

"We're following tracks, Roger. It's got to be them."

"Surely they realized they were on the wrong damn trail and headed back," he said. "I told them about the loop trail three times, McKenna. Three times. How hard can it be?"

"I guess that means Matt didn't find anything?"

"Negative. They missed the cutoff."

"We'll start out at first light, Roger. We'll find them tomorrow."

"Yeah, well, if you don't run into them pretty quick, I'll have to call in air support from the County. I'm going to have about fifteen parents getting hysterical real soon. Call me when you start out tomorrow. I'll be here."

It was fully dark by the time they had the campfire going and water boiling for their dinner. Greg pulled over a downed tree for them to sit on and Chris stretched her legs out toward the fire.

"It's been awhile since I've been out at night," Greg said.

"Me, too. I like it."

In Yellowstone, Chris had often taken her time off to go camping, stealing a few days to get away from the crowds and hike into the backcountry to be alone. In Yosemite, especially during the summers, there were few days off and even then, it was difficult to find a trail that wasn't occupied by a hundred others. She didn't miss the crowds, that was for sure. Sierra City was a great place to unwind after eight hectic years at Yosemite.

She watched Greg silently, searching her mind for a safe topic they could discuss without egos and testosterone getting in the way. She thought of none. So instead, they added the boiling water to their freeze-dried dinners and sat quietly around the fire listening to owls in the distance and the occasional howl of a coyote.

The next morning, as the sun was just creeping over the mountain peaks, they had their horses saddled and were on the trail again. At nine, they heard the high-pitched singing of adolescent boys. They looked at each other and smiled. Ten minutes later, they came upon the group heading their way.

"Hi there," Greg said, leaning over in his saddle.

"Hello. You're rangers, I hope." One of the two adults came forward, relief showing on his face.

"Search and Rescue."

"We missed that loop trail Mr. Hamilton was telling us about. We turned around two days ago."

"You're probably two more nights on the trail," Chris said, swinging out of the saddle. "How're your supplies?"

"We should be okay. I guess some of the parents are getting worried?"

"For sure," she said. "I'll radio in and let them know you're okay." She glanced at Greg. "Feel like camping for a couple more nights? One of us should probably stay with them," she suggested. She really wasn't up to two nights with fifteen young boys and two adult men.

"Sure. I can handle it, McKenna. You run on back."

Chris gritted her teeth but managed a brief smile. "I'll leave the radio with you. Just in case you get into trouble."

She rode fast, putting distance between them, trying to ward off the foul mood that had settled over her. Spending time with Greg usually did that to her. She stopped for a moment when she came to a stream crossing to let the horse rest, then she pushed on. It was well after dark when she arrived at the lodge. Bill and Peggy were always kind enough to let them use their horses and Roger tried to compensate them as best the budget would allow. The stable was already closed for the night so Chris brushed down the horse herself. She had pushed the horse hard but she didn't want to spend another night out on the trail. The horse was munching happily on the grain Chris left out and her own stomach let her know she had skipped lunch. She thought about stopping by the Rock but she needed a shower and she wasn't really in the mood for one of Dave's surprises. Canned soup at the cabin sounded better.

After her shower, she sat on the sofa relaxing with a glass of wine. Dillon was curled in her lap, purring loudly, having forgiven her for leaving him alone the night before. She had J. T. Stone's book out and she flipped it over, looking at the picture on the back. She wondered, not for the first time, how she could be so attracted to someone just from a picture. The author was certainly attractive, but it was more than that. Chris thought perhaps it was the eyes that drew her. Dark eyes that seemed to look right into her very soul. Or maybe the lips that just hinted at a smile but never quite made it. She finally flipped the book back over with a slight laugh. J. T. Stone was probably no one she would want to meet, judging from the stories Roger had told her of Jessie's childhood. She was probably one mixed up adult now. Anyone who wrote about murder all the time had to be a little strange.

The next week, when she joined Annie again for dinner, Chris asked about her daughter.

"Roger's told me some."

"Oh, it's my own fault. I allowed Jack to take her from me. He was obsessed with her, right from the beginning. He wouldn't even allow me to breastfeed. Here I held this week-old baby in my arms and I had to feed her with a bottle."

"You must have loved him very much then."

"Oh, I did, in the beginning. He was very exciting and very handsome. He took me out of the city and brought me here and I loved it. I was happy. Of course, when I found out about his affairs, the first time, I was devastated. But then I got pregnant and I thought it would all be okay, so I just ignored them, you see. He always came home to my bed and I was so young and foolish. I thought that would be enough. Then Jessie came along and he changed. I realized how little he needed me. Even for Jessie, I was just a cook and housekeeper, someone who was here all the time but who wasn't allowed to share in their lives. He taught her that so I can't totally blame her."

"I'm sorry, Annie, for bringing this up. You don't have to tell me," Chris said, mindful of the sadness in Annie's voice.

"Oh, all that happened thirty years ago," she said, waving her hands dismissively at Chris. "That doesn't bother me now." She pushed her plate aside and refilled her wine, this time a dark cabernet. "I found someone to love me, though," she said quietly.

Chris took a sip from her own glass, waiting for Annie to continue.

"His name was Jonathan and he was an attorney in San Francisco. He was older than me, a widower. I went there to inquire about getting a divorce, you see. But I couldn't go through with it. I always held out some hope that Jessie loved me just a little and if I stayed with her father, then I wouldn't lose her completely. Anyway, Jonathan and I started seeing each other and I fell in love with him. Jessie was only twelve then. I vowed to stay with Jack until she graduated high school, then I was going to be with Jonathan."

She held her wineglass in front of her a long moment before finally taking a swallow. Then she smiled and patted Chris's hand.

"Of course, things never turn out the way we plan, do they? Jack found out about Jonathan and he was furious, to say the least. Never mind that he had women all over the state or that we had not been intimate in years." Her voice grew bitter then and she slammed her hand on the table. "He was a bastard all right. Unfortunately, Jessie was home when he decided to bring it all to light. She heard everything and if there was any love in her for me, it died that day. Oh, her eyes looked at me with contempt and hatred. I had made her daddy cry, you see. I had broken his heart." Annie stood up suddenly and took their plates. "Bullshit, of course, but he was a fine actor," she said as she walked away. "A fine actor."

Chris stayed at the table, trying to imagine this woman's grief. All these years to have lived here alone, carrying such painful memories along. Why did she stay here?

Annie came back and reached over the table to fill their glasses. "I find it's best to be drinking whenever I dwell on this subject. Not that I think about it often, Chris. I couldn't survive if I did. But it helps to remember sometimes."

"What about Jonathan?" Chris asked.

"Well, after Jack's death, he wanted to marry me, but there was Jessie to consider. She had not spoken to me since that evening of our fight. Even after the funeral, nothing. It was as if I didn't exist. I couldn't get through to her. Of course, she blamed me for everything and why not? She knew nothing of Jack's affairs over the years. She only knew what he told her and what she had seen. I never went with them on their camping trips or hiking or fishing. She thought, and was told, I'm sure, that I didn't want to be with them. In truth, I wasn't allowed to go, you see. It's my own damn fault for allowing him that control over me but I was young and foolish. Anyway, it was as if I had pushed him myself, for all Jessie cared. We lived in complete silence for nearly nine months, then she left."

"Forgive me for asking, but do you think Jack ever . . . abused her?"

Annie slid her eyes away quickly and Chris saw the shadows of doubt cross her face, but Annie shook her head.

"No. He wouldn't. It wasn't Jack's style. I mean, he had women. Lots of women," she said.

Chris didn't push. It wasn't her business anyway, although she could see the thought had crossed Annie's mind before. Instead, she moved the conversation back to Jonathan.

"You could have gone to San Francisco, started over," Chris suggested.

"No. I would have been no good for Jonathan then. I stayed here with my sorrow. Wallowed in it, actually." She leaned closer to Chris. "I learned a great deal about wine that first year, Chris," she said quietly, then laughed. "But I always thought that if Jessie needed me for anything, she would at least know where I was. If I moved, how would she find me?"

"But she never did?"

"No. Never. She's done quite well for herself, though." Annie leaned forward and nearly whispered, "Have you noticed how often mothers get murdered in her books? Oh, and not a quick death, either."

Chris laughed with her, impressed again that this woman's spirit had not been broken.

"The only thing I know about her life is what is crammed on the book jacket. Not much, but at least I know she's in New York." Then she shrugged. "You take what you can get, Chris. The rest, you leave to your imagination."

Chapter Nine

Jessie parked her rental car in front of the office and took a deep breath of mountain air as she walked around the car. The late-August sun felt good on her skin and she couldn't wait to trade her slacks for shorts. Looking around, she was surprised at how familiar everything seemed. The roads going through town were still not paved and she remembered riding down them on her bike, dust flying, going to meet her father at the ranger station. She looked up at the trees and smiled, remembering how big they looked to her as a child, how she used to put her arms around their trunks and try to touch her fingers on the other side. Of course, she never could. She got out and breathed deeply, letting the still familiar smell wash over her. Sixteen years. Just like yesterday, she thought.

She heard the screen door open and she turned toward the cabin, surprise showing in her eyes. She slipped the sunglasses back on quickly as Mary Ruth Henninger came down the steps, looking every bit of fifty, though Jessie knew her to be in her late seventies by now.

"Welcome, dear. You must be Miss Parker."

Jessie took the offered hand, smiling slightly at the firm handshake of the older woman.

"I'm a little late, I'm afraid," Jessie apologized.

"Just a few hours. I know how traffic can be in those big cities. Come inside and we'll get you fixed up, dear."

Jessie followed her up the steps, knowing it was not the traffic that made her late, but rather a trip to the grocery store and her own hesitation at finally coming back here after all this time. It was as if she were afraid of this place. But she hoped sixteen years were long enough. The last thing she wanted was to be recognized by any of the locals who might remember her. She took off her sunglasses only long enough to sign where Mary Ruth asked. She was proud that she didn't hesitate when signing the strange name.

"You know, you look familiar, dear. Have you stayed here before?"

Jessie coughed, then cleared her throat and answered truthfully. Indeed, she had never stayed at Mary Ruth Henninger's cabins before.

"Well, I've got a nice secluded cabin for you, just like you requested. Number seven. Not quite as far back as cabin eight but a new ranger is living there now."

Jessie nodded and politely listened to the directions, thinking she could still find her way around here blindfolded.

As she drove to her cabin, she had a momentary lapse and a pleasant feeling of contentment settled over her, almost as if she were simply on vacation. But she couldn't keep memories away for long and she was soon a little girl again, chasing after her father, loving life to the fullest.

So unlike the woman she had grown to be.

A hardness settled back over her by the time she found her cabin. It wasn't very far off the road, but it was nestled in the trees and there were no other cabins nearby. None that she could see, anyway. She walked around, some of her good humor returning as she watched not three, but four chipmunks come up for a close inspection of their new cabin guest. She heard a squirrel fussing at her from a low hanging branch and she looked up, watching it as it flipped its tail at her before scurrying up the tree a little higher.

She quickly unpacked the rental car, taking the bags of groceries in first and putting the perishables in the refrigerator. She had picked up quite a few things in Sacramento, including a couple of thick steaks. She didn't envision going out for dinner and she certainly didn't want to go to the local grocery store for food. In reality, she couldn't remember the last time she had cooked steaks outside. She finally came to her most important bag. Wine.

She held up a bottle of cabernet sauvignon and nodded. She would have that with her steak tonight. Other bottles followed and she put the pinot grigio and chardonnay in the refrigerator to chill, the rest lined the small counter space next to the sink.

She went back outside for her two bags of clothes and walking back into the cabin, she finally took the time to look around. The sofa was worn, but looked clean. The small lamp on the end table had been left on for her and it brought a coziness to the room, despite the bare walls. She shrugged. Certainly not the fancy hotel she had stayed in last night in San Francisco, but it had a welcoming warmth that she was never able to find in a city.

She changed into shorts and put on the new hiking boots she had bought. It had been sixteen years since she had on hiking boots. Her exercise these days was jogging in city parks with hundreds of others and she was actually looking forward to a little solitude on the trails. She walked towards the woods behind the cabin and found a small stream, barely three feet across and she jumped it easily. A little farther along, though, she came upon a cabin and stopped. One of the Henninger's, she supposed. She followed the stream until she came to the road, then walked the short distance to a trailhead that she remembered. Elk Meadow Trail, a two-mile hike to the meadow and back would be easy enough. A good way to get back into the swing, so she started out, ignoring the notice that everyone should sign in before going into the forest. She followed the trail, pushing childhood memories away and letting her mind go blank. She tried to remember the names of the trees. Sugar pine, of course. Who could forget a tree with twenty-inch pinecones? She easily picked out a white pine and Douglas fir. Then she stood next to a spruce and the name would not come to her, much to her disappointment. She walked on, finally getting close enough, and she grinned. An incense cedar. Her favorite tree. She stuck her nose next to the bark and inhaled, breaking into laughter at the joy that simple scent brought to her.

She stepped back and looked to the heavens, wondering when the last time was she had laughed out loud. Too many years to remember, she thought. But this was nice and she turned a circle, her arms held out, away from her side, letting this carefree feeling overtake her, relishing in the freedom she suddenly felt.

Then she wandered on, following the trail that she remembered, pausing at the meadow, thinking of all the times she had come here in the spring, running through the wildflowers, chasing butterflies, her father right behind her.

She shook her head. She wasn't ready for that yet. Today, tonight, she just wanted to relax. Tomorrow she would hike up Ridge Trail and remember.

Later that evening, she sat on her porch and waited for the charcoal to heat. Her steak was seasoned and ready and the opened bottle of wine sat conveniently next to her chair. Her mood had changed from apprehensive to dark, to reflective, to melancholy and to just plain content. A feeling she hadn't had in so many years, she hardly recognized it. And she didn't want to lose it now. She closed her eyes and listened to the night sounds. She was thrilled to hear an owl in the woods behind the cabin and she listened as its mate answered from farther in the forest.

The sounds of piano music drifted to her, coming slowly to her senses. She opened her eyes lazily and looked around, wondering who would disturb the night with music. But as she listened, the piano faded into the background, its soothing sound relaxing her as the owls again called to each other. The cabin across the stream, she thought, when she spotted a light through the woods.

Chris sat on her back deck drinking a beer and listening to the soft sounds of the piano. This music always put her to sleep and she yawned now, thinking she should turn it off before she fell asleep right here on the porch. She heard the owl call and looked up into the trees, wondering where he was hiding. She heard Dillon's low mew and chuckled. He, too, was looking into the trees, perhaps looking for the owl.

"You're too fat," she told him. "He'd never carry you off."

She finished her beer in one long swallow and went inside. She turned the music down and picked up the book she was reading. As always, she flipped it over and stared at the author, wanting to ask so many questions. Annie talked freely about Jessie now. Chris suspected that after all these years of keeping her feelings in, this was Annie's way of purging herself. She talked for hours about Jack and Jessie and even Jonathan. Jonathan was dead now, Chris had learned, but Annie didn't seem to grieve for him, not like she did for Jessie.

Chris read only two chapters then stopped, as she did every night. She didn't know why she was prolonging the book, perhaps because this was the fourth book and there were only two more published and she wasn't ready to say goodbye to J. T. Stone. She put it back on the shelf neatly and poured herself a glass of wine before bed. Dillon crawled in her lap and she stroked him, letting him fall asleep as she sipped her wine in the quiet darkness.

Chapter Ten

Jessie stood out on the ledge, looking across the canyon to the other side as the sun's rays broke across the mountain, hitting her face, warming her. She thought she would feel something here and was surprised when it didn't come. Sixteen years ago, her father had stood on this very spot. What had he been thinking? Was he thinking of her? Or was he thinking of Annie and how she had betrayed him? She would never know. Just as she would never know for sure whether he had jumped to his death or simply slipped after coming up here to do some soul-searching. She wanted to think the latter, but she knew in her heart that it wasn't.

This was the first time she had come up here to the ledge since they had found him. She had walked into the canyon the day she left, but she couldn't bring herself to come up here. Now, she looked around, hoping to feel something, wondering why she didn't. Anger. Sorrow. Something. But nothing came. She simply felt empty, like she had these past sixteen years. She sat down on the ledge and leaned over, looking into the canyon some three hundred feet below, imagining the spot where he laid. She couldn't remember exactly where it was, though in her mind she could picture him falling, no scream coming from him, just the resounding thud as he crashed on the rocks below, his broken body empty, her father gone forever.

She took a deep breath and let her tears come, as she knew they would. For sixteen years, she had not shed a one, not once. But she hung her head now and let the sobs rock her until she could cry no more. She sat there for minutes, maybe hours, as the sun rose higher in the sky and the tears dried on her cheeks. She sat up, hugging her knees to her chest and rested her damp cheek on her legs, her eyes traveling across the canyon, resting on the evergreens on the other side, unseeing. She felt sorry for herself mostly. All those lost years.

Jessie sensed a presence seconds before she heard the scuffing on the rocks. She lifted her head from her knees only slightly, surprised to find someone standing there, watching her.

"You're kinda close to the edge there, ma'am," Chris said, wondering who in their right mind would sit on the ledge like that, only a foot from tumbling into the canyon. There had been no sign-ins at the trailhead but that didn't mean anything. Not everyone followed the rules.

Jessie had half a mind to ignore the woman, thinking it wasn't any of her damn business how close to the edge she sat. But she was getting tired, so she stood up and stretched her back, realizing just how long she had been sitting there.

"I was a little close, I guess," she said to the stranger, looking over the edge and into the canyon one more time. Then she turned and easily hopped over the foot-wide gap in the rock and stopped in front of the woman. For the first time, Jessie noticed the Forest Service patch on the stranger's T-shirt and the radio strapped to the woman's hip. With an arch of one eyebrow, she allowed her eyes to travel over the woman, up past scuffed hiking boots, tanned, well-muscled legs, hiking shorts, and the white T-shirt tucked neatly inside. Her light brown hair was layered and wind blown, strands hanging over the blue eyes that looked back at her. Sexy. Jessie gave one of her most seductive looks and smiled.

"Who are you?"

"Search and Rescue."

Jessie grinned. It was just too easy. "And . . . who are you searching for?" Jessie asked quietly, stepping closer.

Chris was amazed at how well she hid her surprise, for there was no mistaking those nearly black eyes looking at her so intently. How many nights had she held the book and looked at them herself? The only thing different was the hair, now much shorter than in the picture.

"I'm looking for hikers that don't sign in at trailheads. It's a huge offense, you know."

Jessie teasingly raised both arms over her head. "Guilty. I guess you caught me then." Jessie met the woman's steady gaze, thinking how beautiful her eyes were. Blue. Blue as a mountain sky. She wondered how long it would take for this conquest. A little diversion from the unwanted task of seeing Annie; this woman would do nicely.

Chris was not immune to the flirtatious looks and gestures of J. T. Stone, but she sensed a complete lack of sincerity and she was much too wise to fall victim to that sort of seduction. And despite her fantasies every night, she never really believed she would meet J. T. Stone. But here she was, unabashedly flirting with her. Well, two could play this old game.

"Now that I've caught you, what in the world should I do with you?"

"House arrest?" Jessie suggested, her lips forming into a seductive smile. "Overnight stay?"

Chris crossed her arms and watched Jessie Stone for a moment, letting her eyes travel the length of her, much like Jessie had done earlier. Then she shook her head. "No. I think I'll let you off the hook this time. First offense and all."

Jessie was a bit disappointed. She'd been so close, she was sure. But the game wasn't over. She would be here at least a week.

"Thank you. I guess I should head down then. Want to escort me?"

"Can't. I'm heading up. Sorry."

Jessie shrugged. This woman clearly wasn't interested. And Jessie wasn't about to beg. The women in New York were so much easier. "Have a nice walk then." She gave one more lingering look, then told herself that the woman must be straight not to have taken the bait. Oh well, her loss.

Chris walked on up the trail, purposely keeping her back to Jessie Stone, refusing to turn around to watch. Only when she topped the next ridge did she stop and lean against a tree. She took a drink from her water bottle, wondering what in the world J. T. Stone was doing up here. Chris was almost certain that Jessie had been at the exact spot where Jack had jumped. The ledge with the split in it, Annie had said. What's she doing here? Maybe to finally see Annie. Maybe to do research for a new book. Then her eyes widened. Maybe to do both.

Jessie passed the trailhead, her mind still on the woman she'd met on the trail. She picked up the pencil, thinking she would have just a little more fun. She wrote: Jennifer Parker. Out safely. It was gorgeous at the top . . . view included.

She smiled as she closed the lid on the box. She didn't doubt the woman would look on her way back down. She passed the dusty Jeep on her way to her rental car, assuming it belonged to the SAR woman. She paused, looking at the neat interior. It suited her, the woman with the wind-blown hair.

Opening the window on her own car as she drove, Jessie let the cool breeze hit her face, drying the sweat from her hike. It had felt good to use muscles that were dormant too long. And it had felt good to cry, she admitted. The hardest part would be facing Annie.

If she could even manage it. She wondered what Annie would be like after sixteen years. She wondered if she had gone and married that man in San Francisco. Probably. Annie may not even be in Sierra City anymore. Wouldn't that be ironic? She finally got up enough nerve to come back and Annie wouldn't even be here. On impulse, she pulled into the gas station and walked up to the phone booth, flipping through the directory. Her fingers found the S's and she held her breath, pausing at *Stone, Annie*. So, she was still here after all. Jessie closed the book and walked away, her heart hammering in her chest.

She made a sandwich for lunch and chased it down with a glass of wine, then lay on the sofa, letting sleep take her. She had not slept well the night before and she was a little tired after her hike. She would have plenty of time to decide about Annie, she thought as she drifted away.

Chris followed the Ridge Trail loop, enjoying the quiet of the weekday. She had met no one since encountering Jessie Stone that morning and figured she would not. Friday, the tourists would begin showing up and by Saturday, there would again be people on the trails, trying to leave the city behind for at least the weekend. She passed the cutoff to Lake Trail and continued down the hill to her Jeep. She was tired and wanted a shower, glad she had worn shorts that morning instead of jeans. But they still clung to her now and she pulled her shirt out, letting the cool air hit her bare waist.

On her way past the trailhead marker, out of habit she lifted the sign-in box and glanced at it, wondering if anyone had gone up after her. Jennifer Parker? Chris smiled. Who was she kidding? Then she laughed. The woman was still flirting, even on the sign-in sheet.

Chris passed her road and went on to the office where Ruth Henninger would be. Maybe Jessie Stone was staying at the cabins. It would be much more private than the lodge and she apparently was looking for seclusion, judging by the alias she used.

Ruth came out to meet her, as Chris assumed she did everyone. She slammed the Jeep door and walked up.

"Good afternoon, Miss Henninger," Chris greeted.

"Oh, please, I've told you, it's just plain Ruth." She turned and beckoned Chris to follow. "Come inside. I have fresh baked cookies, Chris."

At least once a week, Chris stopped by, just to chat. She suspected that Ruth looked forward to her visits now.

"You look hot. Want some iced tea?"

"That sounds great, thanks." Chris sat at the table and took a cookie, still hot from the oven.

"How are all the rangers doing, dear?" Ruth asked, as she always did.

"They're fine," Chris answered, as she usually did.

"How do you like that Robert?"

Robert Hatcher. Chris had to force a smile onto her face. He was probably one of the most handsome men Chris had ever seen. He had been with Roger a little over a year but few liked him. He rarely worked the trails, usually making some excuse or other about staying inside or having urgent paperwork to finish. He pretended to tolerate her, but still, Chris had little use for him. She detested laziness.

"I don't get to see him much," Chris said. "He doesn't get out on the trails a lot."

"Now he's a handsome one, with that moustache of his. I saw him at the grocery store. What about Matt?"

"I like him fine," Chris said. "What's with the questions?"

"Well, a woman your age, you need to be dating. I would hate to see you end up like me, an old maid."

Chris laughed, drawing a smile from Ruth. "I'm serious. And don't tell me they haven't asked you. As pretty as you are, they're probably banging your door down." Then she leaned closer to Chris. "A little too skinny, though, Chris. Men like to have a little to hold on to."

56

Chris laughed again. "Thanks, but I'm not looking for a man, Ruth."

"Women nowadays, think they have to be so independent. I declare, in my day, we wanted a man to take care of us."

"What happened to you, then?"

"I guess I scared them off, what with having a business to run and all," she said wistfully, staring out the back door.

"And how is business, Ruth?"

"Oh, the cabins are full on the weekends, that's all. Now that school has started up again, the families have all gone home. Had a new one come in yesterday, though."

"Really?" Chris asked.

"Pretty girl. Alone, too. I put her up at number seven. She was looking for a secluded place, just like you. Why you young women want to be by yourselves so far back in the woods, I'll never know."

"Number seven? That's across the stream from me, isn't it?" Chris asked innocently.

"Yes, through the woods. Her name is Jennifer Parker. She looked so familiar to me, but she said she'd not been here before."

Yes, Ruth would have known Jessie as a young girl, Chris supposed. No wonder she didn't use her real name.

Chapter Eleven

It was two days later before Chris saw Jessie Stone again. Wednesday morning on her way to the Rock to meet Roger for breakfast, she saw the lone figure jogging ahead of her. She recognized the short, dark hair immediately and she slowed, watching the tan, muscular legs keeping a beat as Jessie methodically pounded the dirt, arms pumping at her sides. With intentions of driving past without stopping, Chris nonetheless slowed. When Jessie looked up and grinned, Chris found herself stopping and waiting.

"Morning," Jessie breathed, wiping the sweat from her brow. She leaned on the Jeep's door to catch her breath and Chris was surprised at her nervousness as she stared back at Jessie Stone.

"Hi," Chris greeted. "Been at it long?"

Jessie laughed. "About fifteen years."

Chris blushed. "I meant this morning," she clarified.

"I know you did. About thirty minutes. Thirty more to go." Then

Jessie straightened and rested her hands on her hips, offering Chris a genuine smile. "Did you get my message on the trailhead?"

Chris smiled back. "Yes. Glad you made it out safely, Jennifer Parker."

Jessie shrugged. "Well, I had no choice. I would hate to have gotten lost or something and have them send some man to find me since you were already out on the trails."

Chris pressed her foot down, stirring the motor just a little before answering. "I'm sure they would have radioed me and I'd have rushed back down to save you."

Jessie showed off even, white teeth as she laughed. "Well, it would have been my lucky day then."

Chris only nodded, deciding that this game had gone on long enough for now. She shifted the Jeep into first gear. "Gotta go."

"Going to work?"

"Breakfast. Then work."

"Rock House?"

"Yep."

"Any good?"

Chris laughed. "If you like greasy food, I guess."

Jessie leaned down and stared into her eyes, making Chris catch her breath. "And do you?"

"Sometimes."

Jessie stood up again, away from Chris. "Well, it's a start."

Chris was wondering if they were still talking about food, but she was afraid to ask, so she pulled away.

"See ya."

"Hey," Jessie called after her. "What's your name?"

"McKenna," Chris said, driving off. She took a deep breath and looked at herself in the mirror, then grinned at the flushed face looking back at her. Shifting into fourth, she thought she might be out of her league with Jessie Stone. All flirting aside, she still suspected that J. T. Stone had major problems. Or Jennifer Parker, whoever she was pretending to be today.

Jessie jogged down to the trailhead of Elk Meadow, then slowed to a fast walk as she entered the woods, smiling to herself as she passed the sign-in sheet without writing down her name. She looked up at the blue sky. Yes, that was exactly the color of the woman's eyes. McKenna. She had a nice smile, too, Jessie admitted. And if she were honest with herself, she would admit that the little game of seek and conquer that she usually played was not working on this McKenna woman. Jessie wasn't even sure she wanted it to work anymore. She suspected that this McKenna was a nice person and if she were in the habit of making friends, she might make one of McKenna. But she had no friends. She had no relationships of any kind in her life, save the seek-and-conquer types she saw once and then never again.

Jessie looked once more to the sky, thinking you could tell a lot from a person's eyes. Warm, friendly blue eyes. She went back to her walk, wondering if she would ever see those eyes again.

Chris watched the steam rise from her coffee cup and contemplated telling Roger that Jessie Stone was back. But it really wasn't any of her business. Jessie obviously didn't want anyone to know or she wouldn't be using an alias, so Chris kept quiet.

"What are you going to eat?" Roger asked, breaking into her thoughts.

"I think I'll just have toast this morning."

"She eats like a bird," he told Margaret, who was waiting patiently for their orders. "Let me have the pork chop with scrambled eggs. Extra hash browns. We know McKenna will be stealing off my plate."

Chris ignored him and sipped from her coffee.

"Awful quiet this morning," he commented.

"Just tired, I guess."

"Hmmm. By the way, Matt has a crush on you," he said.

"I know."

"What are you going to do about it?" he asked.

"Nothing."

"Nothing?"

"He must know I'm gay. What else can I do?"

"Might have been easier to tell him you've got some guy back at Yosemite," Roger suggested.

"Nope. I'm not going to hide, Roger. You know me better than that."

"Yeah. But Matt's a good guy. I hate to see him following you around like a puppy dog."

"He does not. Bobby follows me around like a puppy dog."

Roger laughed. "Yeah. Bobby's got a bad case of hero worship."

"But, I really like Matt, you know. I wish we could be friends and not worry about all that other bullshit."

"Speaking of," Roger said, nodding toward the door.

Matt walked to their table, his long hair tied in the familiar ponytail.

"Morning McKenna, Roger."

"Hey, Matt," Chris said. "What's going on?"

"Roger's got us assigned to the South Rim today."

"Horses?" she asked as she glared at Roger.

Roger smiled sweetly at her. "Got two different groups of backpackers out there. Fifteen total. They're taking the trail up from Tahoe. They should be in our area today or tomorrow, so I thought we'd keep a lookout. They left Tahoe on Saturday."

"You know those backpackers don't want us baby-sitting them, Roger," she said, already hating the idea.

"A lot could have happened between Saturday and now, McKenna. Besides, it's not like we're swamped up here and can't take the time."

"You could have told me this yesterday," she complained. "Now I've got to go back and get my pack."

"If I'd told you this yesterday, then I would have had to listen to you complain for two damn days."

61

"It'll be fun, McKenna. We'll get to camp out. I'll meet you at the stables." Matt left them with a wave and Chris again glared at Roger.

"Thanks a lot," she said dryly.

"I didn't want Matt out alone that far and Robert is . . . well Robert's allergic to horses or something," Roger explained.

"Robert Hatcher is about as worthless as they come, Roger. Matt works his butt off around here and Hatcher sits on his ass acting all important-like in the office, ordering the maintenance guys around like he's the boss. And Matt's been here three goddamn years longer. Hell, I do more around here than Hatcher and I'm SAR."

"Calm down, McKenna. Hell, I know he's worthless, you think I'm blind."

"Then why does he get away with it?" she demanded.

"It's just politics, McKenna. His daddy is some big shot in Washington and his grandfather was some big shot with the department back in his day and that's just the way it goes. Besides, Hatcher moves around a lot. Every couple of years, he requests a transfer, so I figure we'll make it as unpleasant as possible for him and he'll move on and then we can get someone else. Maybe get Bobby hired on."

"Well that's the best news I've heard. Bobby is much more than a volunteer around here."

"Yes, I know. And we take advantage of his willingness to help but that's partly his fault, too."

Chris stood and fished a couple bills out of her pocket, pausing long enough to steal a mouthful of hash browns from Roger's plate.

"Gotta keep up my strength." Then she winked. "See you later. I'll radio when we hook up with the hikers."

"Yeah. And McKenna, I wanted to tell you how much I appreciate everything you do. I warned you your SAR duties would be limited and I'd have you helping out all over the place."

"Roger, I love the quiet here. I wouldn't trade it for Yosemite even if you had me cleaning bathrooms."

"Well, as long as we still have a budget for maintenance, I'll keep you out of the bathrooms. Now get going. Don't keep Matt waiting."

Chris drove back to her cabin to get her pack. She always kept it loaded and ready to go, just in case. She added a couple more freeze-dried dinners and filled the water bottles. Anytime she went out on the South Rim Trail, she packed enough for several nights. Rummaging in the fridge, she found an apple that was salvageable and some cheese. She grabbed a package of crackers. It would have to do.

"Sorry, fella, but you're on your own," she said to Dillon. She filled his food bowl up and scratched under his chin for a second. "Don't eat it all the first day."

Ten minutes later, she was saddling her horse while Matt checked the charge on their radios.

Jessie sat on her porch that evening, listening for the owls. She had not heard the piano music since that first night and she wondered why. As she filled her wineglass again, she thought of Annie. She had been putting it off, she knew. It was the reason she had come here in the first place, to see Annie. Not to hike the trails and meet new people and pretend she was on vacation. She knew Dr. Davies was right. If she was to ever find peace in her life, she would have to talk it out with Annie, get some things off her chest, find the closure to that chapter of her life and attempt to make a life of her own after all these years. Dr. Davies had said she could call if she needed. At the time, it sounded like a great idea and something to fall back on should things get rough. But she felt fine, really. Even the prospect of seeing Annie was not nearly as frightening as it had been. Maybe she would stop seeing Dr. Davies. Maybe she would feel like a whole new person when this was all over with.

She looked to the sky, still pleasantly surprised to be able to see the stars. It had been too many years of searching for them from her apartment balcony for the stars to be familiar to her now. As her eyes scanned the sky, she thought of McKenna and wondered where she lived. And with whom. She unexpectedly thought of her father then, remembering all the evenings he would be called away to look for a lost hiker, the days before search and rescue. She would beg him to let her go along, but he always made her stay, saying one lost hiker was enough. Of course, she knew the trails better than he did.

McKenna? Why did the woman intrigue her so? Perhaps because she had so blatantly ignored Jessie's attempts at seduction. Few women said no. In fact, Jessie couldn't remember the last. Well, she had never been one to pass up a challenge.

Chris and Matt sat around the campfire eating their instant dinners and drinking coffee. Their horses were tied nearby and their tents glowed in the dim light, a backdrop for their shadows that danced in the red embers each time the wind blew.

She felt him watching her but she ignored him, poking instead into the fire. She really did like him and wanted nothing more than for them to be friends. And maybe she was reading too much into it. First Bobby, now Roger telling her that Matt wanted more than friendship, she took everything to mean more than it was. Maybe Matt simply enjoyed her company as much as she did his.

"Can I ask you something, McKenna?"

"Of course." Here it comes, she thought.

"Well, I need some advice. On women," he added.

She cleared her throat. "On women?"

"Well, I mean, you are one and you date them, right?"

It was with difficulty that she swallowed the coffee she had just sipped. Again she cleared her throat. "Well, I do know women, yes."

"It's Donna, at the Rock," he explained. "I mean, I've been here four years now. I've always liked her but she treats me like her pal. You know, like you and me."

Chris nodded, thinking how very ironic this conversation was turning out.

"I've seen her through a terrible marriage and now a divorce and still, she talks to me as if we're just buddies."

"But you're attracted to her?" Chris asked.

"Yeah. I mean, surely she knows. I talk to her all the time."

"Matt, you talk to everyone all the time. I've been to the Rock with you. You make the rounds, you know nearly everyone there, why would she think she's special?"

"I've stayed there past closing before, just talking with her. She's confided in me, I've confided in her. I mean, we are friends, but I want it to progress to the next level and I don't think she knows that."

"Matt, it is very rare for men and women to be friends. I mean, especially straight men and women. And it's just because there is always that sexual undertone lurking. Maybe she's felt safe with you, because she didn't think you were interested in her that way and she's allowed a friendship to build between you. Maybe she sees you treating her the same way you treat everyone. As friends. Maybe she sees you there with me and thinks something's up with us. Who knows?"

He shook his head. "No, McKenna, everyone knows which way you lean."

Chris stared at him. "Everyone? It's not like I have a girlfriend or anything."

"Can we deal with me first?" he asked.

She laughed then and he joined in and she felt herself really relaxing around him for the first time.

"You know, Matt, I really like you. I was actually afraid you wanted . . . well, that you thought we could be more than friends."

"Oh, come on, McKenna, surely you didn't buy into Bobby's matchmaking?"

"No, of course not," she lied. "It's just that we've never talked about it, you know. And I do like going to the Rock and having a beer with you and not having to worry about anything."

"Me, too." Then he nudged her shoulder. "But back to my problem. How should I approach this with Donna?"

Chris laughed, relieved that they finally had everything out in the open. "I would probably invite her over to my place for dinner, which I have elegantly prepared myself. A nice bottle of wine, maybe fresh flowers on the table, some quiet music. But don't lose what's brought you together in the first place." At his raised eyebrows, she continued. "Your friendship. If it's a nice evening, you might sit outside and just talk. Don't leap directly from friendship to dating, Matt. Make it subtle. Let her know that things don't have to change between you just because you start dating. And don't rush things. Have a nice dinner and when it's time to end things, a soft kiss, just to let her know that it wasn't just two buddies having dinner."

"What if she doesn't want me to kiss her? I mean, what if she really only does want a friendship?"

Chris shrugged. "Maybe she's not thought of the possibility of anything else. It may take her time to readjust her feelings, Matt. Like I said, don't rush things. Start doing things together, outside of meeting at the Rock, just the two of you. Get to know each other on another level."

"You know, all of this sounds really good, but I'm not exactly a great cook," he said. "I may run her off just by preparing the meal."

"I'd offer to help, but if I could cook, I wouldn't spend damn near every night eating Dave's crap."

Matt was silent for a moment, then looked up and waited until Chris looked at him. "You know, Hatcher's been talking to her a lot lately. He never paid her the time of day before, but it's like he knows I'm interested so he's making this some kind of competition."

"Hatcher is a bastard. And people around here know it. I wouldn't worry about him, Matt."

"Yeah, but women just fall all over him."

"Hell, you look at him from a distance and he's gorgeous. I'll be the first to admit he's one of the most handsome men I've ever met. But you get close and look into his eyes and they're just empty. And then you get to know him and find out what a bastard he is and you really know the meaning of 'beauty is only skin deep.'"

"You're probably right."

"Can you name one person around here who he's friends with?"

Matt shook his head. "No. He usually eats alone when he comes to the Rock. Other than flirting with the women there, he doesn't really talk to anyone."

Chris slapped his shoulder once. "Right. So don't worry about him, will you?"

They sat in silence awhile longer, one of them occasionally stirring the fire but they were both lost in thought. Chris let her mind drift to Jessie Stone, wondering what she was doing tonight. Sitting alone in her cabin, thinking of her father, no doubt. Or Annie. Why did she really come back here?

It was early afternoon the next day when they came upon the backpackers. The two groups had joined up and all were accounted for. The only problem was an annoying blister one of the women had developed and Chris offered to wrap it for her. Matt radioed Roger and they headed back, leaving the backpackers to finish their hike alone, but only after Matt had sufficiently teased Chris. The woman with the blister was a cutie and she had scribbled her name and phone number down and shyly slipped it into Chris's pocket.

At twilight, they were still some six miles from the trailhead, so they camped again, this time near the creek. They fell asleep listening to the water softly tumble over the rocks and down into the canyon. Chris thought it was the most peaceful night's sleep she'd had in weeks.

They took their time over breakfast the next morning, making it back to the station by noon. She and Matt gladly accepted Roger's offer of an afternoon off, even though the weekend crowds were starting to come into town.

"Ellen's cooking tonight. Why don't you come over?" Roger offered.

"No, thanks. I think I'll stay in and keep Dillon company. Maybe next time."

Chris was tired after two days on horseback and two nights sleeping on the ground. She took a long, hot shower and for the first time, wished there was still a tub. A long soak would do wonders. She was drying off when her cell phone rang and she walked naked into the kitchen to answer.

"McKenna," she said.

"It's Annie. I missed you last night."

"Oh, Annie, I completely forgot. We were out on the South Rim the last two nights. I just got back today."

"Is everything okay? Anyone hurt?"

"No, no. We were just checking on some backpackers coming from Tahoe." She changed ears as she walked back into the bathroom to finish drying off. "Listen, can we make it tonight?"

"Of course. As long as you don't mind leftovers."

"Annie, your leftovers are better than my cooking any day," she said. "I'll be there at six."

Chris hoped Annie didn't bring up Jessie tonight. If there was one person Chris wanted to tell about Jessie being in town, it was Annie. She parked in her usual spot under the juniper and went inside after a brief knock. She had been joining Annie for dinner at least once a week, sometimes twice, ever since Roger had introduced them. She looked forward to their visits and the chance to eat a good vegetarian meal that was something other than Dave's surprises or her own pitiful attempt at cooking.

"Chris, I'm back here."

Chris now knew that was her studio. Annie had two walls knocked out of a corner room and glass installed and it offered her great views of the mountains and trees around her home. She did most of her painting there. Chris made her way back, exclaiming over how much Annie had finished in the last week.

"You're almost done," she said, inspecting the painting Annie was working on. It was of Sierra Peak, the most prominent landmark in the area. It was to be a gift for her.

"Not quite. A few more days, perhaps."

"It's beautiful, Annie." Annie told her that she had never given one of her paintings away and Chris was honored to be the first.

"Thank you, Chris, but I sometimes wonder at your judgment. You like the one I did of the elk and we both know they look more like cattle than elk," she said and they both laughed.

Before dinner, they took their wine to the back deck and watched the squirrels. Annie asked about the backpackers and Chris rattled on, bringing Annie up to date with the happenings in town, all the while keeping Jessie's name at bay. It wasn't until after dinner that Annie brought her up.

"I got my monthly newsletter from the book club and Jessie will have a new one out by Christmas."

"Really?"

"This will be number seven, by my count."

"I've only read four," Chris said.

They were quiet for a moment, then Annie said, "You know, sometimes I have half a mind to just call her up. If I thought it would do any good, I would. But I'm sure she's working through sixteen years of built-up hatred. Maybe if I ever get one of her books where the mother doesn't die, I might take a chance."

"I wish you could, too, Annie. It shouldn't be this way between families."

"What about your own? You've never mentioned them."

Chris grinned. "We don't exactly speak."

"And you're giving me advice? Shame on you."

Chapter Twelve

On her way to the Rock the next morning, Chris again passed Jessie jogging and again she stopped.

"Where have you been?" Jessie demanded as she leaned on the Jeep's door.

"South Rim Trail, in the backcountry."

"Searching for?" Jessie prompted, a grin slashing across her face.

"Backpackers."

"Find them?"

"Of course." Chris thought Jessie was much prettier than her picture revealed, if that were possible. Her eyes weren't quite as lifeless in person.

"You're not working today, are you?"

"Yep."

"It's Saturday."

"My turn," Chris explained.

Jessie nodded. "Where will you be?"

"I'm in the office this morning. Then I'll just be making the rounds, probably end up at Lake Trail this afternoon."

"Maybe I'll see you there, McKenna. I've been wanting to get in a little fishing."

With that she ran on and Chris watched, her eyes lighting on the back of muscled thighs. She finally realized she was still sitting in the middle of the road and she drove off, honking once as she passed Jessie.

After a quick lunch of cheese and crackers, Chris filled her water bottle and headed out to Lake Trail. The ranger station had been busy that morning and she knew that Lake Trail was the easiest and therefore, would be the most crowded. The cabins were full for the weekend, as was the lodge. Bill and Peggy had rented out all of their bikes and the dirt roads around town were crowded with hikers and mountain bikers alike. The beautiful late summer weather contin ued, bringing with it people from the city yearning for the outdoors. She stopped at the trailhead, glancing at the sign-in sheet. Six people in one group; there goes the wildlife, she thought. Another two; bird watchers. They should've started earlier. A group of four, two of them kids. Jennifer Parker. Chris smiled and looked up. Fishing? Two other names were listed below, but Chris scarcely noticed as she closed the lid and headed off down the trail. She hadn't expected Jessie to be here already. She had planned on making Lake Trail her last stop but because of the crowd, she thought she better make a quick run through before heading out to Fire Lookout.

It was almost a half-mile to the lake, then the trail followed the shore and connected back to the start, about two miles total. The Lake Trail cutoff, which hooked up with Ridge Trail, was about a mile into the hike. She walked briskly, coming upon an older couple with a poodle on a leash. She nodded and smiled, then barely got out of the way as the poodle decided to attack. She rolled her eyes as the couple pulled the barking poodle down the trail, disrupting the quiet of the lake for miles around.

Chris kept an eye out along the shore. She spotted Jessie at the first turn, standing by herself out on the point, expertly casting a fly rod. She watched for several minutes before walking up.

"Any luck?"

Jessie turned around and smiled. "Hi, McKenna. I'm afraid not. And I was hoping for fresh trout for my dinner."

"Then the luck's all with the fish," Chris said.

"And here I was going to invite you to dinner."

Chris laughed. "Please don't kill one on my account."

Jessie cocked her head and frowned. "Don't like fish?"

Chris shook her head. "I'm more of a vegetable person."

"Good Lord, a vegetarian? I thought I left them all behind in the city," she said.

"I manage."

"So, you want to come?" Jessie asked.

"Come where?"

"Dinner?"

"Where?"

"Cabin seven," Jessie said, her back still to Chris.

"Henninger's?"

"Yes."

"Okay."

"Six-thirty?"

Chris looked around at the crowds and shook her head. "Seven?"

"Fine. I'll have the first glass of wine without you."

Jessie turned around and their eyes met for a moment, then Chris motioned to the trail with a quick toss of her head.

"Better go."

"McKenna?"

Chris stopped and looked back. "Yeah?"

"What's your first name?" Jessie asked, again capturing her eyes.

"Chris."

Jessie nodded. "I like it." Then she turned back to her fly fishing, leaving Chris staring after her.

It took Chris longer than normal to make the loop as she stopped several times to answer questions and offer suggestions on other hiking trails. She stopped on her way past the point, but Jessie was already gone. At the trailhead, Jessie had signed out just like she was supposed to. Chris laughed at her comment. "No fish died today!"

Chris ran into Bobby later and sent him on Ridge Trail as she took the route up Fire Lookout Trail. There was a large group at the top, all enjoying the view without the benefit of the tower. Since the incident this summer with the two boys, Roger had the steps taken down and new warning signs put up, and they'd not had a bit of trouble.

She spent a little time up at the top, answering questions and just enjoying the views herself before heading back down the mountain, using the shortcut Bobby had shown her.

It wasn't until she was driving home that she realized she had intentionally put Jessie Stone from her mind. She tried to ask herself why exactly she was going to dinner with her, and she had no answer other than she found Jessie attractive and she would be the first to admit that she was extremely curious about this woman's life. And her sudden return to Sierra City. But she just couldn't shake the feeling that she was betraying Annie somehow.

After her shower, she took time to relax on the deck with a cold beer. It had been a busy day and she was feeling the effects of her afternoon hikes. Dillon was attempting to sneak up on a squirrel and she watched him for a moment. Then her eyes traveled on into the woods, thinking it would be so much quicker just to walk to Jessie's cabin. But more polite to drive. It wasn't as if they knew each other well enough for such informal visits.

At a quarter to seven, she picked out one of her few remaining bottles of wine and with a quick pat on Dillon's head, was gone. She drove slowly, enjoying the evening. The days were getting shorter, she noted. And cooler. Wouldn't be long before the snows came and she would trade her hiking boots for snowshoes and skis.

She enjoyed the winter, if only because it allowed a slowdown from the hectic summer. Of course, search and rescue took on a whole new meaning in the snow. And instead of quiet nights on the deck, she would spend quiet evenings in front of the fire.

She found Jessie's cabin without difficulty and parked next to the rental car. She had a long-sleeved T-shirt tucked into jeans and had opted for white athletic shoes instead of her usual hiking boots. She knocked on the door and waited until she heard Jessie call for her.

"I'm back here."

Chris grinned. How many times had she heard Annie yell out those very words to her? She was standing in the kitchen counting the bottles of wine on the counter when Jessie came in from the deck. Eleven bottles. Seems she and Annie had something else in common.

"You certainly didn't have to bring anything," Jessie said. "Least of all wine." She smiled warmly at Chris. "I'm glad you came."

"Thanks for asking. There aren't a lot of opportunities for dinner out around here."

"Well, here, let me pour you a glass of wine. Or would you rather have something else?" Jessie offered.

"Wine's okay."

"And you can take your bottle back with you. I think I have plenty."

Chris followed Jessie onto the deck. Two wooden chairs, identical to her own, were waiting and she sat, stretching her legs out.

"Nice evening, isn't it?"

"Yes. Nice," Chris agreed. "It was a busy day. This time of year, everyone is trying to cram in as many weekends as possible before winter."

"Have you been here long?" Jessie asked.

"Just since summer. I transferred from Yosemite when they opened up a full-time SAR here . . . ah, search and rescue," Chris clarified.

"So I guess you are pretty much on your own then."

"Well, I've known the manager here, Roger Hamilton, for years."

Chris did not miss the surprised look that crossed Jessie's face and she had to stop herself from tossing out Annie's name as well. If for no other reason, Jessie was still Jennifer Parker to her.

"How nice," Jessie murmured.

They sat in silence, both looking out towards the woods, lost in thought. Before long, the owls started calling and Jessie smiled.

"There," she said softly. "Every night I wait for them."

Chris laughed quietly. "So does Dillon."

"Who?"

"My cat. He's terrified of them. He sits in the window while I'm on the deck and his eyes get so big every time they call. I think he's afraid they're going to swoop down and carry him away."

Jessie frowned at her words. "Where do you live?"

Chris pointed towards the trees. "Number eight."

"You're kidding?" Jessie laughed, then nodded. "So, you're the one that likes piano music?"

"Sorry. It relaxes me after a busy day. I didn't realize it carried this far."

"No, it's okay. I liked it."

They sat there with the dark approaching, not speaking, just listening to the quiet. Chris wondered at Jessie's subdued demeanor this evening. She was being polite and friendly, but the teasing, flirting woman Chris had first met was absent. Chris wondered if the mention of Roger's name had thrown Jessie into a tailspin. Chris was about to speak when the timer on the oven disturbed the silence.

"Good. I'm starving," Jessie said.

She got up, leaving Chris to follow. Jessie's empty wineglass stood on the counter and Chris filled both hers and Jessie's and carried them to the table.

"I had to really put an effort into dinner, you know. I've never cooked for a vegetarian before."

"Can't be that hard," Chris said.

Jessie laughed. "You don't cook, do you, McKenna?"

"Not much, no."

"How do you make it out here without cooking? It's not like there are fine restaurants on every corner."

"Well, I eat an awful lot of pasta."

Jessie laughed again. "Guess what's for dinner?"

Chris sat while Jessie lit a candle and placed it between them. A plate of steaming pasta and vegetable casserole followed. Chris bent over her plate and inhaled, smiling as the scent of garlic reached her nose.

"Garlic," Jessie said unnecessarily. "It's on the bread, too, so I hope you don't have a hot date after dinner. You'll run them off."

"A date? In Sierra City?" Chris chuckled. "Not hardly."

"Oh, surely there are lots of eligible . . . people here."

Chris noticed the hesitation and took her cue. "A few eligible men, yes. But if I desire female company, I have to go to Sacramento."

"And do you?"

"Go to Sacramento?"

"Desire female company?"

Chris grinned. "On occasion, I do both."

Their eyes held for a moment and just when Chris saw Jessie's dark eyes begin to soften, Jessie pulled them away, instead motioning to Chris's plate.

"Well? What do you think?"

Chris took a bite and grinned. "Mmm. Excellent."

"Good."

Chris broke into the garlic bread, tearing off a piece as butter ran down her fingers. Without thinking, she brought her hand to her mouth, licking the butter off a knuckle. She looked up and found Jessie watching. Their eyes locked again for a brief second and this time it was Chris who pulled away.

Apparently all those nights of reading J. T. Stone's books and fantasizing over her picture on the back had caught up with her. For the first time since meeting Jessie Stone, Chris had permitted her attraction to a damn picture to surface. As she had told herself on numerous occasions, Jessie Stone was no woman she wanted to get involved with. Having hot uninhibited sex, now that was another matter.

Chris blushed at her thoughts and shoved another bite into her mouth. Perhaps on her next weekend off, she would go into Sacramento and hit the bars and try to curb her suddenly aroused libido.

She fished for something to get the conversation flowing and decided to get a little personal. Maybe she could find out something about Jessie's personal life, something she might be able to share with Annie.

"Where are you from, Jennifer?"

Jessie looked up, apparently surprised at the question or maybe the name, Chris wasn't sure which.

"New York City," she finally said. "I'll be here another week or so."

"Well, you're a long way from the East Coast. Just vacationing or did you come to California on business?" Even to her own ears, the question sounded forced.

"I'm sort of between jobs," Jessie offered.

Chris nodded. "Do you like it here?"

"Very much. I jog Elk Meadow every morning. I've been to Ridge Trail and now Lake Trail," she said. "It's been very relaxing."

On impulse and quite without thinking, Chris heard herself speak.

"I'm off tomorrow and Monday. I was thinking of hiking into the backcountry and camping out. I would love company."

Jessie put her elbows on the table and cradled her chin.

"That sounds like fun. Are you sure you're up to babysitting a city girl out there?"

"I may be wrong, but you hardly look like a city girl. I've seen you out there, remember. Fly fishing?"

Jessie shrugged. "Anyone can take lessons." Then she leaned closer. "Maybe I was trying to impress you."

"And you certainly did." As their eyes held, Chris felt herself drifting into dangerous territory. If it were a game of seduction they were about to play, Chris would most definitely lose. Even now, she felt herself sinking deeper into the dark depths of Jessie's eyes.

It was with difficulty that she pulled away. One deep breath and a sip of wine later, Chris was able to again focus. "So, camping? You up for it?"

Jessie visibly relaxed, leaning back in her chair and twirling her wineglass slowly between her fingers. Chris relaxed, too and moved far enough away from the table to rest her ankle across one knee.

"I don't have a backpack or sleeping bag," Jessie said.

"I have a small pack you can borrow. And a sleeping bag, I'm sure I can round one up."

"In the morning? Early?"

"Well, not at the crack of dawn, but we should be on the trails by nine o'clock. The place I'm thinking of is about a six-hour hike. That'll give us time to set up camp and explore around a bit before dark."

Jessie smiled, excitement showing in her dark eyes. "Sounds like fun. Where should I meet you?"

"I'll pick you up and we'll go to the trailhead from here. I'll bring the food. Nothing fancy, though. Freeze-dried."

Chris left before ten, after they had finished the wine but before they opened another bottle. It had been a pleasant evening, Chris admitted. And the prospect of a camping trip excited her. She fished between the seats and found her cell phone, quickly punching out Bobby's number at the lodge.

"Are you asleep?"

"McKenna? No. What's wrong?"

Chris laughed. Bobby was always on duty. "Nothing. I need a favor," she said.

"Oh? Need me to cover for you tomorrow?"

"I'm off tomorrow," she said.

"I didn't think you took your days off, McKenna. Roger says you're there practically every day."

"Maybe I haven't had anything else to do before. Now, I need a sleeping bag."

"Now?"

"First thing in the morning."

"Why?"

"Why do you think? To sleep in."

"You have one."

Chris sighed. She should have called Matt. She would be off the phone by now. "Maybe I'm taking a friend with me," she offered.

"Really? Who?"

"Jesus Christ, Bobby! Can I borrow the goddamned sleeping bag or not?"

"Okay, okay. Come by in the morning."

"Thank you."

She tossed the phone back between the seats. She would be lost up here without Bobby, but sometimes he could be a pain in the ass.

Jessie opened another bottle of wine anyway. She pulled on a sweatshirt and sat out on the deck, her eyes going immediately to the sky. The owls were no longer calling and it was very quiet, not even a hint of a breeze to stir the trees. The days were still warm but as the calendar marched through September, the nights warned of the winter to come. Jessie was almost sorry she wouldn't be here. She could envision nights by the fire while the snow fell outside.

She glanced to the trees, wondering if Chris had made it home. Jessie liked her. Liked her a lot. For the first time in many many years, she actually felt like she was forming a friendship with someone and she wasn't exactly sure how to proceed. Chris wasn't someone to be played with, that was for sure. Unfortunately, Jessie had made a career out of playing with people's feelings. She was very good at it. But Chris . . . she was different. If Jessie were the spiritual type, she would think that there was a reason for Chris's presence in her life. She had never let anyone in before, but she had a sudden urge to cleanse herself by pouring out all the sordid details of her life. And not to someone who was paid to listen to her. What would it be like to talk to a friend? To tell a friend about past hurts? To share the joy of her childhood? And the devastation of her father's death?

But she sighed. Not exactly a great start on a friendship, using an alias. And Chris knew Roger Hamilton. Now that was a name from the past. Had he been here all these years? If anyone were to recognize her, it would be Mr. Hamilton. Now she would definitely avoid the ranger station. The last thing she wanted was a stroll down memory lane with Roger Hamilton.

Chapter Thirteen

It was nearly ten by the time they signed in at the trailhead. Picking up the sleeping bag had taken longer than expected. Bobby had been full of questions and not in the least bit concerned with the time. Then, on impulse, Chris had stopped at Ellen's to pick up a freeze-dried dinner for Jessie. The meatless ones she had at her cabin weren't exactly her favorites anyway, so Chris thought it would be rude to subject a meat eater to them.

They headed up the mountain, taking the South Rim Trail. Jessie had packed lightly and the one change of clothes, jacket, and few toiletries easily fit into the small pack Chris had brought for her. They were dressed identically in shorts and T-shirts, both of their sweatshirts having been shed shortly after making the first steep hill on the trail.

Jessie was in excellent shape and kept pace with Chris almost effortlessly. She occasionally asked Chris the names of certain trees and shrubs, but mostly they talked of other hiking trips they had been on. Jessie admitted that she had not been in the woods since high school.

Chris raised her eyebrows questioningly.

"I'm thirty-three," Jessie said with a grin. "You?"

"The same." Hadn't Annie told her Jessie's birthday was in the fall? "When's your birthday?"

Jessie's lips twitched, then she finally grinned. "Soon."

"Soon?" Chris nodded. "In other words, none of my business?"

Jessie shrugged. She couldn't remember the last time she had actually acknowledged her birthday. It was a time her father had always made special for her. There was never a birthday cake from her mother, but her father would somehow produce one, throwing an impromptu party at the ranger station, balloons and all. October 10. It never failed to come around, but she wished she could forget. She had such happy memories of her childhood. Why was she always so sad when she thought of them?

"Hey."

"Hmm?"

"Okay?" Chris asked.

Jessie shrugged again. "Just thinking."

Chris nodded but said nothing. It would do no good for her to bring anything up now. Instead, she hiked on, leaving Jessie alone with her thoughts. Annie would absolutely kill her if she ever found out Jessie was here and Chris had kept it from her.

At twelve-thirty, they were getting close to timberline and the rim of the mountain. The views had changed dramatically. No longer were the spruce and pines blocking the surrounding mountain range. Now the terrain turned rugged. Large outcroppings of rocks littered the mountainside and Chris chose a flat one to sit. Jessie laid her pack next to Chris's and stretched her back before sitting on an adjacent rock.

"Lunch?"

"I'm starving," Jessie said. She took a deep breath, finally letting her eyes settle on the view. "God," she whispered. "It's beautiful."

Chris smiled and nodded. "Sure is." Then she pointed to her right. "There's a trail off of the South Rim that goes up a little higher and hits the ridge of the next mountain. You can see Lake Tahoe from there."

Jessie nodded, remembering. Her father had taken her up there once. It was a difficult hike for her at the time, but the view had been worth it.

Chris watched a range of emotions cross Jessie's face but said nothing. She still had no idea why Jessie was back in Sierra City, but maybe this little camping trip would make her open up some.

After their light lunch of cheese, crackers, and an apple, they hiked another three miles before Chris left the trail and followed a stream down a canyon a short ways.

"As a backpacker, you're never supposed to get off the trail," Chris said with a grin.

"But you know a spot?"

"A little flat area beside the stream, just before it cascades over the mountain as a waterfall. Great views from there."

Jessie nodded. She knew the exact spot. Another little secret that her father had shared with her.

"How did you find it?" she finally asked.

Chris shrugged and stopped, balancing on a boulder in the middle of the stream.

"I like to hike along the streams, hop rocks, get my feet wet," she said and laughed as she nearly fell in. "I love the sound of water," she added. "I just found it by accident, really."

"Tell anyone?"

"Are you kidding? Just you."

"Good."

Their eyes locked for a moment, both breaking into slow smiles. Then Jessie followed Chris along the rocks, laughing good-naturedly when she slipped and dunked one boot into the cold water up to her ankle.

They were silent as they followed the stream and before long, Chris loosened her pack and laid it away from the rocks in dry spruce needles. She motioned for Jessie to follow. They walked on, the roar of the falls making its presence known.

Jessie let her mind drift back, remembering the time her father had shown her this place. Their secret place, he had said. They would sneak off and make sure no one followed them, then pitch their tent where they could sit and watch the sun as it fell behind the horizon, listening to the sound of the falls. She wondered if Chris knew there was a trail going down to the falls. You could walk all the way down and stand behind the cascading water. Jessie remembered sticking her face into the cold spray, afraid she would be knocked down by its force, but her father had been there, holding her.

Chris watched Jessie now, saw the small smile touch her then disappear just as quickly. She wondered what it was Jessie was thinking of.

Jessie let out a sigh and shook herself, warding off . . . something. She finally let her eyes slip back to Chris and met her curious gaze.

"It's beautiful here."

Chris held her eyes a moment longer. For a second, Chris was certain those dark eyes had opened to her, revealed some deep truth. Then they closed again, the same mysterious dark gaze that Jessie normally fixed her with securely in place.

"Yeah. This is one of my favorite spots."

Chris walked to the edge where the stream sloped downward before disappearing over the side of the mountain and looked out over the distant canyons, the peaks rising up beyond them in the west. It was a clear afternoon, still warm for early September. The nights had been getting cooler, hinting of autumn, but the days remained warm and cloudless.

There was no sign of a previous campfire, no charred rocks to mark a spot and Jessie watched as Chris gathered some rocks now and cleared an area. One of the rocks that Chris picked up was black on the bottom. Apparently, Chris dismantled the fire ring when she left, leaving no sign that she had been there. Just like her father used to do. Jessie shrugged off the depression that threatened and went about gathering small twigs to start their fire. There was a fallen pine nearby and she broke off larger limbs and hauled them over to the fire ring, breaking them with her foot and stacking them neatly in a pile.

They set up the small tent and took out the sleeping bags, then Jessie surprised Chris by pulling a bottle of wine out of her backpack.

"You packed that?" Chris grinned. "Weren't too concerned about weight, were you?"

"And aren't you glad?" Jessie asked. "Or do you want to have coffee with your dinner?"

Chris laughed. "Tell you what. I'll share my tent if you share your wine."

"Hardly a fair trade, seeing as it's not raining." Jessie clutched the bottle to her chest and raised an eyebrow seductively. "You'll have to do better."

"Okay. I think I have a sleeping bag to bargain with."

Jessie seemed to consider this, her eyes raised into the trees. Then she looked back at Chris, her eyes twinkling with delight.

"Sleeping bag for half my wine? Okay, McKenna, I accept."

Chris nodded, enjoying the unexpected playfulness. By the look on Jessie's face, she was enjoying it too. They worked in silence again, Jessie breaking up sticks for the fire and Chris laying out the few cooking utensils and pots she had brought along.

"I think I'm going to hike the stream a bit," Chris said.

"Go ahead," Jessie said. "I brought a book." She pulled out a worn paperback and waved it at Chris. "I'll just sit and relax."

"Okay. I won't be gone long."

Chris walked back the way they had come, hopping across the rocks until she came to the trail. She crossed over and picked up the stream on the other side. She had been camping here twice before and both times had intended on exploring upstream but had ended up perched on a rock overlooking the falls and canyon. She thought this time she would leave the view and solitude to Jessie. She had lightened up since the first couple of encounters and Chris was beginning to enjoy her company. She wanted nothing more than to confront Jessie with her true identity, to talk about Annie, to find out why she was back, but Chris admitted that it really wasn't any of her business. And if Jessie wanted to be Jennifer Parker for a few days and escape from her real life, who was Chris to haul her back to reality?

She stopped after nearly a half-hour, the trees casting long shadows over the stream as the sun was sinking lower. If she were to catch the sunset, she would have to hurry.

She found Jessie leaning against a rock, book held opened in her lap, but she was looking out over the canyon.

"You're back," she said. She lazily moved her head to glance at Chris, a sleepy smile on her face.

"How's the book?"

Jessie shrugged. "One of those self-help books. Mostly bullshit," she said.

Chris laughed at the sincerity of Jessie's words.

"So you took a nap instead?"

Jessie grinned. "This crap always puts me to sleep." She motioned to the sky. "I was afraid you were going to miss the show."

"Of course not. That's why we're here."

The sun made its way over the ridge, far to the west, shooting oranges and reds their way. Jessie opened the bottle of wine and they each poured some in their drinking cups. They sat against the rock, quietly watching the sun fall from view, their eyes filling with the deep colors of sunset, the western sky aglow as a brilliant burgundy shot through the few low-hanging clouds before fading to a quiet pink. Overhead, the cedars and pines whispered their secrets as the wind caressed the branches and carried scented air into their faces.

Jessie couldn't imagine a sight more beautiful. The colors were even more splendid than she remembered and she shut her eyes for a moment, trying to forever burn it in her memory.

She felt Chris watching her even before she opened her eyes. A faint rosy haze remained where the sun had been only moments ago and she turned to Chris, their eyes locking in the last light a day.

"Beautiful," Jessie whispered

"Yes, very."

"Thank you for letting me share that with you."

Chris's smile was as soft and unhurried as the sunset had been and Jessie felt herself being pulled into those blue eyes. Unfamiliar feelings washed over her and she didn't know what to make of her rapidly beating pulse or the difficult time she had catching her breath. She let her eyes slip briefly to Chris's mouth, wondering if her lips were as soft as they looked.

Chris pulled her eyes away, silently acknowledging the growing attraction between them. She wondered if her attraction was simply a result of finally giving life to a picture on the back of a book. Chris still wasn't certain that she liked Jessie Stone, but she suspected she had yet to meet all of her.

She moved away, leaving Jessie staring after the long-gone sun. She started the fire easily, then put water on to boil for their dinner. With the dark came the chill of night and Chris moved into the tent, stripping off her shorts and pulling on an old, comfortable pair of sweats and bulky sweatshirt.

Jessie did the same, taking the small flashlight from Chris's hand. When she came out of the tent, she was holding up toilet paper.

"Gonna take a trip to the woods," Jessie said shyly.

Chris nodded. "Don't go far."

"Don't worry. If you hear me scream . . ."

"I'll come running," Chris assured her. She watched the light flash into the woods as Jessie disappeared behind a spruce. A short time later, Jessie came back, discreetly tossing her toilet paper into the fire.

"Much better," she said.

Chris watched as Jessie sat cross-legged on the ground close to the fire. She added more wine to each of their cups and handed one up to Chris.

"Thanks."

They ate dinner in relative silence, sharing thoughts occasionally, but mostly content to listen to the crackle of the fire and the sounds of the forest as it came alive after dark.

Jessie washed up their few dishes in the stream and Chris got the fire going again, adding some of the larger limbs Jessie had collected earlier. They sat down across from each other, with the leaping flames the only barrier between them. Jessie held up the wine bottle.

"Enough for one more each, I think."

"It was an excellent idea," Chris said. "Not exactly practical," she added.

Jessie waved her off. "Backpackers have too many rules. A quick up and down trip, there's absolutely no reason a good bottle of wine can't be brought along."

"Had you been packing in the equipment, you might not have wanted the extra weight."

Jessie leaned forward. "But I wasn't. That's what I brought you along for."

Chris laughed. Jessie's eyes sparkled across from her. Maybe that was why her next words nearly caused Chris to choke.

"You're extremely cute, McKenna. You know that, right?"

"Cute?"

"Extremely cute," Jessie corrected.

"Well, I . . . thanks," Chris stammered, hoping Jessie could not see her blush.

"Not beautiful or anything like that, McKenna. I don't want you to get a big head," she teased.

"I'll try to keep the swelling down," Chris murmured.

Jessie let her gaze slide from Chris into the fire. Maybe a pick-up line in another life, but she meant it sincerely now. Not only did she find Chris attractive, she liked her. And she couldn't remember the last time she had thought that about another person. She covered the smile on her face with her hand, amused at her own thoughts. She could pick up a stranger in a bar in two minutes and be inside her panties in five. She had practically hit Chris over the head and still she showed no interest in Jessie at all.

Well, that wasn't entirely true. Chris's blue eyes weren't exactly expressionless and Jessie knew when another woman found her attractive. She just wasn't used to the wariness that Chris showed. Didn't matter anyway. Why ruin what was turning out to be an interesting friendship? A friendship might be something they could carry with them. Anything else, and Jessie would run.

"Ah . . . Jennifer?"

Jennifer? Jessie mentally shook herself. When you used an alias, it helped if you remembered the name.

"How long are you going to be vacationing here?"

Jessie shrugged. She should just tell Chris the truth. She didn't know why she was using a damn alias anyway. If her purpose was to see Annie, what did she care if anyone noticed?

Chris watched the questions fly across Jessie's face, wondering what decision she was coming to, what lie she would tell Chris next.

"Like I said, I'm between jobs, so I'm not really in a hurry. I haven't decided yet."

Chris nodded and held Jessie's eyes in the firelight. She dared her to look away.

"Tell me about yourself," Chris suggested.

"Why?"

"Because I want to know."

"Just like that?" Jessie gave a nervous laugh. "Just because you want to know, I'm supposed to tell you?"

Chris leaned forward, still holding Jessie's eyes captive.

"Yes."

The silence continued as Jessie felt words form and threaten to spill. She fought with herself over what to tell Chris, if anything. It would be so much simpler to pretend to be Jennifer Parker who was between jobs, and not some deranged author named J. T. Stone.

Chris watched Jessie's face, saw the shadows cross it in the soft light of the fire. She could let it go, she knew, but she sensed Jessie's need to talk, even if Jessie didn't. And besides, she'd had quite enough of Jennifer Parker.

"Tell me . . . Jessie," she whispered.

Jessie drew a sharp breath. Had she been standing, she was certain her legs would have failed her.

"How . . . how did you know?"

Chris gave a half smile. "I have your books."

"Fuck," Jessie said. "Well, I feel foolish."

"You could tell me you're just a celebrity looking for privacy, thus the name change," Chris suggested.

Jessie laughed. "Hardly a celebrity."

Chris added a couple of logs to the fire while she allowed Jessie to collect herself. Now it was her turn to keep secrets. Jessie had no need to know that she and Annie were friends. No need to know that Chris already knew everything about her childhood.

"I grew up around here," Jessie admitted after taking a deep breath. "A lifetime ago."

"Tell me."

"Even if I wanted to talk about it, I wouldn't know where to begin," Jessie said.

"Why don't you want to talk about it?"

Jessie leaned forward. "There are some things you just don't talk about."

"Why?"

"Why? What kind of question is that? I hate that word."

"Okay. No questions, then. Tell me about your life when you lived here."

Jessie grinned. "Why?"

It was Chris's turn to lean forward. "Why? I hate that word." She nudged Jessie with her shoulder. "Tell me about growing up here. Please?"

Jessie gave a small laugh, finally giving in. "Okay. Fine." Jessie stared into the fire, remembering. "I had a lovely childhood. As seen through the eyes of a child, anyway. It was pretty pathetic when I think about it now. I grew up out here in the mountains and my father took me everywhere. He was a ranger right here in Sierra City," she explained. "He took me camping and hiking and fishing. Everywhere he went, I tagged along. I was happy."

"What about your mother?" Chris asked.

"I had a mother in name only," Jessie said bitterly.

"What do you mean?"

"She lived in the same house as us, but she was like a stranger. We didn't talk, really. She and Jack didn't exactly have the ideal marriage. She wouldn't even share a bedroom with him. They seldom spoke to one another."

"Jack? You always call him that?"

Jessie shrugged. "He didn't like me calling him Dad."

Chris raised an eyebrow, but said nothing.

"I . . . worshiped him. He was my best friend. My only friend. I went everywhere with him, did everything with him." Jessie looked through the fire at Chris. "He died when I was still here. Seventeen."

"I'm sorry," Chris murmured.

Jessie shrugged again. "A long time ago. I left shortly after he died. I couldn't stand being here with her." Jessie stared into the fire, remembering. "I went to San Francisco, got a job, started college. Writing was just an outlet at the beginning. I never thought I'd actually make a living at it."

"So you're here . . . visiting?"

Jessie laughed. "Hardly. My therapist says I've got unresolved issues that I need to work through."

"And are you?"

Jessie smiled. "Working through them? Not yet."

Chris pressed on. "So you're not here visiting . . . you're just what? Going back in time?"

"She's still here," Jessie said quietly.

Chris said nothing. It was the most difficult thing she could remember doing, but she kept her words to herself.

"I'm a good listener," she offered instead.

Jessie gave a small laugh. "I've paid a fortune over the years and here you are offering a freebie."

"Still an offer."

Jessie let out a heavy sigh. The rehearsed words she'd said over and over again in therapists' offices wouldn't come. Instead, she said something she'd not yet put words to herself.

"I'm scared to be here."

"Scared?"

"Terrified. I didn't even realize it until now," she said quietly, her words taken away with the breeze.

Chris moved around the fire and sat next to Jessie, their knees touching lightly as she settled beside her. Jessie's amused smile and quick nudge with her shoulder surprised her.

"I'm not scared of the dark, McKenna."

"I just . . ."

Jessie's hand reached out and squeezed Chris's thigh.

"No. Stay."

Chris relaxed, trying to ignore the burning of her skin where Jessie's hand still rested. "What are you scared of?"

Jessie searched the blue eyes across from her. She saw understanding, compassion, concern. Things she wasn't used to seeing. Not even when she paid for it.

"I don't know what it is. I feel like there's something here, something watching me maybe. I don't know," Jessie said, her voice turning almost to a whisper.

"Let's talk, then," Chris suggested. "Your therapist told you to come back. It's been what? Sixteen years you said? Why now?"

"To see her. Annie Stone."

"Your mother," Chris stated.

"She gave birth to me," Jessie said. "She was never my mother."

Chris had to bite her lower lip to keep her words to herself. She knew that soon, she would be getting in over her head.

"You said you did everything with your father but nothing with her," Chris prompted.

"For as long as I can remember, it was always him. I mean, Chris, I have no memories of her at all, other than just this figure in the house. As a kid, it was just him. Hiking, camping, dinner. Everything was with him."

"As a kid? What about when you got older?"

"Older?"

"Yeah. Like a teenager."

Jessie stared into the fire, trying to remember. Her memories were always so vivid, like it was only yesterday. But in her memories, she was always a child.

Did they still camp? Fish? Had she still followed him around? She must have. So why couldn't she remember?

"Jessie?"

"I don't . . . I don't remember," she whispered. "I can tell you about my eighth birthday. My ninth." She rubbed her eyes, a headache suddenly forming. "I remember . . . I remember camping. We would hike for miles, it seemed. I was always so tired when we got back. I remember riding my bike from the house to the ranger station, I must have been all of ten."

"And at that age, your mother just let you do as you please?"

Jessie laugh was bitter, short. "Let me? Like I asked her? Chris, she wasn't a part of my life. She was just this silent figure in the house. She never really talked to me, you know."

"Did you talk to her?"

Jessie thought back, trying to remember a time they had actually talked about something tangible. The few times Annie had tried to discipline her, teach her something, Jessie had simply run to her father and that was that.

"I just remember silence. There was always a feeling of resentment there," Jessie said.

Chris frowned. "Resentment? By your mother? Or you?"

Resentment by Annie, of course, Jessie was about to say. But . . . why did Jessie carry that feeling with her all these years? Yes, she resented her mother . . . Annie. But why? For not being a mother?

"I've always blamed her for his death."

"Why?"

"He fell off of Ridge Trail into the canyon."

"Why do you blame her?" Chris prompted.

Jessie sighed. She was getting weary of this discussion. Chris's questions were becoming too much like Dr. Davies's questions and soon Jessie would revert to the practiced lies she'd told all her therapists over the years. It was just so much easier than delving into the truth. A rotten truth, she suspected.

"Jessie?"

"I'm tired. How about a walk? The moon's nearly full."

Chris nodded, instinctively knowing that Jessie had reached her limit for the night. "Sure. We can walk back along the stream, might see some wildlife."

Jessie grinned. "As long as it's not something that'll want to eat us."

"Have no fear . . . SAR is here," Chris teased.

Jessie took Chris's offered hand and let herself be pulled to her feet. She didn't release the warm hand holding her own. Instead, she leaned closer.

"Well, I feel completely safe now."

The sudden jolt of desire caught Chris completely off guard. Jessie was too near, her lips far too tempting in the moonlight. Only inches separated them and Chris fought with herself to close the gap, to take what was obviously being offered.

Jessie captured Chris's eyes, watching as warring emotions crossed her face. It would be so easy, she thought. Just a little more temptation, a little more teasing. Then what? Another conquest?

Jessie finally pulled her eyes away. She didn't want a conquest tonight. Instead, she squeezed Chris's hand and smiled gently.

"Come on, McKenna. Show me the sights."

It was with difficulty that Chris dropped the warm hand clasping her own. She broke up the fire, then brushed away any pine needles that were too close. The embers would catch easily enough when they returned. Then she rummaged in her pack and found the small flashlight. She shoved it into the front pocket of her sweats before motioning with a slight toss of her head.

"Let's go."

They walked in silence as moonlight bounced off the water, enough so that Chris could forgo the flashlight. They followed the stream until they met up with the trail.

"We can hike up the trail," Chris suggested. "There's an overlook not too far from here. Ought to be pretty with the moon shining over the mountains."

"McKenna, I meant to tell you this earlier," Jessie said as she followed Chris. "There's a trail not far from the tent, it goes along the ledge and ends up behind the waterfall."

Chris stopped short. "You're joking?"

Jessie shook her head. "We camped up there before. Jack took me behind the falls."

"I've walked all around there. I've never seen anything resembling a trail," Chris said.

"It was hard to find, I remember. You have to squeeze between two boulders and you think you're going right over the side of the mountain, but there's a ledge there and the trail snakes down, right behind the falls."

"Maybe we'll look for it in the morning. Any more secrets you want to share?"

Jessie grinned. "You found the caves yet?"

"Caves? What caves?"

"Guess not."

"Roger's not said anything about caves, Jessie."

"Roger Hamilton may not know about them. They were already closed to the public when my father started working here. He took me there many times," Jessie said. "Not any big deal, McKenna."

"Where are they?"

"I'm surprised you haven't found them, as much as you like to hike the streams."

"Quit teasing me. Where are they?" she asked again.

"After you meet up with the Nevada Trail, past the South Rim, you cross that little creek. At least, it used to be little."

"It still is. Little Bear Creek. You can hop across it."

"That's the one. Follow it upstream into the mountains, only about a mile, I think. You come to a really flat area, all smooth rock. On the left is some outcropping of granite. There are two caves in the rocks there."

"Real caves?"

"Well, not underground or anything like that. One of them is pretty large, probably one hundred feet deep, maybe eight feet high. That's the one they were afraid of. Too many loose rocks. The other one is just a cozy room. Jack took me there once when it was raining. We always kept firewood inside, just in case. We had a campfire right there and cooked the fish we had caught earlier. Stayed totally dry. They're easy to find, if you know what you're looking for, McKenna. If not, you'll walk right past them."

"So when the mountain collapsed, these are just cavities that formed from the fallen rocks?"

"Probably." Jessie shrugged. "I was just a kid. They may have just seemed huge to me. But Jack called them caves."

"Well, next time I'm up that way, I'll have a look."

They walked on in silence, boots scuffing rocks the only sound. Chris led them higher, towards an overlook. She took out her flashlight and cast the beam ahead. They came near the edge and stopped, both looking out over the moon-touched mountaintops. The distant peaks all but glowed in the moonlight.

"It's so quiet," Jessie whispered. "Beautiful."

Chris nodded. Indeed, it was enchanting. Her eyes strayed from the moon-kissed peaks to Jessie. Jessie stood, bathed in the moonlight, her face aglow as she scanned the horizon. Chris couldn't pull her eyes away. She had never seen anything more beautiful.

Jessie stood motionless, her eyes fixed on a distant mountain peak. A memory tried to crowd in . . . he was beside her, holding her, keeping her warm. What else? Were they camping? Had they been up this high? She closed her eyes, but still, she couldn't remember. Instead, an image came to her of them camping near the river. She was seven, maybe eight and he had taught her to tie flies that trip. They had fished for hours the next day, bringing their catch home. It was one of the few times she could remember Annie having dinner with them.

"What are you thinking about?" Chris asked quietly.

Jessie shook her head. "Nothing really. Just . . . it's so quiet. No owls. No wind. Nothing."

Chris nodded, not wanting to speak and disturb the silence. She knew they should get back. It was getting late. And colder. But Jessie looked so peaceful standing there, her arms crossed against her waist as she stared out into the vastness.

Jessie felt Chris watching her. She turned and caught her eyes, her breath catching at the unguarded desire she saw there. It was at that very moment she realized she was starving for physical contact, for intimacy. And not from a total stranger she'd just met at a bar. She could imagine Chris kissing her, holding her. She wanted her heart to pound with life like she knew it would, should their lips meet.

Chris swallowed hard, the sound echoing in her ears, so loud, she was sure it was bouncing off the canyon walls for all to hear. But there was only Jessie, eyes locked with her own. Chris silenced the voice in her head that urged her to turn and go, leaving Jessie to follow if she chose. Instead, she stepped closer to the eyes that beckoned, unable to resist any longer. Their eyes locked again, then Jessie moved into her arms, her mouth searching for Chris's waiting lips. The flashlight fell unnoticed between them as Chris pulled her closer, her hands on Jessie's hips holding her flush against her. Their mouths moved together, tongues meeting as they let their desire rage unchecked.

"Oh, God, yes," Jessie breathed, pressing her hips more firmly against Chris. She let her desire overtake her, felt her knees grow weak as Chris's hands moved up her sides, stopping just beneath her breasts. Jessie tried to remember a time she'd wanted another's touch this desperately. There was none. The countless, nameless list of strangers paraded through her mind in seconds and then there was only Chris, whose hands stoked the fire within her.

Her mouth opened fully to Chris, tongue moving against tongue. Her hands found Chris's and she slid them the few inches to her own breasts, moaning as Chris's warm hands cupped her. Jessie moved against her, her arms sliding over Chris's strong shoulders to hold her close.

Chris wasn't prepared for this. Staring at Jessie's picture for hours on end and the fantasies that followed did not compare to this. She felt Jessie's fullness and she pushed against her. Then, in one quick motion, her hands slid under Jessie's sweatshirt, touching her warm skin. She finally pulled her mouth away, searching Jessie's eyes, seeing mirrored passion. Chris moved her hands upward, stopping just beneath Jessie's full breasts.

"I want you to touch me," Jessie said softly.

"This is crazy," Chris murmured.

"Yes," Jessie agreed, her eyes never leaving Chris's.

Chris found the lacy bra and let her fingers move over it, feeling hard nipples straining against it. Jessie gave her a gentle nudge and Chris opened her legs, feeling Jessie's thigh slide between her opened legs. She was lost. She quickly shoved the bra aside, her hands closing over warm flesh and her mouth claimed Jessie's with a new hunger. Chris felt herself grow wet with need and she moved against Jessie's thigh, pressing her swollen clit hard against her.

"I want you," Chris breathed into Jessie's mouth.

"Yes. I want you, too."

Jessie's hands moved under Chris's sweatshirt, pushing it away from her flushed skin. She wasted no time as her hands moved up her body, trembling slightly when she found no bra. Her fingers gently grazed swollen nipples and she bent her head back, feeling Chris's lips move away from her own, across her face to find the throbbing pulse in her neck. Insane, she thought. This desire was nearly too much for her to bear. Jessie was always the one to drive women to the brink of desire, not the other way around. Never had she wanted to lie down on a cold forest floor and have someone make love to her. She wanted that now, regardless.

Chris came to her senses moments before she would have pulled Jessie down with her, unmindful of the rocks and sticks beneath them. She pushed Jessie away and held her at arm's length, her breath heaving in her chest.

"Jesus," she whispered. How close? How close had she been to ripping Jessie's clothes off? How close was she to pulling her own sweatshirt over her head.

Jessie licked her lips, wanting Chris's mouth again. It wouldn't take much, she knew, and she could have her. Right here, right now. But instead, she took a deep breath and moved away. It would serve nothing for them to lose themselves in this passion that had nearly swallowed them. Instead, Jessie tried to make light of it.

"Wow, McKenna, you sure know how to show a girl a view."

"I . . . I'm sorry."

Jessie cringed. She didn't want an apology. If anything, she should be the one apologizing.

"Don't you dare," she whispered. "We both wanted that."

Chris nodded. Yes. No doubt they'd both wanted it. Wanted more, in fact. But she knew it was best not to dwell on it.

"We should get back," she said. She bent over, searching for the fallen flashlight. Her hands gripped it, turning it over in her palm as she tried desperately to think of something witty to say. Anything to ease the tension that had sprung up between them. Nothing came.

Instead she turned and headed back down the trail, hoping Jessie would follow. She did.

They walked to their campsite in silence, finding the embers of the fire nearly dead. Chris contemplated starting it again, if only to delay the eventual departure into the tent. Together. Side by side. Chris physically shook herself. They were tired. They would sleep. That's all.

Chapter Fourteen

They hurried down the mountain, trying to beat the rain that was threatening. They had taken time for coffee and a quick breakfast of two muffins that Chris had stuffed in her pack, which were flattened nearly beyond recognition. Neither mentioned the incident of the previous night, nor the mostly sleepless night both of them had endured.

The air was cool and damp, just enough to prevent them from shedding their sweatshirts. By the time they reached the trailhead, it was starting to sprinkle and thunder rumbled overhead. They both tossed their packs in the Jeep, which was still uncovered. Chris had removed the top for the summer and she turned the heater on now as she drove quickly to the cabins.

"I don't guess I could talk you into coming to my place first?" Chris asked. "I could use some help with the top and I don't think I'm going to beat the rain."

"Of course. I don't mind getting wet, McKenna. Why should you have all the fun?"

The canvas top was stored under her bed and Chris ran to get it as the rain fell harder. They were soaked by the time the Jeep was covered and the windows zipped up.

"Come on inside. We'll wait it out," Chris offered.

She found towels for both of them, then left Jessie on the sofa with Dillon perched importantly in her lap. Chris took a quick shower, then changed into dry clothes. Jessie and Dillon were still on the sofa when she returned.

"He likes me," Jessie stated as she pointed to the curled up cat in her lap.

"Well, don't get a big head or anything. That's his favorite position."

"And I thought it was my charming personality he was attracted to."

Chris smiled at the two of them, watching a relaxed Jessie as she petted the cat.

"Listen, if you want to take a shower, I can probably find some clothes to fit you. We're about the same size," Chris offered.

"That's okay. I can wait."

Chris shrugged, then opened the refrigerator and peered inside.

"I'd offer to fix you lunch, but it's kinda bare," she apologized.

Jessie startled her as she leaned over her shoulder.

"Beer, salsa, milk, more beer and . . . cheese?" Jessie teased. "Oh, and an apple. Like I said, you don't cook much, do you?"

"I can open a can of soup and I can do cereal," Chris stated.

"Do cereal? That's really not cooking, McKenna." Jessie reached inside and pulled out two beers. "This will do."

They sat quietly at the table, listening to the rain. Chris wondered when they would broach the subject of last night or if they ever would. Jessie's eyes were veiled, her words guarded. Perhaps she regretted the few minutes of abandon the previous evening. Or maybe she was simply regretting the conversation about her childhood.

"You know, McKenna, I really didn't know how to act this morning," Jessie finally said.

"What do you mean?"

"You know what I'm talking about," she stated. "And I'm not only talking about the episode out there in the moonlight. That was . . . nice. But there's not a single person in my life that knows about my childhood, except several therapists scattered in San Francisco and New York. Actually, there's not really all that many people in my life, period," she admitted. In fact, there wasn't anyone.

"What do you mean?" Chris asked again.

Jessie turned cool, dark eyes on her. Eyes totally devoid of emotion.

"I have a problem establishing relationships, or so I've been told. I'm not exactly a nice person, McKenna," she said.

"You're not? I think you're nice," Chris said.

"But you don't really know me, do you?"

Jessie stood up and walked to the window, her back to Chris. No need to prolong this, she thought. Tell her what a bitch you are. Get it over with. Tell her how close you came to using her last night. There was no need to hang around here, pretending to vacation. She came to Sierra City to find Annie, to talk to her. No other reason than that.

But when she turned around, she collided with clear blue eyes that were filled with trust and understanding. Chris looked back at her, waiting.

"I . . . I use people, McKenna. For whatever I need. Professionally, personally." She shrugged. "For sex."

"And are you warning me or are you confessing?" Chris asked calmly.

"Look, McKenna, I'm just saying that I'm a taker. Not a giver. And for some crazy reason, I don't want to do that to you."

"Why?"

"Because that's just who I am, what I am. I don't know why."

"No. Why don't you want to do that to me? If you just use people for what you need then discard them, why are you warning me?"

Why indeed? Jessie turned back to the window, wrapping her arms across her chest. Because for the first time in so many years, she actually found someone she liked. And that scared her.

"Jessie, if you're upset about what happened last night, let's talk about it. I don't know about you, but it certainly wasn't something I planned."

"Wasn't it? Then why did you invite me along?"

Chris shrugged. "I like you."

Jessie groaned. No. She didn't want Chris to like her. God, nobody liked her. Why in the world would this woman be different?

"McKenna, if you knew me, trust me, you wouldn't like me."

"Why are you so hard on yourself?"

"Because, goddammit, I'm a bitch, that's why. I told you, I use people. And I'll use you, too. Because that's just the way I am."

Chris looked at the woman before her, the woman who was trying so hard not to be liked. Jessie Stone was an attractive woman. She was also a successful writer. Why then, was this woman standing with her arms wrapped around herself, so completely insecure and unsure of herself?

Chris walked over to her and unwrapped her arms, lightly grasping both of Jessie's hands.

"I'm sorry, but I just don't see it."

"McKenna . . ."

"No. I think you've led yourself to believe this and others have told you this so you assume it's true. But underneath all of that, I think you're a very nice, charming person. If you'll let yourself be, anyway."

Jessie wanted to laugh. What the hell did Chris know about it? They were practically strangers.

Chapter Fifteen

Jessie stood on her porch, inhaling deeply, thinking there was no nicer smell than the forest after a rain. The sweet smell of incense cedar drifted around her and she couldn't resist a small smile. She finally gave in to temptation and stepped off the porch, her boots silent on the wet ground as she walked over to the giant tree and shoved her nose against the bark. If there was one smell she wished she could bottle, this was it. It was one of the numerous smells embedded in her memory from childhood.

She settled in one of the chairs on the porch, thinking she should go inside and shower and get into dry clothes, but she was suddenly too tired for even that. The quick trip she'd planned back to Sierra City was not turning out the way she envisioned. She hadn't planned on taking two days for a backpacking trip. And she didn't know why she found the prospect of seeing Annie so difficult. Perhaps because she really didn't know why she was going to see her in the first place.

And McKenna. The woman was creeping into places that Jessie had kept off limits to everyone before. She really liked her. And what scared her more was that Chris seemed to genuinely like her, too. Why on earth, Jessie couldn't imagine.

As she'd told Chris, she wasn't a nice person. Hadn't Dr. Davies told her as much on her last visit?

Jessie wearily leaned her head back, wondering how she had come to this point in her life. She let the familiar depression settle over her like a blanket. When had it started? In high school? Before that, even? This heaviness had been with her so long, she couldn't remember a time that it had not followed her. Certainly as a child, she was happy. She must have been. Camping trips and fishing, he always made them fun. It was always just the two of them. She hadn't had to share him with anyone. Jack was her only friend.

When had that stopped? Why didn't they go camping anymore when she got older? Had they?

She shook her head. She couldn't remember. She couldn't remember anything.

Chapter Sixteen

Chris was just finishing her first cup of coffee when her cell phone rang. She was hoping it would be Jessie, then panicked, thinking it might be Annie.

"McKenna?"

"Yeah." It was Roger.

"We've got a ten-fifty, with fatality."

"Who?" she asked quickly, her heart pounding.

"Not a local."

"Thank goodness." In the three months that she'd been here, she had come to know a lot of the people in this small town. They all accepted her without question and treated her as if she'd been there for years.

"It's out on County Road Twelve and the sheriff's got a crew out, but according to reports, there should have been three people in the car. They've only got one body. They asked if we could give them a hand."

"They were probably thrown out," she said.

"Yeah. Well, they just found the accident about an hour ago. See if you can find Bobby and maybe Greg and meet me out there. Could have head injuries and they wandered off or something, who knows."

Thirty minutes later, they were on their way to the accident, south of Sierra City. The wrecked car was still there, some fifty feet down the side of the mountain, but the body had been removed. Roger came up to meet them, a grim look on his face.

"Very strange," he said. "Harold Jackson, twenty-two, was the only body found. From what they've found out so far, he and his brother, Jeffrey, age twenty, and a girl, Wendy, don't have her last name yet, left a party in Sacramento after midnight."

"Alcohol?" Bobby asked.

"Drugs for sure. They found cocaine in the car. Sheriff thinks the car was pushed off. There are dents in the back bumper that he doesn't think were made on the way down."

"Jesus," Greg said. "Some car rammed them?"

"That's what it looks like. If the other two survived, they might have headed into the woods, scared. Hell, I don't know."

"Let me look around, see if I can find anything, tracks, broken tree branches, anything that might indicate that they took off," Chris said.

"Okay. I don't want to start a major search here if it's not necessary. But the boys, their father is Harris Jackson."

"The senator?"

"That's the one."

Chris slid down the hill, grabbing onto tree limbs to keep from falling. The car was sitting on its nose, the engine shoved practically into the back seat. No way they could have survived the crash inside the car. They were either thrown out, or simply were not in the car when it went over the side. She remembered one accident similar to this, where the body was found nearly one hundred feet from the site, impaled on a tree branch.

She looked around the site, shaking her head. It was another fifty feet at least before it leveled off. If they were able to walk away, which she doubted, they would have had a hell of a time making it into the forest in the dark, even with a full moon, without sliding or falling off a rock the rest of the way down. She made her way down, past the car and looked for signs of rocks being dislodged or branches broken from someone pulling on them. She found nothing. She took her binoculars out and scanned the forest below, but still saw nothing to grab her attention.

She took her radio off her hip and called Roger.

"Nothing. I just don't see it, Roger. They weren't in the car."

"Ten-twelve," he said and she waited like he asked. "McKenna, come on back."

"Ten-four."

It took her nearly twenty minutes to climb back to the top and she was out of breath. She paused, hands on her hips as she breathed deeply. She scanned towards the forest, half expecting to see a body hanging from a tree.

"They found a body, a few miles back. Male."

"And the girl?"

"No. No sign of her," he said. "He'd been shot," Roger added.

Chris just stared at him. Murder? In Sierra City? This had to be a first. In this century, at least.

"Shot? Jesus," Bobby murmured.

"Yeah. My guess is drugs and they got mixed up with the wrong people this time. It's not our affair, thank goodness."

"What about the girl?" Chris asked.

"She'll probably turn up dead or else maybe she's the shooter." He turned to go then stopped. "Either way, it's going to be a big deal. Jackson is on his way out here now from Washington."

They went back to the station, silent on the ride back. She thanked Bobby and Greg for going with her, then went into her office.

Kay came in a short time later. "I've been listening on the police scanner," she said. "It's already all over the news in the city."

"Yeah, it's a big deal, for sure."

"You had a visitor this morning," Kay said. "A stranger."

"And?"

"There was a message." She handed her a white envelope with her name scrawled across the front. "I hope you don't mind, but she said you were friends. I gave her your cell phone number."

"Thanks." She waited until Kay left before opening it. It was an invitation to dinner at cabin number seven. She was surprised. When she had dropped Jessie off the day before, she was noncommittal as to when they might see each other again.

Chris got home late after spending the day directing the media and other interested parties away from town. By two o'clock, Sierra City was buzzing and it looked like the Fourth of July, with all the people milling about. The Rock House was doing a booming business and she couldn't even get close to Steve's gas station. They were to be on the national news at five o'clock and all the locals gathered at the Rock to watch. Chris stopped by, too, joining Roger for a beer after such an eventful day. He was curious why she wasn't staying for dinner, but he didn't press.

Her hair was still damp as she drove to Jessie's. She was fifteen minutes late and Jessie was on the back porch waiting.

"You came," she said. Their eyes held for a moment, then Jessie looked away.

"Did you think I wouldn't?"

Jessie only shrugged. "I hear you had a busy day."

"A nightmare." Chris took the beer that Jessie offered and leaned against the porch railing. "It was a regular circus in town today."

"One of the benefits of not having a TV, I guess. Ellen at the grocery store told me about it."

"Everyone was quite excited about being on television tonight, though."

"You?"

She shook her head. "No, but it'll die down in a day or two."

Chris studied Jessie as she sipped her beer. Jessie seemed a little reserved, guarded. Chris took a deep breath, knowing it was none of her business, but unable to let it go any longer. Annie was her friend. A friend she was scheduled to have dinner with Thursday night. And she was tired of playing games.

"Jessie, what are you really doing here?"

Jessie was surprised by the question and she looked away. Trust Chris to be direct. "I told you, my therapist says I've got issues here."

"Yes, you've said that. But what does that mean, exactly?"

"Exactly? What kind of question is that? I've got issues. If I knew what the hell they were, I'd do something about them."

Chris pushed off the railing and stood beside Jessie, thinking again that she should just mind her own business. But of course, she couldn't.

"I know Annie Stone," she said.

"You've heard of her?"

"No, I mean I know her. We're friends," Chris said.

Jessie's eyes widened. "Friends?"

"Roger Hamilton introduced me. You remember Roger?" she asked.

Jessie nodded, shocked. This, she was not expecting.

"Let's talk. Honestly, okay?"

"Honestly? McKenna, what's gotten into you? I invited you over for dinner and you want to have a heart-to-heart? This has nothing to do with you."

"Aren't you curious as to how I knew your name? Your books don't mention Jessie, just J. T."

Jessie shrugged. "It never occurred to me, really." And it hadn't.

"I was reading your book and Roger came over and saw it. He started telling me about you being from here and all. I was curious about you, I guess."

"Why?"

Chris met her eyes, but ignored her question. She wasn't ready to admit her infatuation over a picture. "Roger told me about Annie. I wanted to meet her."

"Why on earth?"

"I don't know why, I just did. And I like her very much," Chris admitted.

Jessie turned angry eyes to her. "How can you possibly like her? You know nothing about her."

"I probably know more about her than you do. I also probably know more about you than you remember yourself," Chris stated. She was getting into dangerous water, she knew, but the Annie that Jessie remembered was not the Annie that Chris knew.

"How dare you?" Jessie spat. "How dare you pry into my private life like that?" Then Jessie slapped Chris on the arm. "And how dare you let me pretend to be Jennifer Parker when you knew all along."

"What did you want me to do? I figured you had a reason."

"Look, I came back here because . . . because I don't know why, okay. It just seemed like the thing to do. I can't remember anything. All I feel is hatred and resentment for this woman who is my mother and I don't know why," she finished in a whisper.

"Jack had a lot of women, did you know that?"

"What? You believe what she told you? You didn't know him. He wasn't like that."

"Roger said the same thing."

"Jesus Christ! So you've been gossiping about my life?"

"It wasn't like that, Jessie."

Jessie gripped the railing and stared out, seeing nothing. She remembered that night, that night that Jack and Annie had been screaming at each other. Annie accused him and he denied it. She was the one who had a lover. She was the reason for . . . everything.

"Well, who could blame him? There was certainly no love waiting at home for him."

"How do you know that?"

"I lived there. I saw. She never spoke to him. She never did anything with us. She never went anywhere with us. She wouldn't even share a bedroom with him. She didn't love him. She didn't love me."

"Maybe she wasn't allowed to go anywhere with you. Maybe she wasn't allowed to love you."

"That's ridiculous. Is that what she said?"

"Why do you think she didn't love you?" Chris asked.

"She never talked to me. She hardly acknowledged that I was around."

"But you had meals on the table and clean clothes, all ironed for school?"

Jessie turned around slowly, a frown on her face.

"What about when you didn't come home for dinner?" Chris asked gently.

"Like when?"

"Fishing after school?"

Jessie thought back, then cleared her throat. "Jack would pick me up after school sometimes and we would go fishing. We'd cook them and eat them right there," she said in a distant voice, remembering.

"And when you got home, the table would be set for dinner and Annie would be waiting," Chris said.

Jessie looked away again, remembering the times Annie was sitting by herself at the table, dinner long cold.

"What then?"

"I would go to my room," she said quietly. She thought back, hearing her father laugh at Annie as she sat at the table. But she pushed that thought away. She was the one hurting, not Annie. But why?

"Jessie, there's more to it than you're letting yourself remember," Chris said, wondering how much she could coax from Jessie.

"So, do you and Annie just sit around and talk about me or what?"

Chris could tell she had lost her. The brief moment of uncertainty had passed and in its place was the anger. "No. We're just friends. She's been locked in that house for thirty-two years. She needed to talk."

"What do you mean?"

"They call her the 'hermit lady' around here. Ellen owns the grocery store and she's been here five years and has never even seen her. She doesn't leave the house. Roger brings her groceries a couple of times a month. But she has her hobbies," Chris added bitterly.

"Hobbies?"

"She paints. She reads," she said pointedly. She saw Jessie's head turn quickly, but she looked away again.

"I don't care about that. I don't care about her," Jessie said stubbornly. "And if you don't mind, I'm really not in the mood for dinner, McKenna."

"Jessie . . ."

"No. Just leave. I want to be alone."

"I'm sorry."

"For what?"

"I just wanted you to know about Annie. I didn't mean to upset you," Chris said.

"Well, you have, McKenna."

The dark eyes still sparked with anger and Chris lowered her own. She had said too much. She had delved into things that were not her business. And she had destroyed any friendship that she and Jessie had started. For that, she was sorry. But she wasn't sorry for bringing up Annie.

Chris left without another word and Jessie went inside, standing in her small kitchen with her arms wrapped around herself. But she refused to think. Her head was already pounding and she opened the bottle of wine that was to go with their dinner.

"My life's a fucking mess," she whispered to the empty cabin.

Chapter Seventeen

Chris was assisting the sheriff's department the next morning, along with Matt and Roger. It turned out the missing girl was Wendy Dearborne, granddaughter of Phillip Dearborne, the famous San Francisco district attorney. Needless to say, the case had top priority, and all those around Sierra City cursed the fact that the accident had happened in their area. Heads were rolling from the top down, and now they were participating in a search, starting where Jeffrey Jackson's body had been found and covering the forest between there and where the car went off the road. Another group was starting at the accident site and Greg and Bobby were helping them.

Chris was trying to concentrate, looking for any evidence, but her mind kept wandering back to the night before. She had handled it poorly, she knew, but it was too late for that. She could have just ignored the whole thing and gone on like they had been. Have a little fun while Jessie was here, someone to have dinner with, maybe more, she thought. But she liked Annie too much. The woman didn't deserve to suffer any more. And Chris knew that if Jessie would just go talk to Annie, get everything out in the open, maybe they could repair the damage that had been done all those years ago. But what damage? Even Jessie didn't know the answer to that.

They walked until noon, then stopped to rest and eat the lunch they had brought. She and Matt sat on a downed tree and Roger leaned against a rock.

"We're not going to find anything. I can feel it," Matt said.

"Yeah. I agree," Chris said. But they were just following orders.

"We'll be out of it after today," Roger said. "The senator has the FBI on it. Then we can get back to our menial duties of managing the forest."

Chris noticed the bitterness in his voice and knew he hated the fact that his office had been taken over. She did, too.

"Where the hell is Hatcher, Roger? Why isn't he out here?"

"McKenna, don't start with me. You know damn well where he is."

"You know he doesn't like to get dirty, McKenna," Matt said with a grin.

"Somebody had to stay at the office, the phone was ringing off the hook," Roger said. "Might as well be him."

Chris just shook her head, remembering how Robert Hatcher had nearly fallen over himself when the FBI showed up.

"Kay said that his father and the senator are friends. You'd think he would be out here looking, too," she said.

It was another couple of hours before they met up with the other search group. No one had found a thing.

They all stood in a group as the sheriff addressed them.

"I want to thank you all for helping out. Roger, thanks for lending your SAR team. The senator has asked the FBI to take over the investigation so we'll just be assisting them if they need us."

Chris and Roger exchanged glances. So, even the sheriff was being dismissed.

It was after five o'clock when Chris got back. She wanted a

shower and a cold beer. She had told Matt she would meet him at the Rock for dinner. Anything was better than sitting in her cabin alone, even one of Dave's surprises. Dillon met her at the door and she scooped him up and kissed him before filling his bowl with food. She took a beer from the fridge on her way past and undressed as she went. Her clothes were scratched, stained and sweaty and she piled them in the clothesbasket in the corner of her room. It was time to hit Roger up for dinner so she could do laundry, she thought. She stood naked in the bathroom, downing her beer before stepping under the hot spray.

With her head tilted back and the water pounding against her breasts, she thought of Jessie and wondered what kind of day she had. Chris was tempted to drive to her cabin and check on her but she didn't want to take a chance on getting thrown out again.

She changed into clean jeans and a long-sleeved T-shirt. Her hair was still wet and she opened the Jeep window and let the cool breeze dry it as she drove. It was too long, she noted. The bangs were hanging in her eyes and she brushed them away impatiently.

The Rock House was busy for a Tuesday night and she spotted Matt and Bobby sitting at a table with Roger.

"Hey guys."

"McKenna."

She caught Martha's eye before she sat down and raised her hand. "A beer, Martha. Please," she called.

"Yeah, yeah, you and everybody else. Keep your shirt on, McKenna."

"Why does she abuse me?" she asked.

"Abuse? Hell, she's being nice tonight," Roger said.

"But she's not sweet like Donna," Bobby said.

Chris flicked her eyes at Matt and grinned and he pleased her by blushing slightly. But she stopped her teasing there. Matt still had not worked up the nerve to ask Donna to dinner.

Martha brought her a draft beer, sloshing some on the table as she usually did.

"Dave wants to know what you want tonight," she said.

"Look, let's just be safe, okay. How about a baked potato? A little sour cream and cheese?"

Martha grinned. "You're learning, McKenna."

"Bring us another round, too."

"I only have two hands, Roger. Wait your turn."

"If she knew how many damn miles we walked today," Roger mumbled.

Chris laughed. "And you're the jogger in the bunch."

"Jogging is not climbing over boulders and around trees."

"I think you're getting soft in your old age," she teased.

"Soft my ass. I can still run circles around you, McKenna."

"Sure you can."

Chris suffered through three men going on and on about their steaks as she ate her baked potato, trying her best to ignore them.

"Why are you a vegetarian, McKenna?" Bobby asked.

She opened her mouth to give a politically correct statement when Roger chimed in.

"A woman," he said. "I think she was trying to impress her."

"Girlfriend?" Matt asked.

"Wow, McKenna. You'd give up steak for a woman?"

Chris glared at Roger before addressing the questions.

"She was a girlfriend at one time, years ago. And yes, I did give up steak for her, Bobby." Then she grinned. "It was well worth it."

"And where is she now?" Roger asked.

"You know damn well where she is."

"Where?" Matt and Bobby asked in unison.

"She decided she liked a millionaire's son better and married him," Chris said.

"Guess she liked meat after all," Bobby said innocently.

Chris nearly spit her beer out for laughing.

Chapter Eighteen

Jessie grabbed a blanket and a bottle of wine and headed out. The trail would be treacherous at night, but she didn't care. She couldn't escape her thoughts and she desperately needed answers. It was only when the moon went behind a cloud that she remembered she had no flashlight. But it didn't matter. She didn't care.

She stumbled along the trail, her boots hitting unseen rocks and she would have walked into a tree had the moon not shown itself again. She finally found the ledge and blindly jumped across the break, landing only feet from the edge.

So many years ago, her father's life ended right here. She stared out over the canyon into the darkness below. Why had he jumped?

She sat down and let her feet dangle over the edge, part of her knowing she was far too close but she didn't move back. Instead, she reached into her bag for the bottle of wine.

"What happened?" she whispered.

She took a swallow from the bottle and shoved it between her legs, letting childhood memories flood her. Camping. Just the two of them in the tent. Fishing, him teaching her to tie flies. Hiking the trails, she running ahead of him, then him chasing her, finally catching her and swinging her around. Annie was never there. She wasn't there for either of them. Jessie closed her eyes. Annie didn't love him. She remembered him telling her that. Annie wasn't there for him.

Then the tent. It was so hot, he told her she didn't have to put her pajamas on. Jessie took another swallow from the bottle. Annie wasn't there for him. But Jessie was. She was always there.

"Oh God," she whispered.

"Jessie, you're my best girl, aren't you?"

How many times had she heard those words? The best girl. And because Annie wasn't there, she had to be.

"No."

"It's okay, Jessie. It'll be our little secret."

"Oh, no," she sobbed and clutched the wine bottle to her. "No."

Forgotten memories hit her full force and she cried for her lost innocence. The tent. It was so hot. Oh God, and it hurt. It hurt so bad. But he had soothed her, told her it would be better the next time. It wouldn't hurt so much. She was such a good girl.

"Goddamn son of a bitch!" she screamed through her tears. She rocked back and forth, the bottle of wine her only comfort on this dark, dark night.

Chapter Nineteen

Chris drove back to her cabin with the Jeep window open. The night was cool, but the fresh air felt good after sitting in cigarette smoke for the last few hours. She glanced toward the parking area for Ridge Trail like she always did and slammed on her brakes. Jessie's rental car shone in the moonlight.

"Jesus! What the hell is she doing?"

She parked beside the car and felt the hood. It was cold. She let out a heavy sigh.

"Oh, man."

After hiking all day, the last thing she wanted was a quick trip up Ridge Trail. It took her nearly thirty minutes to negotiate the trail in the dark, even with her flashlight. She topped the ridge and stopped to catch her breath and relief washed over her as she saw the lone figure sitting on the ledge. The moon cast enough light for her to see Jessie huddled in a blanket, a bottle of wine sitting next to her. She turned the flashlight off and walked over to her.

"Jessie?" she called softly. There was no answer. No movement. "Can I sit with you?" Still nothing.

Chris took one long stride across the crack in the ledge and sat down behind her, moving the nearly empty bottle of wine away. She spread her legs on either side of Jessie and put her arms around her, pulling her back against her chest. Jessie didn't resist, instead laid her head back against Chris. Chris felt her take a deep breath, then release it slowly.

"You okay?" Chris whispered.

"No."

"Want to talk?"

"No."

Chris only nodded and held Jessie to her, rocking her gently in her arms. After a few moments, she felt rather than heard Jessie crying. Chris kissed the back of her head gently and tightened her hold.

Jessie relaxed into the comfort of Chris's arms, letting her tears fall silently. She had thought that she was cried out, but for the first time in so many, many years, secure arms held her, offering solace, nothing more. And it felt good. But she knew she didn't deserve it. She had nothing to give back. She was just an empty shell of a woman. And emptiness was something she was very used to.

She felt Chris kiss her hair, felt her arms tighten and she squeezed her eyes shut against the feelings that settled over her. She didn't deserve this. No, she deserved to hurt, to feel pain.

She turned her head suddenly, pressing her lips into Chris's neck, then moving to her lips, kissing them hard.

"No, don't say anything," she whispered. "Please. I know you want me. I can see it in your eyes."

She pushed Chris back on the ledge and straddled her, her hands roughly cupping Chris's breasts before her mouth claimed Chris again.

Chris didn't know what was happening, but she had no time for thoughts as her mouth opened and Jessie's tongue entered, driving out all resistance.

Jessie took what she wanted and Chris became a nameless, faceless woman, like so many before her. Just someone she could use to drive out her thoughts. She laid her full weight on top of Chris, pressing her hips hard into the soft body beneath hers, hearing Chris's low moan as her kiss turned hungry. She refused to think, letting her body take over as her hands moved between them, unbuttoning Chris's jeans and slipping easily inside. Her fingers found their target, only briefly acknowledging the wetness she knew she would find. She shook off the hands that cupped her face, denying the tender kiss that Chris placed on her lips.

"No."

The eyes that Chris found in the moonlight were hard, dark, emotionless.

"Jessie . . ."

"No."

Jessie covered her mouth again then roughly grabbed Chris's hand and shoved it inside her own jeans. She rolled over, pulling Chris on top of her, opening her legs.

"Please, take me," she whispered before guiding Chris's mouth back to her own.

Chris tried to pull away, her mind fighting with her body over her desire for this woman. She could take her, right now. But for pleasure? No, it would just be a quick fuck. Jessie's eyes were blank. There was no pleasure there. But Jessie grabbed her hand again, pushing it inside her jeans. Fingers felt wetness and Chris moaned, wanting to be inside her, and she let her body win.

Jessie raised her hips, shoving fingers deep inside her. Her eyes closed as familiar feelings gripped painfully at her heart. Her hips moved roughly against fingers that tried to give her pleasure. She didn't want pleasure. She wanted to hurt.

"Harder," she whispered.

"No, Jessie, look at me."

"No. Please, just fuck me." She closed her mind and saw nothing, only blackness. Then he was there, so big, so rough, callused hands touching her soft skin. *It's alright, baby, Daddy's here.*

Chris saw the tears fall, felt Jessie go limp and she finally pulled her hand away. She stared at her, wondering what had just happened, why she had let it happen. This isn't what she wanted between them.

"Jessie?"

Jessie shook her head as sobs racked her body. She felt Chris pull away from her and sit up. Jessie curled into a fetal position and cried. She cried harder when she felt a gentle hand on her shoulder.

"Jessie, please. Tell me what the hell is going on."

"I just wanted . . . I wanted,"

"I know what you wanted. I want to know why. Why did you do that to me?"

"I tried to warn you," Jessie whispered.

"Warn me?"

"I use people, McKenna. It's the only thing I'm good at."

"Goddamn you, Jessie. I'm not some bimbo you picked up in a bar to take home for a quick fuck. I liked you."

Liked. Past tense. Jessie nodded. This, she was used to.

Chris stood and pulled her jeans up and buttoned them. Never in her life had she been this humiliated. She had thought, maybe, that Jessie liked her, that Jessie wanted to be with her as much as Chris wanted to be with Jessie. But no, she just used people.

"Come on," she said.

"No."

"Yes. I'm leaving and so are you. Get up."

Jessie wanted to argue, but she knew Chris would not leave her here alone. Despite the fact that she had hurt her. Yes, Jessie hurt her. Intentionally. This beautiful woman with such kindness in her eyes, Jessie had turned their mutual attraction into a game. She was very sorry, but she couldn't find the words to explain, so she said nothing.

She followed Chris silently down the trail, several steps behind her. At the trailhead, Jessie stopped at the Jeep but Chris opened the door and climbed in. Their eyes met and Jessie saw none of the warmth that she was used to seeing in her blue eyes. She saw hurt and pain and a hint of anger. She didn't blame her. She stepped aside as Chris pulled away and walked numbly to her car.

Chapter Twenty

Dinner with Annie was the hardest thing Chris had ever endured in her life. Annie was full of questions about the accident and Chris filled her in, but the usual banter between them was missing. Annie commented that Chris was unusually quiet, but Chris passed it off to exhaustion. She so badly wanted to confide in Annie about Jessie, but she knew Annie would never forgive her for not telling her that Jessie was here. The painting that Annie had done for her was finished and it turned out to be beautiful, even to her inexperienced eye, and she told Annie as much. She hung it over the mantel as soon as she got home.

She had not even been tempted to drive to Jessie's cabin. She was still very angry at both Jessie and herself. And for the life of her, she couldn't imagine what had happened. Maybe that was what Jessie was used to. A quick fuck and hey, see you around. But that had never been Chris's style. Even her teasing words to Jessie about making trips to Sacramento to the bars was mostly talk. Only once had Chris taken a woman up on her offer and then, only after several drinks. She had regretted it the next morning and hadn't been back since.

But with Jessie, Chris had allowed her attraction to overtake her good sense. But what they had done, however brief, could hardly be called making love. And on the ledge, for God's sake. Had they actually been in the throes of passion, they could have both tumbled off into the canyon.

But it didn't matter. Lesson learned. And it was true. Jessie had tried to warn her. She just hadn't believed it.

It was after the third day and no sign of Jessie when Chris broke down and drove to cabin number seven. She found it empty. The door was locked and she walked around to the back porch. The chairs were standing neatly against the cabin and she pressed her face against the window and peered inside. Empty. All of Jessie's things were gone and Chris told herself that she was glad, that she didn't want anything more to do with Jessie Stone, but she knew she was lying. She really was worried about her. Without realizing what she was doing, she stopped the Jeep at Mary Ruth's and met her on the porch.

"Oh, she left three days ago. Didn't even see her, though. There was just a note and the key left on the porch here."

Chris figured Jessie must have gone straight to the cabin and packed and left that same night. Well, it was probably for the best.

Her days returned to normal. The excitement over the murders had died down like they knew it would, and their weekends were again busy with hikers and campers hitting the trails before winter came. They were well into September and the first snowfall of the season wouldn't be far behind.

Chapter Twenty-one

Jessie waited in the reception area, early for her appointment for once. She wore black jeans and a black vest, with a wrinkled white T-shirt underneath, comfortable in her athletic shoes. Probably the only one in the building who was. High heels and hose, suits and ties were everywhere. Back in the city, she thought. She had been back nearly two weeks, but she had not left her apartment once. She had sat for hours, just thinking. She thought of Chris a lot, especially of how they had left things between them. She wondered if Chris would ever forgive her. She wouldn't blame her if she didn't. She thought of Annie, too. She wondered what she would be like and she acknowledged that she didn't really know her. They had shared a house for seventeen years, but Jessie had no idea of her likes and dislikes or anything else about her. Chris had been right. She probably did know Annie better than Jessie ever would. She tried not to think about Jack, but long buried memories kept creeping in, memories that she wished she could still forget.

"Ms. Stone, she's ready," the receptionist told her pleasantly.

Jessie walked confidently into Dr. Davies' office and offered a smile.

"Well, so glad you're back. I was surprised to find your name on the appointment list."

Jessie shrugged.

"You look well. Did everything go okay?"

Jessie didn't know where to begin so she just blurted out the words that she still found hard to say.

"Jack sexually abused me."

She expected shock, disbelief. Not the quiet nod that she got.

"What? That's it?" Jessie asked.

"I suspected as much, Jessie. But you had to remember yourself, I couldn't put that idea in your head."

"You suspected? How?"

"Jessie, let's talk about how you discovered this? Did you talk to your mother, to Annie?"

"No. I couldn't bring myself to see her. I met someone who knew her, though." But she didn't want to go over it all again. She had thought of nothing else for the past two weeks. She stood up suddenly, pacing in front of the desk. "What am I supposed to do now?"

"Jessie, sit down."

"No. I don't want to sit," she said, still pacing. "It just came to me. I think maybe I knew, I don't know. Chris kept asking about my childhood, you know, but I didn't remember. I kept telling her I didn't remember."

"Who is Chris?"

"She works there, she knows Annie. She knew who I was," she explained hurriedly. "We had an argument about Annie, about Jack. She told me some things that I didn't know, that I didn't remember." Jessie walked back and forth in front of the desk, her mind reeling.

"That night, I went up on the mountain. Something just pulled me up there. And I sat . . . and I remembered," she finished in a whisper. "I remembered it all."

"Jessie, please sit."

"No, dammit! I don't want to sit. I've been sitting for two weeks. I'm angry. And I want to know why?"

"Why? Why he did it?"

"Yes. I want to know why? Was it Annie's fault? Was it my fault?"

"Jessie, we'll never know why. We just have to work through this and we can, now that you know."

"No. I can come here and we can talk this to death, but what will that solve? It's not going to change anything," she said.

"No, you're right. It wouldn't change anything. But most importantly, you must know that it wasn't your fault. You were a child. You were the victim."

"But why?"

"There could be numerous reasons, Jessie. I can list off clinical answers for you if you want. But let's talk about you. Let's talk about how you feel."

"How I feel? How the fuck do you think I feel?"

"Jessie, I know you're angry. You should be angry. But at least you feel something."

Jessie stopped her pacing and stared at her. Yes, at least she felt something. She couldn't have said that a month ago. A month ago, she just felt dead.

"I'm going back," she stated. "I want to see her."

"That's a good start. Perhaps after we've had a chance to work through this, you'll be able to see her, to talk to her about your childhood. Your mother may have no idea what happened."

"No. Look, I'm not deranged, I'm not suicidal. I don't want to murder my mother, despite what you may think after reading my books." Jessie leaned on the desk and faced Dr. Davies. "I just want my life back."

"And you should, Jessie. You will. But it's not just a matter of accepting this and going about your life. You will have bad moments. You will still remember things that you don't even remember now. We'll work through it and you can still live a normal, healthy life."

"You don't understand. I'm not going to work through this by coming to you and talking about it. I think I only came today to be able to say it out loud to someone. I've been sitting in my apartment for two weeks, working through it. Yes, at first, I thought it was my fault, that I'd done something to deserve it. Then I thought it must be Annie's fault. But last night, I finally realized that Jack was the only one to blame. And I can be as angry with him as I want to be, but he's not here anymore. And you're right. I haven't had a life. Not yet. And I don't want to waste any more time. So I'm going back to see her, to talk to her."

"And I think you should, Jessie. But you need guidance. You need someone to talk to about your fears, and you will have them."

"I think I have someone there I can talk to," she said. "That is, if she'll still want to talk to me."

"Annie?"

"No. Chris. If anyone will understand, it's Chris," she said, hoping it was true.

"How do you know this? She's someone you've known for what, a few weeks?"

"I just know."

Chapter Twenty-two

Chris was out on horseback, following the South Rim Trail. Ever since the car accident, it seemed every nut from the city had decided that Sierra City was the place to be. Two weeks ago, a body had been found. A man in his mid-twenties had been shot in the head and dumped in the forest. Roger and Ellen had stumbled across the body when they were out on their evening walk. He was the younger brother of a jailed drug dealer in San Francisco. Eight days ago, a small plane had gone down, some twenty miles into the forest. There were no trails, and Chris led a group of rescuers and a sheriff's department evacuation unit into where they thought the plane had gone down. It had taken them three days to find the plane. There had been no smoke and no fire. The plane had simply disappeared into the forest. The plane was still relatively intact when they found it, along with about a million dollars' worth of cocaine.

Today, they were searching for a runaway. A teenage girl had left her parents a note and had taken a backpack and enough food for a couple of days. They hadn't approved of her boyfriend and had forbidden her to see him. So, she ran away to be with him. Of course, the boy had no idea. He was safe at home, in a small town about thirty miles north of Sierra City. They had searched every part of the forest that they thought she might have traveled through and had turned up nothing.

"What do you think?" Bobby asked her for the fourth time.

"I think this week sucks," she said. She was tired and she hadn't had a decent meal in eight days. She wondered if she had even left food out for Dillon. She had scarcely seen him in two weeks. "And I thought Yosemite was busy."

They camped near the Nevada Trail that night, their third and her seventh in a row. She radioed Roger when they had the fire going.

"For her to have made it this far in three days, she would have to have been jogging the whole way. We both know that didn't happen."

"I agree," he said. Chris thought he sounded tired and realized that it had been a tough week for him, too. "Come on back tomorrow. We'll concentrate closer to home, even though no one's found a sign of her."

"Ten-four."

The next morning, Roger woke them. "Good news. Found the kid."

"Where the hell was she?"

"San Francisco. She left the note as a decoy and hitched to the city."

"Son of a bitch," Chris said.

"Yeah, I know. Come on home. Let's hope things slow down. Maybe we'll get a snowstorm or something."

They wasted no time and even the horses seemed like they didn't want to spend another night on the trail. It was dark when they got back, exhausted.

Chris stood in the shower, her eyes closed as the hot water soothed her aching muscles. Dillon waited patiently on the toilet seat for her to finish. When the hot water ran out, she turned it off and stepped out, drying herself with a thick towel.

"Miss me?" she asked him as he rubbed against her legs.

She had actually taken the time to stop at Ellen's and pick up something for dinner. She had vegetables sautéing, garlic bread in the oven and linguine ready to boil. After dinner, she sat on the sofa, feet stretched out on the coffee table, sipping wine. Dillon was curled in her lap and she rubbed his ear while he purred.

The knock on the door startled her and she called for them to come in without turning around. Roger stuck his head inside.

"Feel like company?"

"Sure, come on in."

He brought his customary six-pack of beer and he put it in the fridge and took a cold one of hers.

"Hell of a week," he said.

"No doubt," she agreed. "I hope that kid is grounded for life."

He joined her on the sofa and they both put their feet up, staring at the painting over the fireplace.

"Annie?" Roger asked.

"Yeah. You like it?"

"It's good. I'm glad she's found a friend," he said.

"I like her."

"Yeah. Good for you, too, huh?"

"She is. And she cooks. An added bonus."

Chris swirled the wine in her glass absently. Jessie had been weighing heavy on her mind and she was tired of keeping her presence this summer a secret. She wouldn't dare tell Annie, but maybe Roger. She sighed. It had been over a month, but still, she thought of her.

"What's wrong?" he asked.

"What do you mean?"

"You just sighed."

"So?"

"So, you've been . . . I don't know, different."

"Different? I've not been different," she said a little testily.

"McKenna, I know you. What the hell is wrong?"

Chris stared at him, then reached out and grasped his arm.

"If I tell you something, you swear you won't tell a soul? Not even Ellen?"

"What the hell is going on, McKenna?"

"You swear?"

"Okay, I swear," he said dramatically. "Now tell me."

"There was a woman staying here at one of Mary Ruth's cabins a month or so ago. I sort of became friends with her."

"A woman, McKenna? You met a woman and it's a big secret?"

"Jessie Stone."

"What the hell? Are you sure?"

"Yes I'm sure."

"How do you know it was her?"

"Goddammit, Roger, I told you, we became friends."

"Jessie Stone? Here?"

"Here."

"Jesus Christ, McKenna. And you didn't tell Annie?"

"I didn't tell anybody. I first met her out on Ridge Trail, the spot where Jack fell. I knew who she was from her picture, but she introduced herself as Jennifer Parker."

"What the hell was she doing here?"

"You're being difficult, Roger. Let me tell the damn story."

"Sorry. I just can't believe, after all these years, she came back."

"I think she came back with the intention of seeing Annie. She's got some problems, some issues, her therapist says. She can't remember much about her childhood, well her later childhood, anyway. And she damn near hates Annie, although I don't think even she knows why. Something happened to her, Roger and I hate to say this, but I really think Jack abused her. Sexually."

"No, McKenna. I told you, he loved her."

"Yeah, I think he did. I think he *really* loved her, Roger."

"Is that what she told you?"

"No, she can't remember. It's just stuff that you've told me and Annie's told me. And she's definitely got some problems. Sexual problems, too," she added.

"And you know this how?"

"Look, we didn't sleep together or anything, if that's what you're hinting at," she said. What they had done couldn't be lumped in that category, she knew. And she wouldn't tell Roger what had happened on the ledge that night, either. She doubted she would ever tell anyone that.

"So, what happened? Where is she?"

"She left. Right after the accident. We sort of had words, I told her that I was friends with Annie. I tried to make her see that Annie wasn't the one to blame, but she didn't want to hear that. Anyway, I think she may have remembered. Something happened with her, anyway. And she just left. I never saw her again."

"And she never saw Annie?"

"No. And Annie would kill me if she found out that Jessie was here and I didn't tell her."

"Yes, my friend, I think she would."

Chapter Twenty-three

Jessie slipped her light jacket off before walking to Mary Ruth's cabin. It had been cold and damp when she landed in San Francisco, but the sun was shining brightly here. She knocked and heard shuffling in the back of the house.

"Coming," Mary Ruth yelled from inside.

Jessie waited on the porch. Her quick turnaround trip had lasted eight weeks. By the time she made arrangements for someone to look after her apartment, her editor had contacted her with revisions and she worked nonstop, trying to finish the book. She wanted nothing more than to be out of the city. Now, the days were cooler, although still warm for early November. She took a deep breath, loving the crisp smell of autumn.

"Why, Miss Parker, I wasn't expecting you until this evening."

Mary Ruth opened the door and Jessie went inside, where the smell of freshly baked cookies surrounded her.

"I took an earlier flight, Ms. Henninger. Sorry I didn't call, but I didn't think you would mind."

"Of course not. Your cabin's been ready for days. Come into the kitchen, dear. I need to put in another batch." Jessie followed her and her eyes were drawn to the pile of cookies sitting out to cool.

"Try one, Miss Parker. Chris won't mind sharing."

Jessie's heart fluttered at the mention of her name and she looked at Mary Ruth quickly, certain that her face was flushed. "Chris?"

"They call her McKenna. She comes to visit on Wednesdays and I always like to have cookies for her to take home." She put another pan into the oven and turned back to Jessie. "I thought you knew her. In fact, Chris came asking about you after you left."

"She did? Yes, we met while I was here." So, she'd come looking for her. Maybe Chris wasn't as angry as Jessie had imagined.

"Good. She's a lovely girl, so thoughtful. No matter how tired she is, she always finds time to stop by."

Yes, that was Chris. Thoughtful.

"Here, dear. I've got your card all filled out. Just sign at the bottom."

Jessie did as she was asked and wrote out a check. She had to be out by December 20, at the latest, Mary Ruth had told her. All the cabins were booked after that for the holidays.

Jessie left her then, after Mary Ruth had handed her the key and shoved a small bag of cookies into her hands. Cabin number seven was as she had left it, although there was now a small pile of firewood stacked neatly on the porch.

As she unpacked the SUV she had rented, she realized how differently she felt this time around. She wasn't filled with the dread and apprehension that had consumed her in late August. Now, she was actually looking forward to the future, excited about the possibility of seeing Annie and just . . . talking to her. And Chris. She hoped Chris would give her the chance to explain. Jessie was still filled with guilt whenever she thought of that night up on Ridge Trail. And guilt was an emotion she had not experienced in a very long time. But Chris had offered her comfort, friendship, companionship, everything that Jessie had needed that night. And Jessie had simply thrown it in her face. She had made a mockery of their attempted lovemaking. If she were Chris, she wouldn't want anything more to do with her. But then, she wasn't Chris.

That evening, before dark, Jessie put on her running shoes and jogged to the trailhead of Elk Meadow. It had turned colder as soon as the sun faded from view, and she had pulled on sweatpants over her shorts. She ran, the dusk swallowing her, and for the first time in her adult life, she felt free. No long forgotten memories haunted her, no hatred filled her heart. She was starting over. And she would begin by seeing her mother.

It was after dark when she returned to her cabin and the stew that had been simmering all afternoon was ready. She took a bowl and a glass of wine to the back porch and ate there in the silence of the forest. She didn't hear the owls and she wondered if they had left when the weather turned colder and gone to lower elevations or if they had simply moved on to better hunting grounds.

Later, she put on her jacket and walked to the stream, making her way by the light of the moon, her breath frosty in the night air. She peered through the trees and saw no lights from Chris's cabin. Was she at the Rock House having dinner? Was she still working? Jessie shrugged and turned back. It wasn't Chris she was here to see.

Chapter Twenty-four

After Chris and Annie finished their dinner, they sat at the table to play a game of cards. Gin was Annie's favorite and they played that most often. She usually won, too. Chris had been able to put Jessie from her mind, despite the fact that Mary Ruth had casually mentioned that she was back. Chris told herself that she didn't care, that it wasn't any of her business. But Jessie could only be here for one reason. To see Annie. Chris needed to warn her, to prepare her, but she couldn't bring herself to tell Annie.

"I win again," Annie said, displaying her cards.

"I keep telling you, poker's my game," Chris said. She poured the last of the wine into her glass and knew that Annie would open another one. On the nights when she stayed for cards, they went through two bottles, even though Chris complained of a headache all the next day.

"Yes, Roger tells me how you've taken all their money." Annie smiled and dealt another hand.

Chris still enjoyed the nights she visited. After Jessie had left, she had cancelled on Annie for a week or two, not feeling up to discussing her. But now, she usually had dinner with her twice a week, especially now that things had slowed down in the mountains. In the months that she had been coming here, Chris could notice the change in Annie. She smiled over the littlest things now and she showed much more interest in what was happening in town. They still discussed Jessie, but not always. Chris wondered if maybe Annie had transferred her feelings for Jessie to Chris. But that was okay, too. It wasn't like Chris had a mother figure in her life.

"Chris, why aren't you dating any of those nice men in town?" she asked suddenly.

Chris laughed, wondering why it had taken Annie so long to ask. Mary Ruth had asked after the first week.

"Where did that question come from?"

"You spend your free time visiting an old woman. Why aren't you out with some young man?"

"Annie, I'm . . . gay. I thought you knew that," she said easily.

"Gay? Well, I'll be."

"You didn't know?"

"Now how would I have known?"

Chris shrugged. "I thought everyone knew."

"It's not like I gossip with the locals, you know. But it just never occurred to me, I guess." She reached across the table and grasped Chris's hand. "It's okay, of course. It's none of my business what you do in your own bedroom."

Chris laughed again.

"Annie, there's not anything going on in my bedroom. I mean, this is Sierra City, not San Francisco."

Annie blushed. "Well, you know, I read a lot. It's not exactly a foreign concept to me."

"Exactly what kind of books do you read?"

"Never you mind, young lady. Play your hand."

Chapter Twenty-five

Chris met Roger for breakfast at the Rock House Café just like she had been doing nearly every morning since June. He had the Sacramento paper spread out on the table and she tapped his shoulder before sitting down.

"Morning," he said absently. "You're late."

"Thanks, Donna," Chris said, taking the coffee from her. She rubbed her forehead and shut her eyes, ignoring Roger.

"Chris, Dave's got fresh muffins," Donna said.

"Nothing for me, thanks."

Roger put the paper aside and studied her. "Annie keep you up again?"

"Cards." She nodded.

"And?"

"Wine."

He laughed. "You're not as young as you used to be, McKenna."

"Tell me something new."

"Oh, sheriff called me last night. They busted some guy in San Francisco that had the wallets of the Jackson boys."

"You're kidding. Is he the shooter?" she asked. This was the first news they'd had on the murders.

"Too early to tell. He really didn't know much. They've kept him in the dark through the whole investigation."

"Typical," she said.

"Yeah. I think they're hoping to get a lead on the girl."

"Roger, you know she's dead. It's been over two months."

"Yeah. Probably find her in the spring. Some poor sucker from the city will be out hiking off the beaten path and stumble over her."

Chris nodded and finished her coffee. "How's it looking today?"

"Slow for a Friday. The lodge is only half full this weekend. They're predicting a storm by Sunday though. Might be our first major snow storm."

They had had a few light dustings, but not much. Sierra Peak was nearly white, but there was no snow in Sierra City.

"Yeah. Then we can look forward to skiers and those damn snowmobiles. I hate snowmobiles, Roger."

Chris got up and pushed the chair back under the table, grabbing a few stray hash browns from Roger's plate. She fished a couple of bills from her pocket and tossed them on the table.

"See you at the office."

She went out into the sunshine and squinted, then quickly put on her sunglasses. Storm by Sunday? Hard to imagine with all that blue sky staring down at her now. She rubbed her forehead again. Damn Annie! When would she learn?

Chapter Twenty-six

Jessie paused at the trailhead to Elk Meadow, catching her breath. She had jogged at her usual time, hoping to meet Chris on the road. She was oddly disappointed when no Jeep passed her. She shrugged and started up the trail. She would run into her sooner or later, she knew. She also knew that she was hoping Chris could be the one to help her bridge the gap between Annie and herself. That is, if Chris would be willing.

She jogged the two-mile loop without really seeing it, her mind absorbed with the prospect of meeting Annie. She was surprised when she was again back at the trailhead. She slowed to a fast walk to cool down, then finally to a slow walk as she got off the road and hiked the stream to her cabin.

After her shower, she went about unpacking some of the personal things she had brought with her this time. She held up the painting that she had picked up years ago in San Francisco, elk grazing in a meadow, spring flowers all around them, mountains in the distance.

It was this painting that had kept her sane all these years. There was already a nail over the fireplace, so she pulled a chair closer and hung the painting, getting down to see if it was straight.

Too low, but she shrugged. It would have to do. She had a few books, in case she got the urge to read, and she put these on the small bookshelf. A clock for the kitchen and a spice rack that she'd bought in Sacramento went on the counter. Her crystal wineglasses had survived the trip intact and she put those away, along with the few other cooking utensils she had picked up after her flight. She added water to the vase on the table, taking a quick sniff of the fresh flowers. They would last a few more days, she thought.

She made a sandwich for lunch, taking it on the porch along with a glass of tea. Before long, a Steller's jay spotted her and swooped down on the railing, eyeing her suspiciously. She pulled off a corner of the crust and tossed it for the bird, making a mental note to pick up some birdseed and a feeder. She had always enjoyed watching the birds at the feeders when she was growing up. She thought that must be one of Annie's hobbies, because neither she nor Jack ever filled the feeders that she could remember. But they were always full. She remembered now how Annie would sit on the back porch after dinner while she and Jack watched television or she did her homework. What was she doing out there by herself all those evenings? Watching birds? Thinking? Wishing she could enjoy their company in the living room? Jessie again felt a wave of loneliness and guilt settle over her. Her mother had spent most of her adult life in isolation, even in her own home.

Jessie stared out at the trees, wondering why she never asked her mother anything. As a child, was she so consumed with her father that she didn't even notice her mother? And later, so filled with resentment, that she couldn't stand the sight of her? Yes. She knew now what she didn't know then. She blamed Annie for what Jack had done to her.

But she didn't want to think about it now. She took her plate back inside and grabbed the car keys off the counter.

She drove back up Pine Street to the main road and turned

towards town, passing the ranger station on her way. She spotted the dusty black Jeep around back and she was surprised at the tightening in her chest. She shook it off and drove slowly through town, glancing down Nevada Street where the Rock House Café was. Only two cars were parked in front and she figured the lunch crowd had already gone. She turned her attention back to the road, passing the few shops that were still open this time of year. A lot of the tourist shops, those that catered to the biking crowd, closed after Labor Day, not to open again until May. The ones that were still open would probably close after the Christmas holidays. Just outside of town was the Pine Creek Lodge. It had been called the Sierra Lodge back when Jessie was a kid. It looked bigger now and she thought it must have been expanded. In those days, the rental shop was not there, she noted, as rows of mountain bikes stood chained to the rack.

A few miles outside of town, she turned left on the forest road, surprised at how familiar everything was to her. She had avoided this road when she had been here in August, but now, she drove confidently, knowing exactly where she was, remembering every turn. Suddenly, she clamped down hard on the steering wheel. There it was, the house she had grown up in, standing tall on the hill, like always. The trees were bigger, she noted, but little else had changed. The two-story log cabin looked as familiar to her now as it had sixteen years ago. She slowed to a crawl as she passed the driveway, looking at the fading geraniums planted around the mailbox. She sped up then, hoping Annie wasn't sitting on the back porch. She would hate to be caught spying this way. She had originally thought she would be able to turn in and drive right up to the house, but she had been unable to bring herself to do it. Was she embarrassed? Ashamed? It had been sixteen years, after all. She had said some terrible things to Annie then. It wouldn't surprise her if Annie slammed the door in her face. She drove on up the road, past the old bridge that looked exactly the same. She stopped on the other side and got out, remembering the time she had caught hell from her father for going skinny-dipping in the stream one hot summer. Of course, being the only girl with three boys hadn't helped. She must have been all of ten. She smiled slightly, remembering that carefree time in her life where the summers seemed to last forever. She tried to think of their names. Ricky Burton and his twin brothers, but their names wouldn't come to her. They had moved away the following year and she had lost her only playmates. But it didn't matter. That was the last summer she remembered fondly. After that, well . . . things changed.

She drove a little farther on the forest road before turning around. She had lost the courage to see Annie today. She only slowed a fraction coming down the hill, turning to her left briefly to look at the house. She drove back through town, then on impulse, turned onto Nevada Street and stopped in front of the Rock House Café. What she really wanted was a cold beer.

There were only a handful of people in there this time of day. Only one table was occupied, the rest of the patrons sat at the bar. She walked to a corner booth, feeling the eyes of the locals on her. She didn't recognize any of them, but it had been a long time. She wondered if the man Jack used to call Tree still owned the bar. She had her answer when a giant of a man stepped from the kitchen and walked towards her.

"What can I get you, miss?" he asked. His gray hair was cut close in a military fashion and the sleeves of his flannel shirt were rolled to his elbows. He had a white bar towel slung over one large forearm and a pen stuck behind his right ear. She thought he looked every bit the bartender.

"I'll have a draft beer, please," she said.

"Budweiser or Coors?"

"Budweiser will do."

"Coming right up." He ambled away, catching an order for another pitcher without even looking at the table behind him.

"Hey, Tree, did you hear about them catching that man that did in those two boys this summer?"

Jessie looked up at the table where the two men were sitting. Judging by their uniforms, they were two of the many locals who worked in the casinos in Reno.

"No, I hadn't heard," he said as he expertly topped off a cold mug, then proceeded to fill a pitcher with the same.

"I just saw Roger on the street. They arrested some guy in San Francisco who had their wallets. Ends up being some big drug thing, Roger said. Seems Senator Jackson's boys got mixed up with the wrong crowd."

"Folks will forget about that come election time, Ray." Tree put down a napkin and set her mug on top of it. "Here you go, miss."

"Thank you."

"Run a tab?"

"Oh, no. This will be all." She took out a crumbled five-dollar bill from her jeans pocket. "How much?"

"Buck fifty," he said. He smiled at her and she noticed that his eyes were nearly the same color as his hair.

"In that case, I will have another and keep the change."

"Sure thing, miss."

She took a long swallow of the cold beer. She rarely drank beer in New York. Wine was her favored drink. She wondered why she felt inclined to drink it here. Even in August, she had enjoyed a cold beer after her afternoon hikes. She sat there quietly, playing with her napkin. When her beer was finished, she motioned for Tree to bring her the other one.

Just then the door opened and Tree stopped on his way to her booth.

"McKenna," he greeted.

"Tree. Seen Roger?"

Jessie heard the too familiar voice and she sat back against the seat, her pulse pounding. The last place she wanted to run into Chris was the local beer joint.

"Nah. He never comes in before four-thirty. Ray said he seen him out front earlier." Tree brought her new mug and set it down on a fresh napkin. "Here you go, miss."

"McKenna, he was heading out to the campgrounds," one of the men called to her.

"Okay, thanks."

Jessie heard the door close and breathed a sigh of relief. She knew she would have to see Chris sooner or later, but she hoped that meeting could be held in private. After all, the last time Jessie had seen her, they had been on the ledge, Chris wanting to make love to her, and she wanting . . . well, some sort of punishment.

Chapter Twenty-seven

Two mornings later, Sunday, Jessie was jogging on her way to Elk Meadow when Chris's Jeep passed her. Jessie thought she was going to keep going, but at last she stopped, her arm hanging out the unzipped window.

Jessie's heart pounded in her ears and she knew it wasn't from running. She was nervous. She walked the last few feet to the Jeep.

"Hello, McKenna."

"Jessie. Or are you Jennifer again?"

Well, she deserved that.

"I'm Jessie to you," she said quietly.

"Mary Ruth said you were back but I wasn't sure I believed her." She arched an eyebrow at her. "What are you doing here this time?"

Ah, she deserved that, too.

"I want to see Annie," Jessie said. "Did you tell her I was here?"

Chris shook her head. "No. I want no part of it."

Jessie ran a hand through her short hair, wondering how she could possibly begin to apologize to Chris. She knew it couldn't be done in the middle of the road.

"Can we get together and talk? I need to apologize and to . . . explain," she said.

Chris's blue eyes were cool as they met hers.

"No. I don't think so, Jessie. Like you said, you warned me. It just took me awhile to catch on."

Chris gave a humorless smile. And she deserved that, too.

"I can explain," she said quietly.

"I'm sure you can. But I don't want to play."

With that, Chris drove off. Apparently, she had not forgotten or forgiven her.

Chris drove to the Rock House, her hands gripping the steering wheel hard. She thought she had forgotten the hurt and humiliation, but she hadn't. It had been two months and she had tried to put Jessie Stone, the Jessie Stone that she knew, from her mind. But here Jessie was, as if no time had passed at all. She could explain? Sure she could. But Chris was torn. Something had happened that night. The Jessie that she was getting to know was not the Jessie that she found on the ledge. And yes, she wanted an explanation. She deserved an explanation.

She parked beside Roger's old truck, debating whether to tell Roger that Jessie was back. The café was crowded for Sunday breakfast and she joined Roger and Ellen at a booth.

"Morning, McKenna," Roger said over the top of his newspaper.

"Hi." She pushed the newspaper down. "Don't be rude, Roger. I have to look at that newspaper every day of the week. Can't you make an exception on Sunday?"

"Can't a man read the Sunday sports page without you women complaining?" But he folded the paper and put it beside him.

"How do you put up with him?" Chris asked Ellen.

"He has his quirks, but he has his good points, too," Ellen said.

Donna brought over coffee for Chris and refilled Roger's and Ellen's cups. "Everyone want the usual?"

151

"I'll need extra hash browns," Roger said. "You know how McKenna steals mine."

Chris ignored him, knowing it was true. She sipped from her coffee, then decided to confide.

"Guess who I ran into this morning?"

Roger shrugged with eyebrows raised.

"Jessie Stone."

"You're joking. She's back?"

"Apparently. I didn't hang around to talk, but she says she's here to see Annie."

"You should go warn her, McKenna."

"Me? Why me? Why not you?"

"Because you're the only one who's talked to Jessie Stone, McKenna. Remember, you became *friends* with her," he said.

"Is that what I called it?" She still felt a stab whenever she thought of that night on the ledge. She was still pissed off, she knew, but to think that the desire and passion she had felt had not been returned, that it had only been staged, had hit her where it hurt most. Her ego. She wanted to tell herself that the sexual attraction she felt for Jessie was simply a crush on a damn picture, but she knew it wasn't. She had gotten to know her, as much as Jessie would allow, anyway. And she liked her. And that night on the mountain, when they had gone camping, when they had kissed and touched each other in the moonlight, that was not the same Jessie that had used her that night on the ledge. That's the Jessie she wanted to get to know. That's the Jessie that sent her blood boiling. Not the stranger that she found on the ledge with an empty bottle of wine.

"I really wish I knew Annie Stone like you two," Ellen said. "She's just the 'hermit lady' to me."

"She's a wonderful woman, Ellen. She's got a spirit that I can only hope to have at her age. After everything that has happened to her, she's still not broken," Chris said.

"No," Roger agreed. "She's a tough old broad."

After their leisurely Sunday breakfast, Chris headed back to her cabin, hoping to sit on the back porch and read, maybe let Dillon chase chipmunks for awhile. She wanted to sit and relax and enjoy the sunshine while it lasted. It had been a hectic few weeks and she wanted to take advantage of the down time. On the drive, she noticed the storm clouds building in the west and remembered Roger's warning that they might get their first real snowfall of the season. Well, relaxing by a fire was just as appealing. And on that note, she was glad she had taken a day to drive to Yosemite to collect her winter clothes.

By the time she stopped in front of her cabin, the clouds had blocked out the sun and a cool breeze was blowing through the trees. She slammed the Jeep door and looked out at the sky, watching the clouds stream by overhead. The wind seemed to be picking up speed by the second and the pine trees swayed under its force. Firewood. She had not brought any up on the porch yet. The weather had just been too nice to worry about a fire. If it was a major storm, her neatly stacked pile would be buried by morning.

Jessie stood watching from the cover of the woods as Chris brought armloads of firewood to her porch. She moved with efficient grace and Jessie was drawn to her, like she had been that very first day when she'd looked into her sky-blue eyes. She wanted to remember that night up by the falls, when Chris had kissed her so passionately, so tenderly. That night when she had wanted to lie down on the forest floor and make love with this woman. Instead, the memory of their last night together came rushing at her and she tried to push it away, as she had been doing for the last eight weeks. Chris had been so gentle, so caring. Jessie had needed someone that night, yes. But wanted to hurt. The feelings that Chris brought out had little to do with pain. Making love with Chris would have solved little in her quest to purge herself of her father and his hold over her. She wanted to feel pain and anguish. And she did. Only she had transferred that pain and hurt onto Chris and that was very unfair. Chris had offered her consolation that night and Jessie had taken it and run.

She couldn't blame Chris for the way she had treated her this morning. She deserved it, she knew. But that made it so much harder to face her now, and face her she must. She had to apologize, she had to explain. She needed Chris. She needed her to be the bridge to Annie. Jessie knew she could never face Annie alone.

She watched Chris carry split logs up on the porch and drop them beside the back door, then disappear around the cabin for more. Jessie looked up at the sky and wondered if snow was on the way. She had not bothered with a radio since she had been back and knew nothing of the weather. The dark clouds gathered quickly overhead and she felt the wind whip at her hair. She stayed where she was until Chris finally went inside the cabin, then she pushed away from the cedar she was leaning against and made her way to the cabin.

Her palms were sweating by the time she reached the back porch and she rubbed them against her jeans, cursing her nervousness. She took a deep breath before climbing the few wooden steps and stood silently on the porch. She saw through the window that Chris was laying newspaper, then twigs and pinecones in the fireplace, in anticipation of a later fire. She hesitated only a second before knocking lightly on the door.

Chris knew who it was without looking. No one ever used her back door. She turned and their eyes met through the small window in the door. She wasn't ready to face her, she knew. She hadn't had time to sort out her feelings, now that Jessie was back. She stood from her crouch by the fireplace and walked slowly to the door, her eyes never leaving Jessie's.

She opened the door and stood there, blocking the way inside. Jessie had a sudden fear that Chris would refuse to let her in, would refuse to see her. But, after a few seconds, Chris stepped aside and motioned her in. Jessie looked around the cabin, nearly identical to her own. Her eyes were drawn to the painting over the fireplace. Sierra Peak. She would recognize it anywhere.

Chris stood patiently and Jessie finally brought her eyes back to the woman before her. But Chris's face was still hard, eyes still cold.

"Like I said earlier, McKenna, I want to apologize and explain what happened," Jessie said.

"And like I said, I don't really care."

Jessie took a step closer, bravely standing within a few feet of her.

"But the problem with that, McKenna, is that I know you do care." Jessie shrugged and walked over to the sofa and sat without being invited. "We're going to talk so you might as well sit down."

"Look, whatever it is you feel you need to say, forget it. I have."

"No you haven't, Chris. And neither have I."

Chris opened her mouth to protest, then closed it again. This woman left here two months ago without so much as a hint of an explanation and now, she wanted to explain, as if it had been only yesterday.

"Chris, please?" Jessie asked quietly. "I need to explain. I need to tell you what happened. Please?"

Chris finally dared to look into the dark eyes that had been haunting her for two months.

"You're right," she said. "Despite what happened that night, what you made me do up there on that ledge, I do still care. I wish to God I didn't."

"I know. I'm so sorry, Chris. I never meant to hurt you."

"I didn't deserve that," Chris said quietly.

"God, I know. You don't know how many times I've cursed myself for what happened, for what I wanted to happen. I didn't want to make love with you. I haven't been able to make love with anyone. It's always been just sex."

"I don't play that way," Chris said.

"I know. But it was the only game I knew." She patted the sofa beside her. "Please, sit down."

Chris reluctantly moved beside her, settling in the corner of the sofa and facing Jessie, waiting.

For the second time, Jessie was about to confess to someone about her father, about what he had done. Somehow, it was more difficult telling Chris than confiding in Dr. Davies. She didn't want

Chris to think any less of her, she didn't want Chris to judge her. It hadn't been her fault, she knew that, but still, people's reactions could be so different. And she didn't want Chris to think she was tainted in some way, even though Jessie thought that herself.

"That night, out on the ledge, when I was by myself, I had a . . . revelation, I guess. Finally, all of the missing pieces came together. Jack, he . . . he abused me. Sexually," she whispered.

Chris slammed her eyes shut. She had suspected, of course. But to have Jessie whisper the words, to hear her pain, made it all so real. And she felt anger bubble up for this man she had never met, but whose actions had affected two women to whom she had grown close.

"Please say something," Jessie whispered.

"Should I say I'm sorry?" Chris asked. "That seems so trivial." Chris reached across the sofa and took Jessie's hand. "I was afraid it was true. Even before I met you, just listening to Roger and Annie tell me about your childhood, it just sounded too strange."

"You knew? Did . . . did Annie?"

Chris shook her head. "I asked her once if she thought it could have happened. She didn't. Jack had so many women, so many affairs," Chris said. "I think Annie feels like Jack took you away from her as punishment or something." Chris squeezed Jessie's hand tightly. "But I am very, very sorry."

"Me, too. He took away my childhood, my mother." She shrugged. "My life."

"It's not too late, Jessie."

"I hope not. I want to see her. My therapist thinks I'm rushing things, though. I don't think she really believes I've accepted this." Jessie met Chris's eyes, now so different. The coolness was gone and warmth had again taken its place. "That night, when it all came back to me, do you know how close I came to just jumping into that damn canyon?"

"No."

"But then, he would win. He would win all over again. So I just sat there and let it all come, even though I didn't want it to. I just wanted it to go away. I cried and cried. And I felt so ashamed. And when you found me, you offered me comfort. But I didn't feel like I deserved that from you. I didn't deserve to be cared for."

"So you did the one thing that would push me away?" Chris asked softly.

Jessie nodded. "It was all I was used to."

"It doesn't have to be that way, Jessie. You shouldn't feel ashamed for something that someone else did."

"I know."

Jessie stared at the painting of Sierra Peak, drawing comfort from it, much like she did from her own painting all these years.

"I like it," Jessie said, motioning to the painting. "It's Sierra Peak, right?"

"Yes."

"Local artist?"

"Very." Then Chris smiled. "Annie gave that to me."

"She paints?"

"A hobby, but I think she's quite good."

Jessie stood up and walked to the painting, studying it. The detail was very good, the colors perfect. Yes, it was quite good. She turned back to Chris.

"You know so much about her. Do you think she would be receptive to seeing me?"

Chris laughed. "Are you kidding?"

"I wasn't exactly a good daughter, you know. And I think my parting words to her were . . . well, something about her dying," Jessie admitted. "Why didn't you tell her that I was here?"

"I didn't . . . I didn't want to hurt her. Besides, you had already left. What good would it have done to tell her then?"

"And now?"

"Let's just say it'll be a damn shock to her. Jessie, she never gave up hope that you might some day come back into her life. She's told me as much. But there's a lot between you, a lot that you don't know about each other. And you have resentment to work through. Resentment on both your parts. Annie won't admit it, but I'm sure she resents you in some small way for her failed marriage. You know, you came along and took Jack away from her."

"But I never . . ."

"No, I didn't mean it was intentional. Hell, I'm just talking here, Jessie. I just want you to be prepared. Don't think you're going to waltz in there and everything's going to be fine."

"McKenna, I know it's not going to be easy." Jessie reached out and grasped Chris's arm. "I'm just thankful you're still talking to me," she said. "If I were you, I would have probably thrown me out by now."

Chris shook her head. "No you wouldn't."

"You should hate me for what I did to you," Jessie stated.

"Probably," Chris said quietly. "But I'm not really one to dwell on the past."

"Will you take me to see Annie?"

"I'll call her. But you know she's going to be really pissed off at me," Chris said.

"For not telling her in August?" Jessie asked.

"Yeah. This is going to be a shock to her, Jessie."

Jessie watched as Chris grabbed her cell phone and pushed the numbers quickly, as if she dialed them often.

"Annie, it's me," Chris said. She moved away from Jessie, wanting a little privacy as she spoke to Annie.

"Chris, hello. I was just watching the weather. We're getting a storm tonight, maybe twelve inches in the mountains."

"Did you get that firewood delivered?" she asked.

"Yes, I did, and the boys stacked it neatly by the house. Thank you."

"Well, I'll help you bring some inside." She glanced at Jessie, who was sitting on the sofa, trying to listen. "Do you feel like company?"

"I would love to see you, Chris. Dinner?"

"No, not dinner. I won't bother you with that. Actually, I have . . . a friend here that wants to meet you, is all," she said, glancing at Jessie.

"Someone wants to meet me? Oh, Chris, what have you been telling them?"

"Nothing like that, Annie. It's someone I want you to meet."

"Well, then come on over. Hopefully the storm won't catch you."

"Thanks. We'll be over later. And Annie? Get out a good bottle of wine." She disconnected, then stared at the phone in her hand. "You're going to need it," she murmured.

Jessie smiled, having heard most of the conversation. She wondered how Annie would react to her. For that matter, she wondered how she would react to Annie. She had spent the last sixteen years hating her. Could she get past that?

Chris watched Jessie, seeing the different emotions cross her face and the color drain from her face.

"What's wrong?" she asked before she could stop herself. She didn't want to care about her, but she was finding it difficult keeping her distance.

"I think I'm terrified of seeing her, Chris."

Chris nodded. What could she say to that?

Jessie stood, walking slowly to Chris and grasping her arms.

"Thank you for doing this," she said.

Chris tried to pull away. She was doing this for Annie, she told herself. But Jessie's hands wouldn't release her.

"Don't hate me," Jessie whispered. "Please?"

"I don't hate you, Jessie. But I'm doing this for Annie, not for you. It has nothing to do with what happened between the two of us."

Jessie dropped her hands.

"Well, McKenna, I'm glad to see my actions that night haven't affected you." Her voice was hard, Jessie knew, but she wasn't used to apologizing. And she certainly wasn't used to needing people.

Chris watched her withdraw, but she refused to take back her words. Yes, it still hurt when she thought about that night and she wasn't ready to forgive.

Chapter Twenty-eight

The wind was biting when they stepped outside and Chris grabbed her coat from beside the door. The clouds hung low over the trees, promising snow, and she saw Jessie pull the collar of her own coat around her ears.

They drove in silence, Chris occasionally glancing at Jessie who was wringing her hands together nervously. She finally shoved them both between her legs.

"What's wrong?"

"Hell, I'm nervous, McKenna. What do you think?"

Chris was nervous, too. This was a hell of a thing to pull on Annie, and Chris had no idea what her reaction would be. Chris wouldn't be a bit surprised if Annie fainted straight away.

She parked in her usual spot and cut the engine, both of them staring out towards the house.

"Come on," Chris said. "It'll be fine."

Jessie followed her up the steps that were once so familiar to her. She remembered countless times running up them, two at a time. She looked at the front door and watched as Chris raised her hand to knock, wondering why she suddenly wanted to pull that hand back and turn around and leave. She wasn't ready. She didn't know if she would ever be ready.

"Annie?" Chris called as she opened the door.

"Come in, dear. I'll be right there."

Chris met Jessie's eyes before walking inside. She could see the tension and worry in them, and she offered a small smile. "You'll be fine," she whispered.

They walked in and Jessie was practically hiding behind Chris. She knew she wasn't mentally prepared for this, and she wanted to turn and run when she heard footsteps coming from the back room. The room that used to be Jack's study. She looked around quickly, seeing a few familiar things, but not much. The room had been redecorated, thankfully. It hardly looked like the house of her childhood.

"Well, Chris, I was surprised to hear from you today," Annie said and Chris bent to kiss her cheek.

"Hi Annie."

She stepped aside then and motioned to Jessie, who was still standing behind her.

"Oh, dear God in heaven," Annie whispered. Her hand clutched at her chest and she grabbed Chris's arm to steady herself. Her eyes flew to Chris. "Where did you find her?" she asked, her eyes darting between Chris and Jessie.

"Well, she kinda found me," Chris said.

Jessie stood there, speechless. The old, grieving woman she expected was nowhere to be found. Annie looked younger now than she had sixteen years ago. Her eyes were bright and sparkling, no longer the dull blue that Jessie remembered. She stood straight and there was a grace to her walk, not the slow, tired shuffle that she recalled hearing. She raised her head, but she couldn't bring herself to meet Annie's eyes.

"Jessie?"

Jessie looked up at Chris, trying to draw strength.

"This is Annie," Chris finally said.

Jessie at last met the eyes of her mother, clear and blue. She attempted a small smile and nodded.

"Why don't we sit down?" Chris said, leading Annie into the living room. She glanced back over her shoulder and motioned for Jessie to follow. She whispered to Annie then. "Are you okay?"

"Of course I'm not okay," she said quietly.

Annie sat on the sofa and Jessie took an armchair. Chris stood between them, looking from one to the other. She shook her head, then bit her bottom lip. It wasn't supposed to be like this. They weren't even looking at each other, much less talking. She went into the kitchen and found the bottle of wine and brought it back with three glasses. Annie seemed to have recovered from her shock a little by then.

"For so long I've wished for you to walk through that door, though I never thought that you actually would. Now that you have, I'm speechless." Annie looked at Jessie when she spoke, but Jessie's eyes were staring at her clenched hands. Annie saw the relief in them when Chris returned. "Now, maybe you'll tell me how you two know each other," she said, looking at Chris for an answer.

Chris raised her eyebrows questioningly, then glanced at Jessie.

Jessie cleared her throat, then turned pleading eyes to Chris. "Do you mind?"

"I don't believe this," Chris muttered under her breath. She sat down next to Annie and handed her a glass of wine. "Drink up," she said and touched Annie's glass with her own. They all took a long swallow and Chris refilled their glasses again, wondering where to begin. At the beginning, she supposed.

"Annie, I first met Jessie in August," she said.

"August? And you didn't tell me?"

Chris ignored her question, but shot an "I told you so" look at Jessie.

"She said some pretty awful things about you then and I guess I took up for you and told her some things that she either didn't remember or didn't know. Then we sort of had an argument and she left. Anyway, she came back to see you, to talk, so I brought her." She spread her hands out. "Is that brief enough?" she asked Jessie.

"Any more brief and no one would have followed you," Jessie murmured. "Including me."

Annie saw Chris's quick smile and wondered how well they knew each other. There was a familiarity between them, yet it couldn't be. Surely Chris would not have kept this a secret from her.

"Look, I'm going to leave you two alone, okay?"

"No!" they said in unison, then looked at each other for the first time.

"I mean . . . there's no need, Chris," Annie said. Truthfully, she was afraid to be alone with Jessie. She remembered the last words Jessie had spoken to her all those years ago.

"Really, please stay," Jessie said, her dark eyes again pleading.

"I just think, if you're going to talk, it really doesn't concern me, is all."

"Oh, bullshit," Annie said, slapping her knee. "You already know all the family secrets anyway." She looked at Jessie then. "That is what you want to talk about, isn't it?"

"I just . . . I just wanted to see you. To talk. To ask some questions," Jessie managed. Never in her life had she been short of words. She was always in control of every situation. Always. Only now, for some reason, she couldn't seem to voice her thoughts. She swallowed down her nervousness and looked to Chris for reassurance. She was surprised at the warmth in Chris's eyes.

"Annie, she doesn't remember . . . much of her childhood. Or she didn't."

"You don't remember what?" Annie asked.

Jessie closed her eyes. She wasn't ready for this. Dr. Davies had been right. She was rushing things. She wanted to bolt from the room rather than tell this woman, this stranger, what her father had done to her. Then warm hands settled on her shoulders and squeezed lightly and she let out her breath. When she opened her eyes, Annie was looking at Chris whose hands still rested on her shoulders.

"Listen, why don't you come back tomorrow for lunch," Annie suggested. "That'll give us both time to get used to this. We'll talk then."

Jessie finally recovered, knowing she had been given a reprieve. "I'm sure this is a shock to you," she said. "It's a shock to me, too," she admitted. "I never thought I would see you again, or at any rate, talk to you. Especially after the way that I left."

"Yes," Annie nodded. Then she smiled. "I guess that's why the mother is always the first one killed off."

Jessie's eyes widened. "You've read them?"

"Oh, yes. Every word." She looked up at Chris who still stood behind Jessie with hands resting lightly on her shoulders. "Better take her back now, Chris."

"Okay. Do you need anything?"

"Oh, no. I'm fine. I'm sure I'll have the rest of that wine, though," she said with a laugh.

They were nearly to the door before Annie called to them.

"You've grown into a beautiful woman, Jessie."

Jessie smiled at her, but said nothing. They shut the door and Jessie let out a long breath. They both looked at the sky, then hurried to the Jeep as snow flurries fell around them.

"It's freezing," Jessie said and slammed the door.

Chris started the engine and turned the heater on. She turned to Jessie who was still looking out the window towards the house.

"Are you okay?"

"She's not what I expected."

"What do you mean?"

"She's prettier than I remembered. She looks younger, even. She used to look so tired all the time, she used to walk so slowly around the house." She turned back and faced Chris. "Thank you for staying, for being there. I know you only did it for Annie but I was glad you were there."

Chris cringed at her earlier words, knowing they were a lie. She didn't only do it for Annie. She wanted to explain to Jessie, but now wasn't the time.

"In case you haven't noticed, I'm not very good at apologies . . . or thank you's," Jessie continued. "Sincere ones, anyway."

"You don't owe me explanations, Jessie."

"Of course I do. If I'd never met you, I wouldn't be here today. I'd have run back to New York and stayed. And continued with my so-called life."

"What about tomorrow? Will you be okay?"

"I think so. She's right. We both need some time."

"Annie is a fine lady, Jessie. Give her a chance."

Jessie met her eyes and did not look away. "I hope she gives me a chance. I'm the one who left. I'm the one who practically threatened her life when I left."

Chris drove away finally, not knowing what else to say. They were silent on the return trip and Chris drove to Jessie's cabin, parking beside the rental car, this time a four-wheel-drive SUV.

"Thank you again, Chris. I do appreciate it."

"No problem," Chris said.

"Do you want to come in?"

Their eyes met briefly, then Chris looked away.

"No. I've got some stuff to do," Chris said. She tapped the steering wheel lightly with her thumbs.

"Okay, McKenna. Maybe some other time?"

Jessie made no move to get out. She didn't want to be alone, but she wasn't going to beg Chris to stay.

"Supposed to snow tonight. Do you have any firewood?" Chris asked.

"There's a little on the porch. I guess Mary Ruth had some put there."

"The lodge sells it, if you need more. And I've got plenty. You're welcome to some of that," Chris offered.

"Thanks."

"Well, listen, I need to get going," Chris said again.

165

"Of course." Jessie opened the door and stepped out into the cold.

Chris raised one hand as she drove away. She knew Jessie wanted her to stay and she had been tempted. But she was worried about Annie. She drove straight back to her house and went in after a light knock.

Annie was still sitting on the sofa, her wineglass full. She raised startled eyes to Chris, then patted the sofa next to her. Chris sat down obediently.

"Explain," Annie said softly.

"I'm so sorry," Chris said.

"Oh, please." Annie dismissed her apology with a wave of her hand. "You came back, like I knew you would." She took her hand and squeezed it. "I know you care about me, Chris. And I know you wouldn't intentionally do something to hurt me. Now, tell me about August."

"I ran into her up on Ridge Trail. I recognized her immediately from the pictures on her books, but I didn't say anything. She was using a phony name. Jennifer Parker. I wanted to tell you, Annie, but I didn't know what to say. I wasn't sure she was here to see you and I certainly didn't know what to make of the fake name."

"How long was she here?"

"A couple of weeks, I guess. Maybe three. I don't know how long she was here before I ran into her. We got to know each other a little, had dinner a couple of times. I took her on an overnight backpacking trip and I finally told her that I knew who she was."

"And?"

"And I think maybe Jessie should tell you the rest," Chris said.

Annie studied her for the longest time, finally looking away and sipping from her wine.

"You said she didn't remember her childhood," Annie reminded her.

"She's been seeing a therapist, apparently several different therapists, for awhile now, I guess. I think because she didn't remember, her therapist suggested she come back here." Chris bit her lip, wondering how much to tell Annie. It really wasn't her place to talk about Jack. If Jessie wanted to confess to Annie, that was one thing. But Chris wasn't going to be the one to bring all that to light.

Again Annie watched her.

"There's something you're not telling me."

Chris shook her head.

"I found her up on Ridge Trail that last night she was here, same ledge that Jack fell from. She was just sitting there alone with a blanket and a bottle of wine," she said.

"Dear God, she wasn't going to jump?"

"No, Annie. But she had been crying when I found her and we . . . talked some. That's the last time I saw her. Until today. I'm so sorry I didn't tell you, Annie, but she was already gone. What good would it have done then?"

"Chris, it's okay. I'm not angry with you," she said. She filled their wineglasses again. "I guess I'm still in shock. I really never expected to see her again, much less talk to her. She has changed, though. She looks softer, somehow. She was a very bitter teen. And her books are so dark, even her picture on the back. But the woman I saw today wasn't the same woman in the pictures."

"No, I think maybe that woman is gone," Chris said. "But she has a lot to talk about, Annie. And she may say some things that you don't want to hear."

Annie reached over and patted Chris's knee.

"I'll be fine. I just don't want to end up in one of her books, you know?"

Chris laughed, then stopped when she realized Annie was serious.

She left a short time later, after hauling enough logs inside for a couple of fires and stacking more on the back deck. The snow was still light, barely sticking, but the temperature had dropped into the twenties already and the wind howled through the trees as she walked to her Jeep. Snow by morning, for sure.

Chapter Twenty-nine

Jessie rolled over and glanced at the clock. Nine-twenty already. She closed her eyes and pulled the covers to her chin, trying to ward off the chill that had settled in the cabin. She could not get to sleep the night before and only after drinking an entire bottle of wine did sleep come. Her thoughts alternated between Annie and Chris. She should feel relieved that she was finally going to talk to Annie, to get everything out in the open, but she couldn't get Chris off her mind. The attraction she felt for Chris was completely foreign to her and she didn't know exactly what to do about it. But did it matter? Any feelings that Chris may have had for her were surely killed that night on the ledge. Anyway, it was probably best left alone. Who knew what was going to happen? Even if she and Annie talked and cleared the air, then what? She would most likely return to New York and her empty apartment and try to make a life there. But she didn't want to go to New York. She didn't belong there. She wasn't certain she belonged anywhere.

She suddenly remembered the snowfall of the night before. She threw off the blankets and hurried to the window and the sight outside her bedroom took her breath away. How many years since she'd seen anything this beautiful? Branches heavy with snow drooped to the ground, shining bright in the sunlight. Yesterday's wind had stilled and the only sound came from the melting snow as it fell from the trees. A squirrel scampered over the blanket of white and up the cedar tree next to the cabin. She again wished she had a feeder there.

She closed the blinds, conscious of the smile on her face. She didn't bother with clothes, she simply pulled the robe tighter and hurried out the door. She grabbed a handful of snow and brought it to her mouth, laughing out loud as she bit down. She tossed the snow down and looked around, taking in deep breaths of the cold mountain air. Beautiful.

She went back in and showered, then had a bowl of cereal with her coffee. She wished she had gone to the lodge for more firewood, or at least taken Chris up on her offer. She had enough wood left for a small fire this morning, but it wouldn't last long. She made a mental note to pick some up when she was out. Before long, she heard snowplows and knew they would be clearing the side roads as soon as the county roads were done. She was again glad she had rented a four-wheel drive. If a major storm were to hit, they would be unable to keep the roads clear for long.

Jessie broke off the end of a loaf of French bread and scattered it near the cabin so she could watch the jays bicker over it. She settled back on the sofa, an unopened book lying beside her, and watched as a squirrel came up and fought with the jays over the last few remaining bread crumbs. She intended to read and try to relax some before meeting Annie, but an hour later, the book still lay unopened.

It was Chris. She wanted to call her. She still had her cell number. Jessie thought she could call on the pretense that she needed reassurance before she saw Annie. Actually, she just wanted to see her and she hated the fact that the woman had gotten under her skin. She rolled her eyes. This she was not used to. If there was one thing she was used to, though, it was being alone. And she did that very well. Or so she thought.

"Get over it," she said aloud. "McKenna doesn't need you in her life." And she didn't need McKenna, she firmly told herself.

She wore one of the new sweaters that she had bought in New York on her last shopping expedition. She owned little that was suitable for fall or winter in the mountains, so she had spent two whole days buying jeans and sweaters and sweatsuits and even wool socks for hiking. She didn't bother with makeup. Even in the city, she rarely wore much, if any. She brushed her dark hair, then fluffed it in front with her fingers. She met her eyes in the mirror and knew she was nervous. Yesterday, Chris had been there but today, they would have no buffer.

Annie was waiting nervously for the knock on her door. She had decided on a thick vegetable stew for their lunch and she had spent the morning chopping vegetables, trying to keep busy. She had debated whether or not to serve wine with their meal, then decided she might need it after all. She selected one of her favorites from the rack in the basement and it was sitting on the counter, waiting. She was thankful Chris had brought wood up for her. She had not bothered with a fire last night, but this morning, it had helped calm her. She still couldn't believe that, after all these years, Jessie was going to walk through that door. She almost wished that she had insisted Chris join them but knew they needed this time alone. Whatever had compelled Jessie to seek her out, it had nothing to do with Chris and everything to do with Jack, most likely.

The light knock on the door brought her around quickly and she stared at the door for several seconds, unable to make her feet move.

Jessie knocked a second time before she heard footsteps approach. Was Annie nervous, too, she wondered? She took a deep breath and let it out slowly as the door opened and Annie stood there, an uncertain smile on her face.

"Jessie. Come in."

"Hello, Annie."

Jessie stepped inside, pausing beside Annie, who stood several inches shorter than she did. There was a pleasant smell coming from the kitchen and a warm fire welcomed her into the living room.

"Please, sit down. The stew is nearly ready. Just let me put the bread in the oven."

Annie hurried into the kitchen, leaving Jessie standing by the fire. She looked around at the paintings on the wall and some that were stacked in a corner. She hadn't noticed them yesterday, but they were all very good and they all had Annie's name slashed on the bottom. She was very talented for it to be just a hobby.

"Don't look too closely," Annie said as she returned with a glass of wine for Jessie.

Jessie accepted the glass despite the protest of her stomach and the memory of the slight headache she had this morning. "I think they're very good," she said, motioning to the paintings.

"Chris thinks so, too, but it's just a hobby," she said, dismissing the compliment.

"When did you start painting?" Jessie asked.

"Oh, I always dabbled, just with charcoal at first. I guess you were probably five when I started with paint."

"I never knew that."

"No, I don't suppose you did," Annie said quietly. They stared at each other for a moment, then Annie looked away. That wasn't fair, she thought.

The old Jessie would have lashed out, but she held her tongue. That would be no way for them to start.

"I like the one you gave Chris. Sierra Peak."

"Oh, that fool! She hung it where everyone could see," Annie said.

Jessie noticed her discomfort and thought she was embarrassed over her paintings. Well, you're always your own worst critic.

"I was actually going to ask you for one for myself," she said, sur-

171

prising even herself with that admission. "I suppose you find that hard to believe, after the way I left here, after what I said to you on that last day."

"Yes," Annie nodded. "I hope you're not here to carry out your threat."

"I'm really sorry I said that," Jessie said softly. She sank onto the sofa, taking her wineglass with her. She was thankful she had it now.

"Jessie, you don't have to apologize. You were a child. It was as much my fault as anyone's."

Jessie shook her head. "You were never around. Jack said it was because you didn't care about us. He said you didn't like it here in the mountains, that was why you never went with us."

It was Annie's turn to shake her head. "I wouldn't have stayed here all these years if I didn't like it. From the first day he brought me here, I knew I had come home," she said.

"So it's true what Chris said? Jack wouldn't allow you to come with us?"

"Jack loved you very much, Jessie. I think he just wanted you all to himself."

"Why did you let him?"

"Jack was a strong man, Jessie. He could be very persuasive," Annie said, meeting Jessie's dark eyes, so much like her father's.

"He hit you?" she asked, her words barely more than a whisper.

Annie was about to deny it. She had never told Roger and certainly not Chris. But what good would denying it do? If they were here to talk about the past, no sense beginning that with a lie.

"A few times," she admitted. "But I was a very quick learner," she said, a touch of the old bitterness returning. She saw Jessie pale and wondered what thoughts were going through her mind. "He never hit you, did he?" she asked quickly.

"He never hit me, no." She raised her eyes to Annie. "Why did he hit you?"

"Why? I didn't obey him, I guess. The first time was when I tried to breast feed and he insisted I use a bottle. Then again, once, when

I took you to Sacramento with me shopping. You were barely two, I think. We were late getting back and he was worried, I guess. The last time he hit me was when I took you out walking on one of the trails. You were, I don't know, four or five. He told me that I was never to take you out again. That was his job to take you out." She stared into the fire. After all these years, she didn't think that it would be so hard for her to remember, but she still felt the pain that she endured as a young mother.

"I'm sorry I didn't stand up to him, Jessie. But by that time, you were following him everywhere and it didn't seem to matter to you, anyway."

Jessie couldn't meet her eyes and she, too, looked into the fire.

"I don't have any memories of you ever doing anything with me. Was that the last time?"

"Oh, yes," Annie nodded. "After that, he started getting you ready for school, tucking you in at night and taking you with him every chance he got. I was here to cook and clean and do laundry. It was around that time that we stopped sleeping together and he moved into the spare room."

"He had . . . other lovers?"

"He had women, yes. But it wasn't like we had been intimate, Jessie. We hadn't . . . slept together in years."

Annie got up suddenly and went into the kitchen. She'd had enough talk of Jack for the moment and she found it very uncomfortable talking this way in front of Jessie, who was practically a stranger to her. She could confide in Chris without worrying about her reaction. But Annie wondered if Jessie, subconsciously or on some deep level, might believe she was lying about Jack. He was dead and his story buried with him.

"Annie?" Jessie followed her into the kitchen and she watched now as Annie's trembling hand poured more wine.

"I just needed to check on the bread," she lied.

"I'm sorry. I didn't mean to come here and talk about him, really," Jessie said.

"Yes, you did, Jessie. We need to talk about him. He's all we have between us," Annie said. "And you probably think I'm lying about all of this. To you, he was a wonderful man. Unfortunately, I never got to see that side of him." She turned and lifted the lid on the pot and stirred. "Well, I shouldn't say never. He was very nice to me when we were courting and when we first got married. But that was so long ago, Jessie."

"Why didn't you ever talk to me about all of this?"

"Oh, Jessie, you were too young at the beginning to understand. Then, later, well, you idolized your father. There was nothing I could say then. You would never have believed me."

"Why did you stay with him? Why didn't you leave?"

Annie turned and met her eyes. They were open and trusting, so she let the words come.

"I was afraid . . . for you," she said quietly.

"For me?"

"Jack had an unnatural interest in you, Jessie. And as you got older, I was so afraid he would . . . abuse you."

"Sexually?" Jessie whispered.

"Yes. And I couldn't leave you. I didn't know if you would come to me for help, but if you needed someone, who else would you go to?"

Jessie felt her eyes prick with tears and she tried to blink them back, but they came anyway. Annie had been here for her and Jessie never knew it. Sobs shook her shoulders as she remembered his words. *It'll be our little secret. You're my best girl.*

"What is it, child?" Annie walked to her and grabbed her shoulders. "What?"

"He did," Jessie stammered between her tears.

"He did what?"

"He . . ."

Annie stared at her, realization dawning of what she was trying to say.

"Oh, no, Jessie," Annie whispered. She took the crying woman into her arms, the woman who was her daughter, and held her. "Oh, no."

Jessie leaned into the comfort of her arms, then just as quickly pulled away. She wiped at the tears on her face, unable to meet Annie's eyes. She had to finish. If she didn't get it out now, then when?

"I blamed you," she said. "Jack said you weren't there for him and I believed him. And I resented you for what he was doing to me but, I couldn't make him stop. And so I just blocked it out. And when he died, I had to get away from you, from here. I hated you so much," she whispered. "So I ran. I ran from my life here and I buried all of that away and pretended that it never happened. And then it didn't happen. I didn't remember it anymore. I was ten," she said. "That's the last time I remember being a kid. After that . . ."

Annie tried to hold her tears back, but she couldn't. That bastard! She tried to reach out to Jessie, but Jessie moved away.

"No. Let me finish," she said. "I need to finish."

Annie nodded, unable to speak.

"I was never able to let anyone get close to me. I didn't have friends. Even in college, I was always alone. And sex became a game to me. It wasn't for pleasure, not mine or theirs. It was an act performed as some sort of ritual, I think. Over the years, it became that, anyway. But I didn't really know why. I started seeing a therapist after college and that's when I realized that I couldn't remember anything anymore. All I held on to was my hate and resentment for you. And the only reason I could come up with was that I blamed you for his death. I always had my memories of my childhood and they were happy and he was there. But you never were. I've seen six or seven therapists over the years and none of them could help me. When Dr. Davies suggested I come back here and see you and maybe find answers, I couldn't deny that I wanted to come back. I so badly wanted my life back.

"I met Chris out on Ridge Trail. We became . . . friends. She knew that I couldn't remember. She said some things about you, told me some things that you had told her, and bits and pieces started coming back. But Annie, I didn't want them to come back. Not when I realized what it might be. But they came and I remembered everything and I just wanted . . . to die."

"Jessie . . ."

"And when I remembered, I couldn't stay here another minute. I had to get away."

Annie didn't know what to say, so she said nothing. She just watched this woman with tears in her eyes stare back at her.

"I spent two weeks alone in my apartment. I went back over everything and I realized that I wasn't to blame and you weren't to blame. It was just him," she said quietly. "And so I had to come back to see you. To tell you why I left all those years ago."

When Annie reached out this time, Jessie didn't pull away. She cleared her throat before speaking, hoping her voice would follow.

"I'm so, so sorry. I should have realized. Maybe deep down, I . . ."

"No. You can't blame yourself. It was him, not you."

"Now what do we do?"

"I don't know. I honestly don't know," Jessie said. "Is it too late to start over?"

"Of course not. You can stay here with me," she said without thinking.

But Jessie shook her head.

"I don't think so, Annie. Neither of us are ready for that. I've got a cabin rented until mid-December."

"Mary Ruth's?"

"Yes."

"Is it close to Chris?"

"Yes."

"Good. She can be a good friend, Jessie. She has been to me."

"I know. I probably wouldn't be here today if I'd never met her," Jessie admitted. But she didn't know if Chris wanted to be a friend to her anymore.

"She came back here yesterday, after she took you home," Annie said. "She was worried about me."

Jessie nodded. "I thought she might."

"She told me a little about your time here in August. I think she's worried about you, too."

Jessie nodded. Maybe.

"I've had about enough for one day, Jessie. How about lunch?"

"Yes." Jessie, too, felt drained. And relieved. She had been preparing herself for this day for nearly two months and it had been easier than she thought it ever could be. Annie had simply accepted everything she had to say and expected no other explanations. They could never undo what Jack had done, but they could start fresh with each other.

"The table is already set. Just grab yourself a bowl there," she said, pointing to the two stacked on the counter.

They filled their bowls and took them into the dining room, where Annie had already placed hot French bread. Jessie had taken several bites before she realized there was no meat in the stew.

"Are you a vegetarian?"

"Yes. It'll do you good," she said, motioning to the stew.

"For how long?"

"Nearly seventeen years now," she said with a smile.

"No wonder Chris enjoys having dinner with you," Jessie said.

"Well, I like to think it's my company as well as my cooking."

"I didn't mean it like that, Annie," Jessie said quickly. "I know how Chris feels about you."

"Yes, Chris and I get along well, despite the differences in our ages. She's been very kind to me. Roger Hamilton brought her around one day. Do you remember Roger?"

"Yes. Has he been here all these years?"

"Oh, no. He went to Tahoe for awhile. Then Yellowstone. When he came back here, he looked me up. He was a lifesaver," she said.

"Chris says you don't go into town," Jessie stated.

"No. I withdrew for awhile, and it became a habit. If I needed something, I went to Sacramento or San Francisco. Then Roger came back and started bringing me groceries and I made fewer and fewer trips to the city. But it was my choice, Jessie. I've managed."

177

There were so many things Jessie wanted to ask, but she thought she would save that for another day. After lunch, Annie asked if she wanted to look around the house, but Jessie declined. She wasn't ready for that.

Chapter Thirty

Chris and Roger were sharing a booth at the Rock House. Chris shoved her plate away and reached for her beer instead. It had been a slow day. She and Bobby had taken their cross-country skis out, but there wasn't enough snow in most places to actually ski. The clear skies and rising temperatures had turned the snow to slush and they ended up hiking back down in their ski boots.

"If you're going to eat here, McKenna, you should just stick to potatoes. What the hell was that, anyway?"

"I don't know. I only recognized the pasta," she said.

"Maybe you could at least do chicken, McKenna."

Chris ignored him. She wasn't in the mood for his teasing tonight. Her mind was with Annie and Jessie, where it had been all day. She had picked up the phone a half dozen times to call Annie, but she convinced herself that it really wasn't any of her business. This was between Annie and Jessie. If they needed her, they knew where she was. And apparently they didn't.

"What's wrong with you?"

"Nothing, Roger."

"You've hardly said two words tonight, McKenna. What, the snow got you down?"

"What snow? It'll be gone by tomorrow," she said.

"Yeah. Probably back to Indian Summer. Hasn't this weather been something?" he asked. "It's been decades since we've had this little snow at this time of year."

"Are you so anxious to get into winter? After what happened last year?"

"That's what you're here for," he reminded her.

They both looked up when the door opened and Roger showed his surprise as the woman approached them.

"My God, it's her," he whispered. "I can't believe it."

Jessie walked purposefully to their booth, then casually shoved her hands in the pockets of her jeans.

"What the hell were you eating, McKenna?"

Chris smiled and raised her eyebrows at Jessie.

"I wish I knew." Then she moved over. "Sit down," she offered. "Do you mind?"

"Of course not. Do you remember Roger Hamilton?" she asked as Jessie slid in next to her.

"Mr. Hamilton, it's been a long time."

"Jessie Stone," Roger said, sticking out his hand. "Your pictures don't do you justice."

Chris noticed the light blush that crept up Jessie's face, and she laughed.

"Don't give her a big head, Roger."

"Be quiet," Jessie murmured and nudged Chris with her leg.

Roger raised his hand as Martha walked by.

"A couple of beers for the ladies, please," he said.

"Ladies?" Martha asked. "That's McKenna you're talking about."

Chris endured their laughter, and she leaned her elbows on the table.

"I think she hates me," she said.

"I think she has a crush on you," Roger countered.

"Don't you have to get going?" Chris asked.

"Yes, I do," he said. Then he turned to Jessie. "I'm glad you're back. Have you seen Annie yet?"

Jessie was stunned by his question, then realized that Chris had most likely told him about this summer.

"I actually saw her today."

"Good. Well, I'll leave you two to talk, then."

"I'm sure Chris will fill you in later," Jessie said lightly.

Chris and Roger exchanged glances.

"I didn't mean . . ."

"It's okay," Jessie said. "Small towns and all. I'd forgotten."

"No offense," Roger said. "But you being here is big news, although I don't think anyone knows except me and Ellen," he said. "Annie's a good friend of mine."

"Yes, I know. No offense taken."

Roger hesitated, then glanced again at Chris.

"See you tomorrow, Roger," Chris said.

After Martha brought over fresh mugs, Chris turned to Jessie.

"I had to tell someone," she explained. "And it couldn't be Annie."

"It's okay. I'm not really in hiding anymore."

"How did it go today?" Chris finally asked.

"It was . . . good, I think. We talked about a lot of things," Jessie said.

"Did you tell her?"

"Yes. And we had a good cry." Jessie put her elbows on the table and regarded Chris. "It's funny, really. I spent so many years hating her and now I can't even muster up resentment anymore. And I think I like her."

Chris nodded, surprised at how easily Jessie had accepted what had happened to her all those years ago.

"I was actually a little worried about you two today," Chris admitted.

"Just a little?" Jessie teased.

Chris shrugged. "But I told myself that it really wasn't any of my business."

"McKenna, I know you care about Annie. She's quite fond of you, too. In fact, we talked about you some."

"Oh?"

But Jessie didn't elaborate. She sipped from her beer instead. She had gone to Chris's cabin earlier, looking for her. She thought that she wanted to talk, to tell her everything that she and Annie had discussed. That's why she had driven to the Rock House, hoping to find Chris here. But she didn't want to turn their light conversation into a heavy discussion of her life. She was talked out. She was enjoying the easy companionship that Chris was offering tonight. There wasn't even a hint of the bitterness in Chris's eyes that she'd found the other day when they saw each other.

"You know, McKenna, you know more about me and my life than anyone else. And I don't know a thing about you," Jessie said, inviting Chris to tell her a little about herself. She really just wanted to spend some normal time around her, and she wasn't blind to the attraction she felt for her. Every time their thighs brushed, she felt it. She wondered if Chris could feel it, too. She wondered if Chris would allow herself to feel it.

"There's not much. Pretty boring, really," Chris said.

"Compared to mine?" Jessie laughed.

"Especially yours."

"Tell me," Jessie encouraged.

"Life story in a nutshell, huh? Shouldn't take long," Chris said. She drank a long swallow from her draft beer and motioned to Martha for another round. She should really go home and get some rest, but the thought of going home to her empty cabin with only Dillon for company wasn't appealing. What was appealing was the woman sitting next to her. Despite her vow a few months ago that if she ever saw Jessie Stone again, it would be too soon, she found herself drawn to her once again. And this time, when Jessie's thigh pressed against her own, she didn't pull away.

"I grew up in Wyoming with one older sister," Chris began. "My parents stayed together until after I was in college. Twenty-four years of marriage down the drain."

"What happened?"

"They just didn't love each other anymore, I guess. I knew it in high school and I don't know why they waited so long to end it, but they did. Dad remarried and now lives in Chicago."

"Do you see him?"

"No. His wife doesn't approve of my lifestyle so I'm not exactly welcome there. We talk a couple of times a year, though."

"And your mother and sister? Where are they?" Jessie asked.

"Mom lives here in California . . . San Diego, with her current beau. She's fifty-four and he's thirty, if that tells you anything about her taste in men."

"Her current beau?"

"Well, they've been divorced, what . . . twelve years and I'd say he's about the fifth live-in." Chris thought about her mother, who was trying so hard to make up for all the lost years while she was married. Chris sometimes got the feeling that her mother blamed her for them staying together as long as they did. "Then there's Susan, my dear sister. I haven't talked to her since I was twenty-three."

Jessie grimaced. "Your lifestyle again?"

"Oh, yeah. Now that was a fun time. I was working at Yellowstone, my first summer there as a full-timer and she came to visit. She's two years older, by the way. Anyway, she came in a little earlier than expected and walked in on me and Kathy." At Jessie's shocked expression, Chris raised her hand and smiled. "No, not in bed," she said and laughed. "We were in the living room and I was kissing her goodbye." Chris lowered her voice and leaned closer. "It wasn't exactly a peck on the cheek, either."

Jessie laughed, enjoying Chris's story. "Go on."

"Well, you'd have to know Susan to appreciate this. She was Miss Goody Two-Shoes growing up. She never did a thing wrong, made good grades, never drank alcohol or dared touch a cigarette.

Nothing. Straight as they come. I, on the other hand, never followed my parents' rules, and I wasn't afraid to party," she said and laughed again. It had been years since she'd told anyone this story. "Susan screamed when she saw us and clutched her chest in a mock heart attack, all the time her eyes were about to bug out of her head. She was so ashamed of me, she said." Chris leaned her elbows on the table and looked at Jessie. "Actually, I was surprised she even knew what was going on."

"So she left and you haven't spoken since?" Jessie guessed.

"Oh, she didn't leave until the next day, after she told me how humiliated she was and disgusted and all those other wonderful words she threw at me. But I was young and really didn't give a damn what she thought. I told her to mind her own fucking business. Of course, she didn't. She left and immediately called Mom and Dad and they actually came together to talk some sense into me. It was all so dreadful, them wondering where they had gone wrong and all that. But we've gotten past that over the years, I think. But we're not close. And Susan, well, she never got over it. I haven't talked to her since. She's married to a minister and has two kids and I doubt they even know they have an Aunt Chris."

"That's sad, McKenna. Does she see your parents?"

"She sees my father. I think she's embarrassed by Mom, though. She doesn't quite fit into Susan's perfect little world."

"And how often do you see your mother?"

"I see her maybe once a year. She's fine with it now. Probably because I've never brought a woman with me, I don't know. But she's got her own life. When I talk to Dad, he pretends I have no personal life and I pretend he doesn't have a wife who hates me."

"So, what about this Kathy?" Jessie asked with a grin.

"She was just a summer fling. She went back to college, and I never saw her again," Chris said with a wave of her hand.

"Do you make a habit of summer flings?" Jessie asked lightly.

Chris met her eyes and teasingly raised an eyebrow. "When I was younger, stuck at Yellowstone, summer flings were quite appealing."

"And now?"

Chris drank from her beer before answering. "And now I'm getting too old for summer flings," she said.

They paused when Martha brought them fresh beers.

"Run you a tab, McKenna? Don't you have to work tomorrow?"

"Thanks for keeping me in line, Martha. I guess this will be it, then."

"Maybe Roger's right," Jessie said when Martha left them.

"No, I think she just likes picking on me," Chris said.

"Well, you are quite fun to pick on," Jessie teased.

"I am, huh?"

Jessie rubbed the frost on the side of her mug with her thumb, so glad she had come looking for Chris tonight. If nothing else, she might be able to salvage a friendship. And that would be something new for her.

"Chris, I want to thank you for everything you've done. Seriously," she said.

"Seriously?"

"I told Annie today that if I'd never met you, I doubted that I would have ever found the courage to see her."

"I think you would have, Jessie. Because, deep down, you really wanted to."

"I wonder if I would have even remembered everything if you'd not been here to push me, Chris. And I really don't think I would have gone to see Annie," Jessie said, knowing it was true. "So, thank you," she said quietly. "You were there when I needed you."

"Please don't say you're talking about that night up on Ridge Trail," Chris said softly, unable to meet her eyes.

Jessie leaned closer, trying to catch Chris's eyes. "Will you never forgive me for that?"

Chris allowed her eyes to be captured by Jessie's dark ones. She'd had too many beers, she knew, because she was having a hard time remembering that night on the ledge, remembering how humiliated she felt. And it was nice to just sit and talk. She really didn't want to remember it anymore.

"Should I forgive you?" she finally asked.

"Yes. You gave me what I needed that night," Jessie whispered. "I don't ever want it to be like that again."

Chris felt her breath catch and she was unable to pull her eyes from Jessie's. She wasn't immune to her, she knew. The thigh that pressed firmly against her own had not moved, and she did not want to break the contact. But tonight was not the night to take this any farther.

"I'm glad you came here tonight," Chris said.

"Me, too."

"But it's time I got going. Dillon is probably starving."

"Okay, McKenna. Let me get your beer, at least."

Chris was going to decline, but Jessie had already pulled out her money. "Okay. I guess famous writers make a little more than search and rescue folks, huh?"

Jessie laughed. "Maybe a little."

They walked out into the cold night air, the snow crunching beneath their boots and their breath frosty in front of their faces. Jessie looked up into the night sky, watching the stars twinkling overhead.

"I have missed this sight," she said. "There are no stars in the city, you know."

"No?"

"Nope. Not a one," she said quietly.

Jessie leaned against the post railing and Chris watched her. She had the face of an angel. Beautiful wasn't quite the word to describe her and Chris felt the familiar pounding of her heart whenever she allowed her thoughts to move in this direction. It was as if in slow motion Jessie turned her head and effortlessly captured Chris's eyes.

"Thanks for the beer. And the company," Chris added.

"It was my pleasure," Jessie said. She pushed off of the post and walked close to Chris, stopping only inches away. "And thank you," she whispered, moving closer, touching her lips lightly to Chris's.

Chris didn't pull away and she sighed when Jessie left her after only a brief touch. She wanted so much more than that. She stood there long after Jessie's taillights had faded, the flame still flickering inside her.

Chapter Thirty-one

Jessie had just come outside and closed the cabin door when a car drove up. Mary Ruth Henniger climbed out gracefully and walked over to her.

"Mary Ruth, how are you today?" Jessie asked pleasantly.

"Very good, thank you."

She had a folded piece of paper in her hand and Jessie raised her eyebrows questioningly.

"What brings you out?" she asked.

"Well, I just had the strangest phone call. Annie Stone, who hasn't called me in all the years she's lived out here, rang me up to give a message to her daughter. She insisted Jessie Stone was staying at one of my cabins. She described you and I told her you weren't Jessie Stone. Why, Jessie Stone hasn't been here since her daddy died. But she insisted I give you a message."

Jessie laughed nervously, wondering how to tell this kind woman that she had been using an alias.

"Actually, I am Jessie Stone. I'm sorry."

"Well, I'll be," Mary Ruth murmured. "You've cut your beautiful long hair off. No wonder."

Jessie laughed again. It was the first thing she had done when she'd moved to San Francisco all those years ago. Her hair had reached nearly to her waist when she'd lived here. Jack always said he liked her with long hair.

"I didn't want anyone to know who I was when I came here in August," she explained. "I'm sorry about the Jennifer Parker thing."

"Well, imagine that. We all assumed you had left for good," she said. "What in the world are you doing here?" she asked bluntly.

"I came to see my mother," she said simply. She pointed at the note in her hands. "What's the message?"

"Oh, here," she said, handing her the note. "She's wants you to call her. That's her number there. You're welcome to use my phone," Mary Ruth offered.

"Thanks, but I've got a phone. I appreciate you coming all the way out here though," Jessie said politely. She waited for Mary Ruth to drive off before calling Annie.

"It's Jessie. Is everything all right?"

"Yes. Nothing's wrong, I just didn't know how else to reach you," Annie explained. "I tried calling Chris, but I can't find her."

"Oh. I didn't think to give you the number to my cell phone."

"Well, we didn't really talk about when we would get together again and tonight is my normal night to have dinner with Chris. I thought, well, you should join us. I'm sure Chris won't mind," Annie said. "I so want the two of you to be friends," she added.

Jessie smiled and nodded, wondering what Annie's reaction would be if she knew just how close they had been this summer.

"I understand. And I don't think she would mind, other than me cutting in on her time with you," Jessie said lightly. "I actually saw her last night at the Rock House. We had a chance to visit."

"Good. So that means you'll come?"

"I'll come, Annie. Thank you."

After the call ended, Jessie stood staring into the trees reflectively. Would Chris mind? She didn't think so. After all, they'd had an enjoyable visit last night. Then Jessie remembered the quiet, fleeting kiss she had given Chris when they parted. The soft sigh that Chris uttered had been nearly enough to make Jessie deepen the kiss, but she had not dared. Instead, she pulled away after the briefest of touches but not before she saw the thinly veiled desire that Chris had tried to hide.

She doubted they would have any time alone tonight. Besides, with Chris there, she and Annie would most likely not get into any heavy discussions, which was just fine with her. After yesterday, her emotions were still a bit raw.

Jessie drove into town, finishing the task she had started before Mary Ruth had come by with the message. Firewood. Chris had said the lodge sold it, and she filled the back of her SUV for a mere thirty dollars.

She stacked it neatly on the back porch but after making the many trips to and from her car with armloads of wood, she was too tired for her afternoon jog. Instead, she stretched out on the sofa, a deep sleep claiming her almost instantly.

Chapter Thirty-two

Jessie tapped her fingers on the steering wheel to the beat of a country western song that she'd never heard, but it was the only station she could pick up. She glanced forlornly at the CD player, wishing she had thought to bring a couple, at least. Then she glanced at her phone. She should really call McKenna and warn her that she'd be there. But her eyes flicked back to the road. Surely Chris wouldn't mind.

She knocked on Annie's door a short time later and heard Annie call to her. A feeling of familiarity settled over her as she opened the front door and walked inside.

"I'm in the kitchen," Annie called. "Jessie or Chris?"

Jessie laughed and shook her head. Who would have thought that just a few months ago her life had been so dark?

"It's Jessie," she called.

She glanced around the living room, her eyes traveling to the stairs. Maybe today she would tour the house, see what became of her old room. And Jack's study. It was the only place she was not allowed. She closed her eyes briefly, remembering the sound of the front door slamming and her running feet taking the stairs two at a time on her way to her room after school. She also remembered that she never called to Annie in those days, to let her know that she was home, to ask about her day and tell Annie about hers. She opened her eyes to push the memories away and was startled by the voice behind her.

"Jessie?"

She turned around quickly. "Hello, Annie."

"You're welcome to look around, Jessie," she offered gently.

"Oh, I don't know," Jessie said, dismayed that she was blushing.

"Suit yourself," Annie said with a smile and disappeared again into the kitchen.

Jessie stood there, arms wrapped securely around herself, but she couldn't stop her eyes from traveling up the stairs again. Before she knew it, her hand rested on the banister, and her right foot paused on the bottom step. Two of Annie's paintings hung on the wall along the stairway, and she glanced at them briefly before continuing up. At the top, she looked left and down the hall, which led to the master bedroom and the spare room where Jack had slept, then she turned to the right and stared at the door to her old room. The door was closed and her hand settled over the knob tightly. She paused only a second before opening it and she stood there in the doorway, her breath catching. She felt tears gather in her eyes, but she ignored them as she stepped inside. Annie had left it just the way Jessie had that morning she had walked out all those years ago. On the wall, her high school pennant still hung along with a ribbon from a game, announcing Go Bears! Beat the Lions! On the opposite wall, tacked up over her old desk, was a map of the National Forest and Sierra City. She had highlighted all of the different trails that she had hiked and her eyes traveled over them, remembering. Her bookshelf was still neatly stacked with her childhood books, save the few she had crammed into her suitcase when she left.

As she looked around the room, it dawned on her that she had not adorned the walls with posters like most adolescent girls would have. Actually, there was nothing else in the room. No pictures, no personal items. Then she noticed the hardback books propped up in one corner of her bookshelf. Her books. She pulled one out and glanced at her photo on the back, her eyes nearly lifeless in the picture. She wondered what Annie had thought. She put the book back and walked to the bed and gently touched the quilt. In all the years she had lived here, she had never once made up her bed, but every day when she'd returned from school, it was neatly made up again.

"Are you okay?" Annie asked from the doorway.

"Why did you leave all this?" she asked, waving her arms around the room.

"I always hoped you would come back, I guess. After awhile, when I knew you wouldn't, I had plans to clean it out and give your stuff away, but I never could. It's been so many years now . . ." She shrugged, leaving the thought hanging between them.

Jessie turned around and faced her.

"What about Jack's stuff?" After he had died, Jessie wouldn't allow Annie to disturb his study or his bedroom.

"I gave most of it away, Jessie. I did keep some things that I thought you might like, though. They're in a box in the basement along with a few pictures of the two of you."

"No. I don't think there's anything that I would want," she said quietly.

"Well, it's there if you change your mind. If not, we can get rid of it." Annie turned to leave, but Jessie called her back.

"Annie, why did you hang onto me all these years?"

Annie turned back around and faced her.

"You're my daughter. I gave birth to you, brought you into this world. Jack couldn't take that away from me."

"I'm so sorry," Jessie whispered, letting her tears flow.

"Oh, Jessie. Don't cry, honey. It's not your fault." Annie walked into the room and stood before Jessie and took her hands. She was afraid Jessie would rebuff her offer of comfort but she pulled her into her arms anyway.

Jessie fell into to the hug, but only briefly before pulling away. She wiped at her cheeks and like any good mother, Annie miraculously produced a tissue from her pocket, and they smiled at each other as Jessie dried her eyes and blew her nose.

They walked together into the room that used to be Jack's and Jessie was surprised to discover that Annie had turned it into a library. Every wall was lined with shelves overflowing with books. In the center of the room was a recliner, a floor lamp and a small end table.

"Wow. You've read all of these?" Jessie asked as her eyes traveled over the numerous books, some classics, but most just popular fiction, from mysteries to romance.

"Oh, yes. I love to read. In the winter, especially, I'll sit nearly all day in here or by the fire."

They went back downstairs, and Annie went into the kitchen to check on dinner. "Go ahead and look in the study," she called.

Jessie was about to decline, but she shrugged. It wasn't so bad after all, this tour of her old house. She walked through the living room and down a short hallway. This was where Jack had spent most of his time at home. Occasionally, she would be allowed to join him, sitting on the sofa doing homework while he sat in his big chair and smoked a cigar, the daily paper spread out before him.

She pushed open the door and her eyes widened in surprise. The room had been turned into a studio for Annie. The two outside walls had been replaced with glass that offered spectacular views of the forest and Sierra Peak, now white with snow. Annie had several finished paintings stacked against one wall, but other than that neat stacking, the rest of the room was a mess. Her easel stood empty in the center of the room, a stained drop cloth lying beneath it. On the only table in the room, jars of brushes and containers of paint littered the top. This room was so different from the rest of the house, which was orderly and neat.

"I don't even try to keep it clean anymore," Annie said from the doorway.

"The view is incredible, Annie. I like it."

Annie walked into the room and peered up at Sierra Peak. "I didn't know how you would react to the house, Jessie. I didn't leave any reminders of Jack. I hope you understand why."

"Of course I understand, Annie. I wouldn't have expected you to." She met Annie's eyes for an instant. "I'm sorry it took me so long to . . . remember, to get back out here. It seems we've wasted so many years between us."

"I'm not that old," Annie said with a quiet laugh. "I hope we still have a few good ones left."

"I'll admit, I didn't think it would be this easy being here, being around you. You're not at all like I remember."

"If you had come here a few years ago, especially before Roger moved back here, things probably would be different. I was a very bitter woman for many years. Roger gave me an outlet to talk about the past and try to put everything in perspective. Now, there's Chris. She's been such a joy to me. She comes over a couple of times a week and we play cards and talk and drink wine."

Annie gently pushed Jessie from the room and closed the door behind her. Jessie settled on the sofa while Annie bent to get the fire started. Jessie was curious as to just how much Annie had told Chris about the old days. The look on her face must have said as much.

"Oh, don't think we sat around here and talked about you all the time. She was reading one of your books when she moved here and Roger told her who you were and that I lived here. She was naturally curious and on our first couple of visits we talked about you, but we've become friends. She keeps me up on the local gossip now," Annie said and laughed.

"I'm glad you invited me tonight, but I don't want to cut in on your time with her," Jessie said.

"Nonsense. I want you two to get to know each other better. I really hope you'll be friends."

"I think we'll be fine, Annie. I like Chris a lot."

"Good." She bent again to stick a match to the paper and they watched as it caught.

"Annie, tell me about the man you were seeing in San Francisco," Jessie said suddenly.

"My, where did that question come from?"

Jessie shrugged. "Chris told me some."

"His name was Jonathan and he was the attorney I went to see," she said.

"Why did you see an attorney?"

"I was going to divorce Jack. You were twelve and I was lonely," Annie said simply. "Only I couldn't go through with it, but Jonathan and I had become friends and he was someone to talk to. I would see him once or twice a month and eventually we became more than friends." Annie looked into the fire, seeing nothing, picturing Jonathan's warm face. "He was quite a bit older than me and a widower, but such a gentle man, Jessie, and I fell in love with him."

"Why didn't you go through with it?"

"Oh, I don't want to place any more guilt on you, Jessie, but I was worried about you. I didn't want to leave you alone here with Jack, in case you needed me. I was going to wait until you graduated high school, then go be with him."

"Only Jack found out first," Jessie said.

"Yes."

"Why didn't you go after Jack died? After I left?"

"After Jack died, I wouldn't see him at first, wouldn't even talk to him. It was very difficult at that time."

"You mean, I was difficult," Jessie stated. She did feel guilty. It was her fault that Annie had never had a life.

"Not just you, Jessie. The whole situation. Regardless, we stopped seeing each other," Annie said.

"What about later?"

"We talked occasionally, after you left, but it was never the same. He died a few years later," she said softly.

"I'm sorry."

"Don't think it's your fault. It's just life, is all. Some things, we can't control. Remember that."

Jessie nodded and again felt tears prick her eyes.

"Anyway, I made out just fine."

Annie left, saying she needed to check on dinner, and Jessie suspected she had tears in her own eyes.

Ten minutes later, Chris tapped on the door and let herself in. Jessie was sitting on the sofa, flipping through a magazine. Her eyes flew up, meeting Chris's questioning ones easily.

"Hi," she said. She put the magazine down and stood, lightly crossing her arms.

"Hello, Jessie." Chris closed the door but stood there, unmoving. "I didn't expect to see you here," she said. "Everything okay?"

"Yes, fine. Annie invited me," she explained. Then lowered her voice. "I guess I should warn you, she intends for us to be friends," she said with a smile.

"I see. Guess we don't have a choice then." She walked slowly over to Jessie and stood in front of her, her lips forming into a smile. "I'm glad you're getting along. You are getting along, right?"

"Oh yes. It's been fine. I never would have believed it possible," she confessed. "It's almost as if we've not been estranged all these years, you know. I mean, there's still a lot we've not discussed, but I don't know if we even need to. What good will it do? I think maybe just starting fresh with us is the way it should be."

"I think if that will work for you both, then go for it. You might be right. What good will it do to drag out all the old history and get you both upset?"

"I guess. Although my therapist would probably think that was a terrible idea. She likes everything out in the open and hashed over a hundred times before she's satisfied."

Chris nodded and allowed her eyes to be held by Jessie's before looking towards the kitchen.

"What's she whipping up?"

"Spaghetti, I think."

"Oh, goody. My favorite."

Chris walked to the kitchen and Jessie followed.

"Why, Chris, I didn't hear you come in," Annie said, when they walked into the kitchen. She lifted her cheek for Chris's kiss and smiled up at her.

"Smells good, Annie."

"Oh, please. You'll say that about anything," she said and laughed. "You two go visit," she said, pushing them from the kitchen. "I'll be out in a bit. Here, take the wine." She shoved the bottle into Chris's hands and the glasses into Jessie's.

Any pretense that Chris had of ignoring her attraction to Jessie fled the instant their fingers touched as she handed Jessie a glass of wine. She knew Jessie felt it, too, for her eyes locked on Chris's.

"I hope you're not upset with me," Jessie finally said.

"Upset? Why?"

"I didn't really plan on kissing you last night. But . . . well, it was just too tempting," Jessie said lightly.

"Oh, that," Chris said just as lightly. "It was nothing."

"Nothing? Well, I'll have to do better next time."

Chris held Jessie's gaze before lowering her eyes to Jessie's lips.

"Will there be a next time?" she asked.

Jessie leaned closer, feeling the heat that radiated from Chris, suddenly wishing that they were alone.

"Yes. Without a doubt," Jessie stated.

Chris tried to break the hold that Jessie had on her, but she failed miserably. Despite what had happened between them before, she knew she wanted another chance with Jessie. A chance at what, she wasn't really sure. One night of passion? But what if it ended like the last?

Jessie saw the doubts cloud Chris's eyes and she knew she was remembering their last aborted attempt at lovemaking. There was so much she wanted to tell Chris about her feelings that night, about what had driven her to do that, what always drove her to that. But now was not the time. Instead, she changed the subject away from them.

"You know, I wasn't sure if you'd mind that I came tonight or not. I know this is your normal time with Annie. She thinks the world of you, by the way."

Chris smiled and sipped from her wine before answering.

"We usually finish the evening with her beating me in cards and she makes me drink another bottle of wine and I feel like shit the next day," she said with a laugh, acknowledging Jessie's subtle shift in their conversation. "Maybe I can get her to cut me some slack tonight."

"What's so funny?"

They both looked up at Annie who held an empty wineglass. Jessie reached for the bottle to fill it.

"Chris was telling me how you force her to drink two bottles of wine while you beat her at cards," Jessie said.

"Oh, please. I could beat her at cards if she was stone sober," Annie laughed.

Chris smiled, pleased that Annie was so relaxed this evening. She had a glow about her, and Chris knew it was because of Jessie.

They were quiet as they looked from one to the other, then Annie smiled broadly.

"I can't remember the last time I've been this happy. My two favorite girls here at the same time. Thank you both."

Jessie blushed and looked at Chris who smiled quietly while watching her.

"Girls, huh?" Chris murmured.

"Yes, girls," Annie said. "I've been thinking. You know Thanksgiving is coming up," she said shyly. "I haven't actually celebrated it in a lot of years, but I thought this year, well, I have so much to be thankful for. Perhaps Roger and his Ellen might come, if you two thought we could have a dinner together."

"I think that's a great idea," Chris said.

"Yeah. That would be nice," Jessie agreed. She couldn't remember the last time she'd celebrated it either.

"I might even break down and cook a turkey. I doubt Roger would come otherwise," Annie said.

She was nearly beaming and Chris couldn't hold in her laugh. She doubted Annie had planned a dinner party in forty years.

"What?" Annie demanded.

"Nothing," Chris said, hiding her smile with her hand. "It's just . . . well, I've never seen you like this."

"Like what?"

"Well . . . happy, Annie."

Annie blushed and busied herself with the fire while Chris and Jessie shared smiles.

"I'm happy, too," Jessie said. "And I think I have the most to be thankful for."

Annie turned around and Chris watched the warm smile transform Annie's face as she looked at Jessie.

"Let's eat, huh?"

Chris was the only one who went back for seconds but was not the least bit shy while she piled her plate high a second time.

"I think she starves herself in between our dinner dates," Annie explained to Jessie. "She eats likes she's starving, anyway."

"I think you're right. Last night, I saw her plate at the Rock House. I don't think she even knew what it was."

"I don't think it's polite to talk about me as if I'm not here," Chris said around a mouthful.

"Why do you insist on eating there?" Annie asked.

"Because I can't cook, as you very well know."

"Nonsense. How hard can it be?"

"Okay, I don't like to cook. Is that better?"

Annie reached across the table and patted her hand.

"I'm just teasing you. It does my heart good to cook a decent meal and have you consume it with such gusto."

Jessie watched the exchange between them, feeling a stab of jealously at the easy banter they enjoyed. She looked up, startled to find Chris watching her.

"Did you ever get any firewood?" Chris asked suddenly.

"I picked some up at the lodge today."

"Good. We're getting a storm in a couple of days. I was going to take Bobby and Greg out for training tomorrow, while things are fairly slow here, but Roger said he got word that we might get ten inches down here in town."

"But not tomorrow?" Annie asked.

"No. But we've not put out all the cross-county ski markers yet so I'll help with that tomorrow. I'm sure if we get a good snow, we'll be packed with skiers this weekend."

"It seems every year around Thanksgiving we get a storm. But it'll be fun to pull out my snowshoes." She turned to Jessie then, to include her in their conversation. "I love to hike and I don't like winter to slow me down."

"Do you ski, too?"

"Oh, no. I tried those long skis but ended up on my butt more than my feet," Annie said and they laughed. "I stick to walking." She paused. "Do you ski?"

Jessie shook her head. She had learned to cross-country ski as a kid, but had not been out since she had left.

"No, I've really not had the opportunity," she said, not wanting to explain her avoidance of anything that would remind her of the mountains.

"Well, if you feel the need to try, you can go out with me," Chris offered.

"Thank you. If we get the chance between now and December twentieth I'm in."

"The twentieth?"

"That's when I've got to be out of the cabin," Jessie explained.

Chris nodded slowly. She had known that Jessie would be leaving, of course. Back to New York.

"But that doesn't mean you have to leave then, does it?" Annie asked. "I told you . . ."

"That's more than a month away, Annie. Let's just see what happens."

An uncomfortable silence settled around them and Chris absentmindedly twirled the uneaten spaghetti on her plate. Annie finished the small amount of wine in her glass and Jessie stared at her own empty glass. Chris tried to think of something witty to say to break the tension, but nothing came. Annie finally stood up and took the empty bottle of wine into the kitchen. Chris knew she would return with another one.

"I'm sorry," Jessie said softly.

"You don't have to apologize to me," Chris said.

"She offered a room here," Jessie explained. "But I just think that would be too strange. I mean, it's been so many years."

Chris met her eyes across the table and held them.

"If you want to leave, then leave. But don't use the excuse that you don't have a place to stay."

Jessie's eyes flashed, but she knew she should not be angry with Chris. She had spoken the truth. In fact, it had been a comfort that she had to be out by the twentieth. It gave her an excuse to flee if she needed it.

Annie came back in and stood at the table with another bottle of wine. She looked at Chris first before addressing Jessie.

"You just came back into my life," she said. "The idea of you leaving again so soon is painful. I'm sorry. But you do what you have to do. You have a place here if you'd like to stay longer."

"Thank you, Annie. We'll see when the time comes."

"Good. Fair enough. Now, let's take the wine into the living room and enjoy the fire."

Their conversation moved to less personal things and Chris filled Annie in on what was happening in town and Jessie listened quietly, only occasionally interjecting her own thoughts. They stayed nearly another hour before Chris yawned and stood.

"I should really get going. I'll be hiking all over the place tomorrow, I'm sure. Thanks again for dinner, Annie. It was delicious, as always." She bent quickly and kissed Annie's cheek.

"I should get going, too," Jessie said. As much as she was enjoying her visit with Annie, she wanted a chance to finish her conversation with Chris.

"I understand," Annie said.

"Tomorrow may be my last day to get a run in before the snows come," Jessie offered as an excuse.

"I didn't know you jogged," Annie said as she walked them to the door.

"My lone form of exercise, I'm afraid. I'm not a serious runner, though. I usually only do five miles or so."

"And that's not serious?" Chris asked. "Just give me a hiking trail and I'll be fine."

"Thank you for inviting me to dinner, Annie. You've got my phone number, right?"

"Yes. And you've got mine."

Chris and Jessie walked out together, then stopped between the Jeep and Jessie's rental car, their backs to the house. The cedar blocked out the light from the porch and they stood in the shadows, watching each other as their breath frosted around them.

"Was that rough on you?" Chris asked. "I mean, about your leaving in a month."

"A little. It's not like I'm in a hurry to get back, that's not it. I've got my apartment there, but nothing else. I'm just not sure staying here with her would be a good idea. Not yet, anyway."

"Well, like you said, you can decide when the time comes."

They were quiet and Chris shifted her feet, not wanting the evening to end but knowing she should go.

Jessie glanced up at the house to see if Annie could see them, then moved closer to Chris.

"When can I see you again?" she asked quietly.

"See me? I'm sure we'll see each other, Jessie."

"That's not what I meant and you know it."

"You mean, like a date?" Chris asked with a small smile.

"A date? Well, if that's what you want to call it. I just want to see you, to spend time with you." It was Jessie's turn to fidget and she shifted from one foot to the other. "In case you haven't realized it . . . I'm extremely attracted to you."

"Extremely?"

"Yeah, McKenna, extremely."

Chris searched Jessie's eyes, trying to figure out what game Jessie was playing, if any. Her breath caught when she saw desire in Jessie's dark eyes, desire that she didn't even try to hide. She shook her head slowly but was unable to look away. Those black eyes were drawing her close, pulling her in and she tried to resist their power, but she was paralyzed. She stood there, as unmoving as the mountains around them, watching as Jessie moved closer, her head bending to Chris's ear.

"If you don't stop looking at me that way, I'll be forced to kiss you right here," Jessie whispered into her ear. She pulled back slowly, breathing deeply, remembering the unique smell of Chris from other nights. Was it perfume or simply the sweet smell of cedars and the mountains? She saw Chris's pulse throbbing rapidly in her throat and she wanted to put her mouth there. And it was all so new to her, this attraction. For the first time in her life, she ached to wake up with a lover in her bed. Not alone and with all the emptiness that usually followed after her trysts with strangers.

Chris moved her head without thinking, taking the lips that were so close to her own. Jessie's lips were soft, tender . . . so unlike the bruising kisses that she remembered from that night on the ledge.

Jessie moved into Chris's arms, sliding her own over Chris's shoulders. She pressed her body tight against Chris, her eyes closed as her mouth opened to the kiss, and she searched out Chris's tongue, pulling it inside her own mouth.

"I want you so much," Jessie whispered. "Please, come home with me," she pleaded, uttering the one phrase she had never said to anyone before.

"Jessie . . ."

"Please. Make love to me. Let me make love to you." Her hands slid down and cupped Chris's small breasts, her hands as hungry as her mouth.

Chris lost her resolve and pulled Jessie up against her, her hips pressing into Jessie's. She felt herself grow wet and she ached for Jessie's touch.

"I'll follow you," Chris whispered into Jessie's ear. "Hurry."

Chris drove without thinking. She wanted her. She had wanted her since the first time they met, since before that even. She couldn't stop what was about to happen even if she wanted to. She refused to think about the last time.

When the cabin door closed behind them, Jessie pushed Chris against the wall, her mouth starving for her kisses. They pressed together, lips and tongues moving wildly as they struggled to touch through their clothes.

Jessie grabbed the bottom of Chris's shirt and pulled it over her head in one quick motion, then tossed it carelessly to the floor as Chris pulled Jessie's head to her breasts. Jessie's mouth opened and she sucked a nipple into her mouth, her tongue grazing it as Chris gently held her head to her.

"Yes," Chris whispered. She had wanted this for so long, she wasn't sure her legs would support her now as she watched Jessie at her breast. She felt her wetness soak her jeans and she reached blindly for Jessie's hand and pressed it hard against herself.

"Oh, Jesus," Jessie murmured. "You're so wet."

Her hands fumbled with Chris's jeans, finally pushing them down enough to touch her. Her fingers glided through her warmth, dripping wet as she touched her. Chris moaned loudly and clutched Jessie to her as Jessie's fingers plunged deep inside her. Jessie withdrew slightly, then buried herself again inside her as her tongue battled with Chris's. She finally pulled out and stroked her, feeling Chris throb against her fingertips. Chris's hands dug into Jessie's shoulders and Jessie felt her tremble seconds before her orgasm hit.

Chris leaned her head against the wall, her breath coming in rapid gasps. Too fast. It was just too fast, but she couldn't hold back another second.

Jessie's own chest heaved, her body throbbing with need as she pressed against Chris. Had it ever felt like this? Had she ever wanted to scream in pleasure as someone touched her? Had she ever wanted to give pleasure? No, it was just a means to an end. But this was different. The thought of Chris touching her, making love to her because she wanted to make love to her, was almost more than she could bear. She dipped her head lazily and lightly kissed Chris's breast, her tongue coming out to tease a nipple.

"Jessie," Chris whispered. "The bedroom."

Jessie pulled away, her eyes clouded with desire as she took Chris's hand and led her silently into the bedroom. Chris pulled Jessie's top off with ease and her hands lightly brushed her nipples through her bra before removing that as well.

They shed their jeans quickly, then Jessie pulled Chris after her, feeling her weight settle on top of her aroused body. She wanted Chris to hurry. She wanted her to take her now, quickly. But Chris simply touched her, hands moving lightly over her stomach then up, brushing her nipples, making her want Chris even more.

"Chris, please. Touch me," she whispered.

Chris had a brief flash to the other time Jessie had begged her to touch her, but she knew it would be different this time. Her hand slid slowly down Jessie's body, feeling her tremble at her touch. She dipped her head and took Jessie's nipple into her mouth, suddenly hungry for her, not wanting to wait any longer.

Jessie arched and held Chris's head to her breast, waiting as Chris's hand parted her legs.

Chris found her wetness and moved slowly into it, moaning against the breast in her mouth as Jessie whimpered softly against her head.

"Oh, yes," Jessie breathed and her hips moved to meet Chris's fingers. "God, Chris, please, I want your mouth on me," she whispered.

"Yes. I want that, too."

Chris left her breast and kissed her smooth belly before settling between her thighs. She nudged them farther apart, then cupped her rounded hips, letting her tongue move over her thighs, teasing.

"Please," Jessie begged and her hips rose, searching for Chris's mouth.

Chris breathed deeply, savoring her scent, and she closed her eyes and touched her, her mouth opening over her, her tongue diving into her wetness.

"God, yes," Jessie whispered. Her hips moved, meeting Chris's plunging tongue as it moved within her.

All gentleness gone, Chris wanted to devour Jessie and her lips sucked hungrily at her, her shoulders pushing Jessie's legs farther apart, higher on her shoulders and she took Jessie into her mouth, her face covered in her wetness. Her tongue stroked her swollen clit and Jessie wrapped her legs around Chris and held her to her, her hips rising again to press Chris more firmly against her. Chris felt the trembling under her mouth as Jessie's legs tightened around her head.

Jessie exploded, her eyes shut tight against the blinding flash that consumed her, and she felt herself pulse into Chris's mouth as she continued to stroke her. Wave after wave washed over her, and she screamed out with pleasure, nearly embarrassed by the sounds that came from her throat. Finally, her legs fell limply to the bed and she was too spent to even hold Chris to her.

"Dear God in heaven," she whispered. "I knew it would be like that with you."

Chris lay beside her, resting on her side as she took Jessie's hand and kissed her palm gently. Yes, she had known it, too.

Jessie rolled over onto her elbow and touched Chris's face with her fingertips.

"I want to make love to you that way. I want to know what you taste like."

"I don't know if I could stand it," Chris said with a gentle smile. "I feel like a teenager around you."

"Hush, lie back," Jessie whispered.

Chris rolled onto her back, eyes closed as she waited for Jessie's mouth to touch her. She was surprised when soft lips touched her own, gently moving against her. She opened to them, inviting Jessie's tongue into her mouth. Warm hands cupped her breasts and she moved into them, loving the feel of Jessie's hands on her. Jessie's mouth took her nipple and her teeth gently nipped at her and Chris moaned low in her throat, her legs parting even before Jessie's hand moved to her.

"You're so wet," Jessie murmured into her breast. "I can't wait to taste you," she said and she moved down her body, teasing Chris, letting her tongue wet her inner thighs. But she didn't tease long. Chris shoved at her shoulders, urging her to hurry and Jessie gathered Chris's thighs around her and lowered her mouth to her wetness.

They moaned together as Jessie covered her and Chris grasped at the sheets, her fists pulling them from their moorings as she surged up to meet Jessie, her hips rising off the bed.

Jessie's tongue licked at her, stroking her fast, but she felt Chris nearing orgasm and she pulled back. She wasn't nearly ready for it to end. She heard Chris whimper, and she went back to her, her tongue delving inside her warmth, her mouth covering her again. She slowed, wanting it to last, but Chris grasped her head, holding her hard against her and Jessie's tongue moved over her quickly, feeling Chris swell inside her mouth. When Chris arched her hips, Jessie sucked her swollen clit inside her mouth, her tongue taking her at last, feeling Chris's release as she pulsed against her mouth, as she cried out into the night.

Arms wrapped together as Jessie covered Chris with her body, feeling her heart beating wildly in her chest.

Chris was afraid to speak, so she lay with her eyes closed, holding Jessie to her as she drifted off to sleep, exhausted.

Chapter Thirty-three

Jessie stirred as she felt Chris pull out of her arms. She rolled over, noting that the sun was already shining into the window. It did nothing to warm the room, though. She had forgotten to turn on the heater last night and now the early morning chill surrounded them.

"Where are you going?" she asked sleepily, reaching out to touch Chris's bare back as she sat on the edge of the bed.

"Busy day."

"Chris?"

"Yeah?"

"Do we need to talk?" Jessie asked. She sat up, too, moving behind Chris and wrapping her arms around her. Her nipples hardened as she pressed her breasts against Chris's back. She closed her eyes and sighed, the lingering scent of their lovemaking arousing her again, like it had done a few hours earlier.

Chris squeezed her eyes shut, wanting nothing more than to lie back down with Jessie and make love to her once again. But in the light of day, reality showed its face, and she felt her fears surface.

"Talk to me," Jessie whispered. "Please don't just leave."

"Last night was . . . beyond words, really," Chris finally said. "When you left this summer, I thought about you a lot. I thought about making love with you. I wanted to make love with you. But when you came back, I was afraid to be near you. I was so afraid that if we tried, it would end up like that last time and I couldn't do that again. That's not how I wanted it to be with us."

Jessie pulled back a little, but her hands continued to rub slowly across Chris's back.

"It won't ever be like that again. Chris, I'm sorry about that night, but there is nothing I can do to change it. Not now. You know, I thought about you, too, while I was gone. But when I thought about you, about us, it wasn't that last night together that I remembered. It was the night we went camping. It was just the two of us. It was all so innocent and for the first time in my life, I wanted to make love with someone. There was no agenda, no games being played in a bar, no need to have unsatisfying sex with a stranger , no underlying need to hurt," she finished in a whisper. "It was just us and when you kissed me, for the first time in my life, I felt an attraction to someone that was so strong, I was ready to forget everything about myself and just . . . make love."

Chris turned around to face Jessie, seeing the glistening of tears in her eyes.

"I don't know what you want from me," Chris said softly. "I'm scared. I mean, you're here for at least a month. If we spend that time being more than friends, being intimate with each other, then when you leave, I don't think I'll be able to just dismiss it as a summer fling, Jessie. I'm too old for one-night stands."

"Why does everything have to be so complicated?" Jessie reached up and lightly ran her fingertip over Chris's eyebrows then across her cheek. "I just want a chance," Jessie whispered.

"A chance at what?"

"A chance at a normal relationship," she stated. "I don't know how, McKenna. All these years, there's just been one person after another." She felt tears prick her eyes again, but she held Chris's gaze steadily. "So many, I couldn't even begin to count. And I couldn't tell you one of their names. Then I met you up there one day," she said, motioning out the window with her head. "And I liked you. I mean, I liked you as a person. And that scared me," she said with a smile. "I never like anybody. But I'll admit, I wanted to play my little game with you, see how long it would take . . . but I liked you. And it mattered what you thought of me. That's why I curse myself for using you that night, for lumping you in with all the others. But in my eyes, it wasn't you anymore. You were just a woman that would make me forget everything. And I desperately needed to forget everything that night."

"I'm sorry," Chris said quietly.

But Jessie smiled.

"I'm apologizing to you, McKenna. You're not supposed to say you're sorry. I am."

"Okay." Chris nodded and leaned over to kiss Jessie lightly.

"Thank you. And thank you for last night. It was a first for me, by the way."

"A first?"

"A first to invite someone to my home, to my bed. A first to wake up with someone in my arms," Jessie said shyly. "I liked it."

"Well, you want to try for two nights?"

"Two nights, McKenna? Won't Dillon disown you?"

"Shit! I forgot about him. He probably froze his ass off last night," she said as she stood. "I better get going, anyway. We have a lot of trails to mark today."

Jessie watched as Chris walked naked to the heater and turned it on before bending to retrieve her jeans from the floor. Jessie left the warmth of the covers and walked to Chris, her hands moving over Chris's exposed breasts. She couldn't stop herself as she lowered her mouth to capture an aroused nipple.

"Jessie . . . oh," Chris breathed, her hands leaving the jeans undone as they roamed over Jessie's naked back before settling over her hips. She pulled Jessie close against her, hearing the low moan come from Jessie. When Jessie raised her head, Chris found her mouth, kissing her hard before pushing her away. If they didn't stop now, they never would.

"Do you have any idea how much I want you?" Jessie asked, but she turned away from Chris and grabbed her robe. "I'm not used to this, McKenna. Sorry."

"Don't be sorry for wanting me. I'm sorry I have to leave."

"How about if we cook something at your place tonight?" Jessie asked as she tied her robe tightly around herself and followed Chris into the living room. She was unusually nervous, she realized. As she had said, she wasn't used to this.

Chris slipped the sweatshirt over her head and tried to tame her hair by running impatient fingers through it. She looked at Jessie, who stood in her bare feet waiting for her answer. Then she smiled and walked closer, taking Jessie's hands in her own.

"You know, Jessie, I'm not exactly used to this either. I'm not sure how I'm supposed to act this morning . . . but last night was incredible. And I definitely would love to repeat it often," she said before touching her lips lightly to Jessie's. "And I wish like hell I didn't have to leave this morning," she murmured against Jessie's lips as their kiss deepened.

Jessie finally stepped away when she realized she was on the verge of begging Chris to stay. And that, she was definitely not used to.

"I'll tell you what," Chris said. "I'll leave the back door unlocked. You can go over whenever you want, if you feel like cooking. I'll try to make it an early day," she said.

"So, I have free range of your kitchen?"

"Yes. But you've also seen what my fridge has to offer, so . . ."

"I'll bring the food, McKenna."

"Good. I'll see you soon."

Chapter Thirty-four

Chris listened to her messages while she drove the short distance to her own cabin. Two from Roger. The first reminding her that they were marking trails today and the second demanding to know where the hell she was. The third was from Bobby, wondering if they needed to send out SAR for her.

"Very funny," she said out loud. But she needed to hurry. It was already after nine.

Her cabin was frigid, and she ignored the nearly screaming Dillon while she started the heater in the bedroom.

"I'm sorry, okay, but I forgot about you," she told him. He followed her into the kitchen and watched as she filled his food bowl, then flipped his tail and walked away without touching it. "Spoiled brat," she called after him.

She hurried through her shower, then changed clothes twice before leaving. The sky had been nearly cloudless when she left Jessie's. Now, the clouds covered the sun, and the temperature was still in the low twenties. Silk longjohns went under her jeans, and she put an extra layer under her sweater, too.

She called Roger as soon as she left her cabin. She was hoping to avoid his questions until later, but she didn't know if she needed to go to the ranger station or just meet Matt out on the trails.

"Where the hell were you?" Roger demanded. "Bobby was ready to send out a search."

"You know, I have a life, too, Roger. I'm sorry I didn't check in with you first."

"It's damn near ten o'clock, McKenna," he pointed out.

"I'm sorry. Something . . . came up," she said lamely.

"Dinner at Annie's last night? What, is she getting to be too much for you?"

Chris was tempted to just tell him the truth, but she didn't know if Jessie was ready for that. For that matter, she wasn't sure she was, either.

"Look, is Matt already out? Should I just meet him somewhere?"

"He and Greg are out doing Ridge Trail. I sent Hatcher out with Bobby to finish up the South Rim."

"Hatcher? Good God, no wonder there's a storm coming," she said.

"Yeah. I'm sure he's plenty pissed at you."

"About damn time he does some field work."

"Well, you'll be happy to know he's asked for a transfer. Apparently, cold weather is not his thing. He's requested Florida."

"Well, good for him. Maybe his daddy can put him on a boat to patrol the Keys or something. I'll be there in a second, Roger."

She hung up without waiting for his response and tossed the phone between the seats. The first flakes were falling by the time she got to the ranger station. A day early.

"What's with the snow?" she asked Roger when she walked in.

"Oh, they gave me some meteorological bullshit about the jet stream dropping and pulling in moisture from somewhere. All their damn computers, and they miss the storm by a day."

213

She followed him into his office after accepting a cup of coffee from Kay.

"The mountain will be crawling with skiers tomorrow and Sunday," he said. "You're late," he stated as an afterthought. "You're never late."

"I was . . . busy."

"Busy? My God, McKenna, you're blushing. Get lucky?" Then he lowered his voice. "I hope it wasn't a local, McKenna. Can you imagine the scandal?"

Chris rolled her eyes. A local?

"Want to tell me about it?"

"No."

"Come on," he coaxed. "I always tell you."

"About you and Ellen? Please, I don't need details."

"Jessie?" he guessed.

Chris tried to remain expressionless, but she felt the blush creep up her face. The automatic smile gave her away.

"I'll be damned. Well, come on, out with it. I want details," he teased.

"Roger, please, it just . . . happened."

"Sure it did. Does Annie know?"

"No! Of course not."

Roger grinned.

"Well, she called here this morning and invited us over for Thanksgiving dinner. When I mentioned that you weren't in yet, she said that you and Jessie had left together last night," he said, still grinning. "She also said that you two had stood outside talking for a very long time. She couldn't quite see through the window, though, to see what was going on."

Chris gave him a humorless smile.

"Are you enjoying yourself?" she asked.

"Very much." Then he laughed. "Damn, McKenna, you're too old to be making out in front of someone's house."

"We were not making out," she hissed. "We were . . . talking. And then we decided to talk some more at her place. And I fell asleep," she finished. Then she laughed, too. "Roger, please don't tease me about this. I really . . . like her."

Roger leaned back in his chair, a satisfied grin on his face as he watched her.

"Okay, McKenna, I won't tease you." Then he leaned forward again. "Do you want to tell me what's going on?"

"No, I don't." At his hurt expression, she softened her words. "I'm not really sure what's going on, Roger. I mean, she's probably going back to New York within the month."

She felt the impact of her words, and her chest tightened. Back to New York. Out of her life again. And maybe this time for good. She met his questioning eyes across from her, wondering how much he suspected. He was no fool and she was never very good at hiding her feelings. She was very close to falling in love with Jessie, and she realized she was powerless to stop it.

She spent the rest of the morning putting out trail markers along the Lake Trail. She would mark Elk Meadow in the afternoon. They were the two most heavily used trails for cross-country skiing in their area, although the South Rim got a lot of traffic, too, especially early in the season when the snow level wasn't down to the lower elevations yet.

She worked quickly, trying to beat the storm, but it was slow going in the cold and wind. She had to take her gloves off each time she placed a marker, and her hands were frozen by the time she finished the loop around the lake.

She was sitting in her Jeep trying to get warm when Roger radioed her.

"McKenna, what's your ten-twenty?"

"Lake Trail. Just finished," she replied.

"Come get me," he said. "I'll help you mark Elk Meadow. Just heard from Matt up on Ridge Trail. They've had two inches in the last hour, probably four since this morning."

"Ten-four."

Roger was waiting as she pulled up, the hood of his parka pulled up to cut the wind.

"Damn, McKenna, that wind is a bitch," he said as he crawled inside.

"No shit. My hands are still frozen."

"Well, it's a quick mover. Should be over by tonight. Nice and sunny tomorrow or so the experts say."

"How much snow?" she asked.

"Ten to twelve up on the mountain. There's another low pressure system off of Alaska. We need to watch that one," he told her.

"You sound like a damn meteorologist, Roger."

"Yeah. And I can probably predict the weather just as good as they do."

With both of them, they made quick work of Elk Meadow, but it was snowing heavily by the time they finished. They sat in the Jeep, hands held to the heater as they tried to warm up.

"Want to stop by the Rock? They'll have a roaring fire going," Roger offered.

"Can't."

"Plans?"

Chris grinned and nodded. She had done a pretty good job of keeping thoughts of Jessie at bay, but now she let them in and the memory of last night nearly overwhelmed her. She felt the heat down to the tips of her toes.

"Be careful, McKenna."

"What do you mean?" she asked cautiously.

"This one could be a heartbreaker."

She nodded. Yes, she knew that already.

Chapter Thirty-Five

Chris was surprised to see smoke coming from her chimney when she drove up. She was suddenly nervous, knowing Jessie was inside.

Jessie was standing with her back to the fire, waiting. Their eyes met across the room and identical smiles touched their faces.

"Hey."

"Hi."

"Nice and toasty in here," Chris said as she moved to the fire to join Jessie.

"Yes. I've made Dillon quite happy, I think," Jessie said, motioning to the cat who was curled up contentedly on the sofa. He opened one eye and scowled at Chris before closing it again.

"I see he's still pissed at me."

They were quiet and Chris let her eyes travel around the room, noting that the table was set for dinner, wine already opened and ready. She finally let her eyes rest on the anxious ones of Jessie, trying to read them, but they were guarded, probably much like her own.

"Did you have a busy day?" Jessie finally asked.

"Yes. And cold. The snow's coming down pretty good now. Should be great skiing this weekend."

"I guess there will be a lot of people in town, at the lodge," Jessie added.

Chris nodded, wondering why they were having this inane conversation, knowing it wasn't what either of them wanted to talk about. She sighed, not knowing where to start.

"McKenna, why don't you get a shower," Jessie suggested, wrinkling up her nose.

"And what are you saying?" Chris asked with a grin. "I stink?"

But Jessie had moved to the kitchen, making a pretense of checking on dinner. Chris left her without another word, wondering why the conversation seemed so strained between them. If she wasn't so damn hungry, she would drag Jessie into the bedroom and strip her naked. That was really want she wanted to do. But, probably uncivilized, she thought. Then she grinned. Dinner first, then bed.

She lingered in the shower. The hot water felt too good after being cold all day long. She slipped on baggy sweatpants and a long-sleeved T-shirt, donning only thick socks for her feet.

Jessie was again waiting by the fire, this time with a glass of wine. She motioned with her head to the table and Chris picked up her own glass before walking over. She stopped just short of Jessie, then took the remaining step to her, slowly bending her head and kissing the lips she had tried so hard not to think about all day.

Jessie closed her eyes and sighed, savoring their first kiss. She wasn't sure how to greet Chris, what Chris expected of her, so she did nothing. She was oddly disappointed when Chris arrived and did nothing as well. She didn't want to take the time for small talk and dinner. She only wanted what they'd shared last night. After a lifetime of one-night stands, she was nearly insatiable for Chris's gentle, tender lovemaking.

"Okay?"

"For now." Jessie nodded. "Are you hungry?"

"Are we talking about food?"

"We're talking about anything you want."

Chris raised an eyebrow.

"Is dinner ready?"

"It can be. Or we can turn the oven off," Jessie suggested.

Chris leaned over and touched her lips, this time lingering, her tongue licking off the trace of wine on Jessie's lips. Jessie's mouth opened, capturing Chris's tongue and sucking it into her mouth. That was all the encouragement Chris needed. She blindly set her wineglass on the mantel, taking Jessie into her arms and holding her tight against her.

"Chris, please," Jessie whispered into her mouth. Her hands moved under Chris's shirt, touching warm skin before moving to her breasts, lightly raking her fingers over taut nipples.

"I vote we turn the oven off," Chris said, her voice husky with desire. She took Jessie's hand and led her to the bedroom, pausing at the oven on their way.

They stood in the darkness of the bedroom, listening to each other draw breath. Chris reached out slowly and touched Jessie's cheek, lightly running her fingertips across her skin, trying to memorize every line.

"You're so beautiful," Chris whispered. "Before I met you, I used to stare at your picture, wondering what you would feel like, what your lips would taste like," she confessed. "You looked so sad."

"I was. I was dead inside. There was no joy in my life. I never thought I could feel this way. I never thought someone could touch me the way you do," Jessie said quietly. She reached for Chris, pulling her mouth to her own. Their gentle kiss turned hungry, and she slipped her tongue into Chris's mouth, swallowing the moan that followed. They broke apart long enough to shed their shirts, then mouths reunited as their breasts pressed together.

Chris pulled her to the bed, not bothering with the covers and

Jessie settled her weight between Chris's opened thighs, pressing hard into her.

"This was the longest day of my life," Jessie whispered. Her mouth moved wetly down Chris's throat, stopping only when her lips closed over an erect nipple.

Chris arched into her, her hands cupping Jessie's hips and pulling her more firmly against her. She rolled her head back, eyes closed tightly as Jessie feasted. Crazily, she wondered how she had ever lived without this. A low moan escaped as Jessie moved to her other breast and she moved her hands lightly across Jessie's bare back before clutching her head and holding her closer against her breast. She felt Jessie take more of her breast inside and she moaned again, her hips rising again to meet Jessie's thrusts as she ground into her.

Jessie's hand slipped easily inside Chris's sweatpants and she found what she wanted. Hot wetness surrounded her fingers, and she drove them deep inside Chris, feeling her tighten around them. Oh, so wet, she thought. She wanted her mouth there but Chris's hips rose again to meet her thrusting fingers. Instead, her mouth found Chris's waiting lips, her tongue mimicking her fingers as she plunged harder and harder inside Chris, riding the wave with Chris as her hips bucked against her hand.

Chris's hips moved frantically as she met each thrust of Jessie's fingers, driving them harder into her until she simply exploded under Jessie's weight. Her scream was primal, long and hard, and she clutched Jessie to her as her tremors subsided.

Jessie felt the perspiration cool on her back as she rested against Chris, her breath still coming hard as the needs of her own body clamored to be heard. She reached down and unbuttoned her own jeans, shoving them haphazardly down her legs as she pulled Chris's sweats completely off. Cotton briefs followed and she pressed her naked body to Chris, hips grinding hard against Chris as she sought her own release.

"Let me, sweetheart," Chris whispered and her hand moved between them. She was nearly overwhelmed by the wetness she found and her fingers moved into hot fire, stroking the swollen center quickly as Jessie's hips moved against her.

It only took one touch and Jessie felt herself slipping, tumbling over the edge quickly. She came hard and fast, her cry loud to her own ears as she lay spent on top of Chris.

"I'm sorry," Jessie whispered when she found her breath. "I couldn't wait."

"Please don't tell me you're sorry. That was beautiful." She kissed Jessie's damp forehead. "We've got all the time in the world."

"There'll never be enough time," Jessie said softly as she curled next to Chris. "I could make love with you every day for the rest of my life . . . and it still wouldn't be enough."

Chris took a sharp breath. Those words, she was not expecting. Unconsciously, she tightened her arms.

"You know, I was a little nervous about tonight," Chris confessed. "I didn't know if last night could be repeated or if you would even want to."

"I wanted you to walk in that door tonight and drag me off to the bedroom without a single word spoken," Jessie said lightly. She stroked the smooth skin on Chris's belly, wondering at her sudden need to talk, to share her feelings . . . and her doubts. "Can I tell you something, Chris?"

"Of course."

"You're the first person that I've ever been with twice." She looked up, just able to see the expression on Chris's face in the darkness. It was one of sadness. "You're also the first person who's ever made love to me because they truly wanted to. It wasn't just sex. And you're the first one I've ever made love to," she finished in a whisper. "What I'm feeling is so completely new to me, I'm not sure what to call it." She swallowed hard before continuing. "I don't know what love is, Chris. But what I feel when I'm with you is complete happiness, contentment, joy. And passion. Passion I didn't even know I had. And not just when we're like this, touching. Sometimes I look into your blue eyes, and I just want to go there, go inside you, let you surround me and protect me. And I know you would. You've been the one person I could count on, the one person who hasn't let me down."

Chris quietly rubbed Jessie's back while she spoke, her words touching Chris in places no one had been before. Her heart ached for this woman who had so much pain in her life. And so little love.

"Jessie, I'll always be someone you can count on. No matter what happens here or what happens when you leave, if you need me, you just say the word."

"Why, Chris? Why would you do that?" Jessie pulled away, trying so hard to read Chris's eyes.

"Because I . . ." *I'm in love with you.* Chris's throat closed completely, stifling the words that threatened to spill out. *In love?* "I care about you, Jessie. What happens to you matters to me."

Chapter Thirty-Six

The pasta casserole was great for a midnight snack, which was when they finally managed to get out of bed. Chris ate quietly as she watched Jessie moving around her kitchen, refilling her wineglass as she passed by.

"Why are you watching me?" Jessie asked, her back still to Chris.

"Can't I watch you?"

Jessie wanted to tell Chris she could watch her for the rest of her life, but she didn't want to scare her off. She suspected she had already disrupted Chris's orderly life with her timid declaration earlier. Not a declaration of love, exactly. That was still a foreign concept to her. But she knew what she felt for Chris was not simply sexual attraction. Chris had come into her life and captured her very soul. But was that love? She turned around and found Chris still watching her. She met those blue eyes head on, searching for what, she wasn't sure. Love? Did Chris's feelings for her go deeper than this physical attraction? With Chris, it was hard to tell. She was affectionate in so many ways with so many different people, it was hard for Jessie to tell if her feelings ran deeper. Oh, but when they made love, the way Chris touched her, surely . . .

"Jessie?"

Jessie blinked, focusing again on the blue eyes staring at her. Chris arched an eyebrow.

"Sorry, McKenna. I guess I spaced out."

"Is everything okay? I mean, do you want to talk?"

"No, no, I'm fine. I was just thinking." She grinned as she sat down at the table and resumed her dinner. "I guess I'm tired. We haven't exactly gotten much sleep in the last few days."

"We can sleep in today," Chris offered.

"Well, I promised Annie I would take her to Sacramento. She wants to shop for Thanksgiving. That is, if the roads are clear."

"They should be. It stopped snowing." Chris shoved her plate away and sat with her wineglass in front of her. "You know, Jessie, I'm really glad you and Annie are taking the time to get to know one another again. I was afraid you would come here and talk to her and leave again, and just go on about your life. I'm glad you're letting Annie into your life."

"Maybe that was my intention, originally. I don't know. Honestly, I never really had a plan, McKenna." Then she laughed a little. "I never have a plan when it comes to my life."

Chapter Thirty-seven

Chris's boots crunched across the snow on the sidewalk and she scraped them off before going into the ranger station. The roads were clear and traffic was heading into tiny Sierra City. The weather was perfect for skiing and the lodge was packed when she drove past earlier. She glanced at her watch. Nearly noon. Jessie and Annie were probably on their way to Sacramento by now. She had talked to Annie on the phone, who sounded as excited as Chris had ever heard her. The meal she was planning for Thanksgiving would feed twenty, Chris was sure.

"I'm going to ask Jessie to take me to dinner at one of those fancy restaurants, Chris. It's been years since I've dined out. Oh, and we're going to the mall, too. I can't remember the last time I shopped for new clothes."

They would be back late, Chris knew. She was disappointed she wouldn't get to spend the evening with Jessie, but she was glad Annie was getting to spend this time alone with her.

"Hey, McKenna," Roger greeted her when she stuck her head in his office. "Didn't expect to see you today."

Chris shrugged. Her cabin was lonely.

"Thought I'd help out. I see Hatcher's being tour guide," she said, motioning with her head to the group of skiers Robert Hatcher was talking to.

"You know, McKenna, he probably likes you even less than you like him. What's up with that? I don't think I've ever seen you two even have a conversation before."

"He's useless. He's lazy. And he thinks he's God's gift to women."

Roger smiled. "He hit on you, didn't he?"

"Yes, he did. First time we met. When I turned him down, he called me a fucking dyke. I was forced to agree with him," she said with a grin.

"Hey, McKenna, just the woman I need to see."

Chris turned at Matt's greeting, offering him a smile.

"Hi, Matt. What's up?"

"Can I talk to you a minute?" He glanced at Roger. "Privately?"

"Sure. I'll talk to you later, Roger."

She followed Matt down the short hallway to the makeshift kitchen in the back. Matt glanced back down the hallway before closing the door.

"What the hell's going on?" she asked and she perched on the edge of the table, crossing her feet at the ankles. "Secret?"

"Sort of. I finally invited Donna to dinner. Last night. We had a great time," he said.

"What did you cook?" she asked.

"It doesn't matter, McKenna," he said impatiently. "That's not what I want to talk to you about."

"Well, was it at least nice? It wasn't hamburgers, was it?"

"I got one of those frozen lasagna dinners at Ellen's. Garlic bread and a salad."

"Wine?"

"Beer."

"Beer? Matt, you served beer with lasagna for your romantic dinner? I thought I taught you better," she teased.

"Will you stop with the menu already?"

"Okay, I'm sorry. What's on your mind?"

"I kissed her."

Chris grinned and playfully punched his arm.

"Well, way to go, man. And?"

"And I think it surprised the hell out of her. But, well, it was just the one and it's not like she slapped me or anything. In fact, she invited me over tonight," he said.

"Well that's great. What's the problem?"

"What does it mean?"

"It means she likes you, I guess," Chris said. "Isn't that what you wanted?"

"What is she expecting?"

"Well how the hell should I know?"

"You're a woman, McKenna! What does she want?"

"Matt, maybe she just wants to spend the evening with you, have dinner again, talk, get to know you better. Are you afraid?"

"What if she wants sex?"

"Bring condoms," she teased.

"McKenna!"

"Will you lighten up? What if she does?"

"I'm not ready," he said. "I don't want it to be like that."

"You don't want a sexual relationship with her?"

"Yes. Just not on our second date." He looked at the closed door again before continuing. "McKenna, I think I love her. I mean, I think I might want to marry her."

"Good God, Matt. You've had one date. Are you trying to scare her to death?"

"We've had one date, but we've known each other since I came here. We've talked for hours. I feel like she's the one I was meant to be with."

"That's fine, Matt, but slow down. Last night was her first hint that you wanted more than friendship. Give her a chance to get used to this before you propose, okay? And what the hell is wrong with having sex? Please don't tell me you plan to wait until your wedding night?"

"No, of course not. But I don't want to make it into some cheap affair, either."

"You know, Matt, you are a rare breed." She stepped closer and gave him a hug. "Donna is a lucky woman."

"So, if I don't do anything more than kiss her again, she won't think I'm weird?"

Chris laughed. "She won't think you're weird. She'll think you're a gentleman."

"Thanks, McKenna. And you'll just keep this between us, right?"

"Of course."

Chris watched him nearly skip down the hall and she laughed. Love was in the air for sure.

"What was that all about?" Roger asked when Chris plopped down in the chair across from him.

"Private," she said. "Secret. Can't tell."

"Come on," he coaxed.

"Nope."

"Fine. I don't want to know, anyway. I've got enough to worry about. There's another damn storm out there," he said.

"This one wasn't bad, Roger. Only four or five inches in town."

"Yeah, but the mountain is full of skiers today, tomorrow will probably be worse as people from Sacramento drive up for a Sunday afternoon."

"The weather's fine, Roger. Will you quit worrying?"

"This spring, McKenna, when we lost those three skiers, that did me in. I mean, you hear about it all the time, but we were so helpless here."

"Sometimes, you can have the best SAR around and still be helpless."

"We didn't know how to respond. It started snowing and didn't stop for three days."

"Roger, if I'd been here, do you think I could have found them? They could have had radio transmitters, and we still wouldn't have gotten to them in time. It's not your fault."

"Yeah, but I've been dreading the season all the same. Damn jet stream," he murmured.

"Would you feel better if I went out on the trails?"

He smiled. "Bobby's already out there. He went up Ridge Trail. That's where they were," he said. "It shook Bobby up pretty good."

"Well, I'll take a stroll around Lake Trail, then."

"Ellen and I are having dinner at the Rock tonight, if you want to join us," he called as she walked out.

"Yeah, I might do that."

Chapter Thirty-eight

Chris stood silently in her kitchen, impatiently watching the coffee drip. She drummed her fingers on the counter while Dillon watched her.

"I know. Should have set the timer," she said.

But after the four beers she shared with Roger and Ellen, she'd gotten home last night and went straight to bed. As Jessie had said, sleep had not been a priority the last few nights. She wondered how the shopping trip had gone. Jessie had not been home yet when Chris went out for dinner and she didn't call her. She didn't want to interrupt her time with Annie.

"Finally," she said when the coffee stopped dripping. She poured a steaming cup, then took it back into the bedroom where the heater was still on. She dressed quickly, noting with some concern that low clouds were already drifting in from the west, obscuring the early morning sunshine. It was supposed to be another sunny day, perfect for skiing, but the clouds made liars out of the forecasters. Again. Maybe Roger's storm was making an early entrance.

She wasn't surprised to find Roger already at the ranger station. She met his worried eyes as soon as she walked in.

"What's up?"

"Goddamn storm," he said. "Low pressure in the Pacific moved ashore already. Ten hours early."

"What's the word?"

"Hell, like they know. The lodge is full, that's all I know."

"Roger, we can close the trails fairly quickly. Don't panic on me, okay?"

"We can close Lake Trail and Elk Meadow, sure. I'm worried about the back country."

She wanted to tell him not to worry. She'd worked many winters in Yosemite where storms had come up suddenly. And she could remember only two times where skiers didn't make it back in time and they had to go out and find them. Most skiers were aware of changing weather patterns and didn't take chances. But the type of skiers they had here were recreational, at best. Most of them wouldn't carry backpacks in case of emergencies. Most were families, just out for a quick few miles, then back to the warmth of the lodge or cabin, then maybe back out for another run in the afternoon. Only the most experienced skiers took the South Rim trail. And experienced skiers would watch the weather.

"You think I'm overreacting?"

"A little. Let's just watch the weather and wait for another update," she suggested.

"At ten," he said.

"Roger, you can't do this every time a storm comes up. You'll drive yourself crazy."

"I know. But it would really make me feel better if you went out and checked on the activity, see what's going on."

"Sure. I'll check the trailheads."

She grabbed a radio off of one of the chargers and left him as he flipped on the TV, searching out the Weather Channel.

She drove to the South Rim trailhead first. Skiers who would use this trail would normally start out early. She was happy to see only six names on the list, although two had listed the Nevada Trail instead of the loop that would take them back around by the Fire Lookout Trail. By the time she got to Ridge Trail, twenty-two skiers had signed in. It was seven miles to the loop and she thought that even if the storm hit early, they would still have enough time to ski down. She drove through town to where Lake Trail began. She didn't even bother checking the register. The parking lot was nearly full and she could see skiers across the lake as they made their way over the fresh snow. She assumed Elk Meadow would be the same.

The wind picked up suddenly, a gust shaking her Jeep as she drove back through town. She slowed, peering out the window at the low clouds, waiting for the first flakes to fall. The ringing of her cell phone startled her.

"McKenna."

"It's me."

"Jessie. Hi," Chris said, her voice softening. She had meant to call her this morning but that was before Roger and his storm worries.

"Bad time?"

"No, sorry. There's a storm coming. I'm just out checking trailheads. How was your trip?"

"It was fun, actually. And I normally hate shopping, but Annie was like a kid out there."

"Good. I'm glad you had a good time." She paused, then said what was on her mind. "I missed you. A lot."

"I missed you, too," Jessie said quietly. "I came very close to pounding on your door at midnight."

"That would have been a nice surprise. Much better than the dream I had to settle for."

"Can I see you tonight?"

Chris grinned. She had to ask? Damn, she felt like a teenager, sitting here with a silly grin on her face.

"Want me to cook for you?" Chris offered.

"I'm not really in the mood for cereal, McKenna. How about a pizza?"

"Frozen?"

"No, I'll call the pizza place in Sacramento and see if they'll deliver, smart ass."

Chris laughed. "I love frozen pizza. Where and when?"

"My place. As soon as you can, okay?"

"Can't wait. I'll call you when things settle down around here."

"And McKenna?"

"Yeah?"

"Wear something that comes off easily."

Chris acknowledged the happiness that settled over her. Love? Well, even if it wasn't, it sure felt good. She glanced up and met the sparkling eyes in the mirror. Love.

It was just after ten when she parked the Jeep in front of the ranger station. There were skiers coming out with maps, and she hoped they were taking one of the short trails.

"McKenna, how was it out there?" Roger asked anxiously as soon as she came in.

"Busy. At least in town. What's new with the storm?"

"A wet one, for sure. They have torrential rains all along the coast. It's picked up speed. Could mean blizzard for us. They haven't posted warnings yet. They're going to let me know at noon."

She met his eyes and saw his concern. It was serious. "Have you checked South Rim? There were only six skiers signed in this morning," she said.

"Thirteen now."

"Lake Trail and Elk Meadow were packed," she said.

"We can get those closed if need be. We can get people out of there within an hour. South Rim though . . ." He shook his head. "Who knows? There are too many side trails from there. Not to mention the Nevada Trail. There were four skiers that listed that as their destination. Hopefully they'll know enough to turn around."

"Shit," she said quietly. "How long do we wait?"

"We'll wait until the next report to decide if we need to close the trails. My gut tells me we should do it now, but I don't want to over-react."

"Well, I've got a pack in my Jeep. I think I'll go out and see if I can round up Bobby and Greg. Just in case," she said. Bobby would be busy at the lodge, but she was certain Bill wouldn't mind her taking him for a few hours.

"Fine. Hatcher's on his way in. Matt was at Ridge Trail."

She tried calling Greg as she drove to the lodge. He didn't answer and there was no machine. She drove over to his shop before going to his house, but it was closed up. At his house, Greg's truck was there, but his snowmobile was missing. She left him a note to call Roger, then drove to the lodge.

She found Bobby in the rental shop.

"Busy?"

"Yeah, but judging by the weather, they'll be heading back in soon," he said.

"Storm's coming faster than expected. Roger's thinking we might have to close the trails. There are thirteen skiers out on South Rim," she told him.

She saw his eyes widen and knew he was remembering the three skiers they lost last season.

"Do you think it'll be a problem for you to leave if we need you?"

"Of course not. I'll tell Bill. Just let me know."

"Thanks, Bobby. I'll call."

She drove back to the ranger station, hearing on the radio that the winter storm watch had just been changed to a warning.

"Well?" she asked as soon as she walked in.

"Winter storm warning but we heard that on the damn radio. The weather service hasn't called and I can't get through," Roger said. "The guys?"

234

"Bobby's a go. Greg's out on his snowmobile, I think. I left a note." She looked into the concerned eyes of Roger and knew they were going to be in for a long day.

Just before noon, the call came from the National Weather Service in Sacramento and both she and Matt waited anxiously as Roger nodded into the phone. He hung up a short time later.

"ETA two o'clock. Blizzard conditions expected. He said we could see the first snow in an hour. They've got sixty-mile-an-hour gusts down there. It doesn't look good."

"Let's close the trails right now and get as many people off as we can," Chris said quickly.

"Yes, but what about South Rim, McKenna. What if they reached the Nevada Trail, there's not enough time."

"Matt, call Bobby and try Greg again. Roger, when Hatcher gets here, have him and Matt close Elk Meadow and Lake Trail. If skiers are on Ridge Trail, they'll have enough time to get back down, but you need to have someone ski the trail to make sure. I'll take Bobby and we'll head up South Rim," she said.

"Okay. It's a plan, at least. When Bobby gets here, you head out. There's only the four we're really worried about. Right?"

Chris gripped his arm hard and squeezed.

"Right, Roger. It's going to be okay."

"Damn, McKenna, I hate days like this," he said and he ran hands through his already unruly hair.

Bobby arrived with his full pack within fifteen minutes, but there was still no word from Greg. Chris thought how ironic it would be if they ended up searching for Greg as well.

She grabbed a fresh radio, then led Bobby to the back room to add ropes to their packs and get the folding aluminum rack. Just in case, she told herself.

"Keep in touch, McKenna."

"Don't worry, Roger. We'll be fine. Just take care of things down here."

They left, with Bobby strapping the aluminum rack to his pack and Chris taking the extra rope. Their packs weighed more than forty pounds with the added gear—no easy feat on skis. They posted the closed sign at the trailhead and checked the sign-in sheet. Of the thirteen, six had signed out.

They started out, both looking up at the sky, already steel gray with a heavy overcast. The wind was steady, not gusting, but the temperature was barely twenty degrees.

"Man, I'm not looking forward to this," Bobby said as he lowered his eyes from the sky.

"Me either. I'd rather be sitting by the fire with a bottle of rum," she said. "And, you know, maybe some female company." She pushed off with her skis, trying to set a rhythm.

They followed the tracks made by the other skiers and had barely rounded the first hill when two skiers approached. They stopped and waited.

"Looks like a storm coming," one of them said. "Better not head up."

"We're Search and Rescue," Chris said. "Where were you headed when you signed in?"

"Nevada Trail," the other man said. "But there's a skier up there that got separated from his buddy. We were on our way to the ranger station."

Chris and Bobby exchanged glances.

"He's up at the split where the trail becomes the Nevada Trail."

"I'll radio it in. Stay off the mountain. It'll be snowing like hell in an hour."

"Yeah. We're done for the day. But that guy, he's plenty scared."

"We're on our way up," Bobby said.

They watched the skiers go down, then Chris radioed Roger with the news.

"Be careful, McKenna. Keep an eye to the sky."

"Ten-four."

"Easy for him to say," Bobby mumbled.

They trudged slowly up the trail until it leveled off, then continued following the tracks. They wove their way in and out of the trees, up and down hills, all the time maintaining a quick pace. They both knew that if they had any hope of finding the skier, they must do it before the snow started. Tracks would be covered up quickly in even a light snowstorm and this promised to be anything but light.

They stopped once to catch their breath and to check their progress. The junction of the South Rim and Nevada Trail was still two miles away. Chris pushed her parka sleeve up and looked at her watch. One-thirty. They had made good time. She looked at the sky, and as if by doing so, the clouds opened up and the first snow flakes fluttered down around them.

"Shit," she said and pulled her gloves on again. "Let's go."

"I don't like this, McKenna," Bobby said as he, too, looked up at the sky. It was a dark gray, with swirling clouds hanging low on the mountain. It looked like it could burst open at any moment and engulf them.

"I know, but we gotta hurry."

They kept up their even pace as the snow fell lightly around them. The wind had not picked up, thankfully, and they covered the next two miles in near silence. Standing alone, waving at them, was the skier. He slid down the trail to them, nearly wiping them out as he tried to stop.

"Are you rangers?" he asked breathlessly.

"Search and Rescue," Chris said.

"Thank God. I didn't know what to do. It looks like a storm."

"No shit," Bobby said. "We can't waste time. Where did you split up?"

"At the trail up there," he said, pointing.

"Why?"

"We weren't sure which one to take. We didn't have a trail map," he said, glancing at them both.

"Jesus," Chris murmured. "What time?"

"About eleven, I think. Maybe a little later."

"You were both going to take a trail and ski back to meet up?"

"Yeah. We wanted to take the Nevada Trail but we didn't know the way."

"Okay," Chris said. "What's his name?"

"Kenny. Kenny Walker. We're staying at the lodge."

"What color is his jacket?"

"It's blue. Bright blue, just a little ski jacket."

Chris nodded. It was warmer this morning and sunny. They would not have thought to wear heavy parkas.

"Okay. We're going to look for him. You've got to get off the mountain. There's a hell of a storm coming. You've maybe only got a half-hour before it hits full force. Is it your car parked down there or his?"

"It's his."

"Great. And I don't suppose you have keys to it?"

He shook his head.

She pulled a glove off and dug in her pockets, fishing out the keys to her Jeep.

"Take my Jeep. Drive it to the ranger station. I'll radio in and tell them you're coming down."

"Don't you think I should go with you and look for him?"

"No. Now get down as fast as you can."

"But Kenny, I can't just leave him."

"We'll find him. We don't have time to look out for you, too. Now, get your ass down the mountain."

He looked at Bobby, as if for help, but Bobby motioned for him to go. They watched him ski off and Chris unhooked her radio and called to the station.

"This is Kay, McKenna. Everyone's out."

"Ten-four. Listen, we're at the junction to Nevada Trail. We sent a skier down. His partner is not accounted for. He was last seen heading east on Nevada Trail. Kay, he'll be driving my Jeep. I told him to go there so you'll know he made it down safely."

"Ten-four."

She hooked her radio back on her belt, then with a glance at

Bobby, headed out. The Nevada Trail started out going downhill, which could fool you if you didn't have a map. She could see how the skiers thought this trail might take them down the mountain. Actually, it went downhill until it crossed a small stream, then went abruptly back uphill into the forest and beyond. If you stayed on it long enough, you'd end up at Lake Tahoe.

They were still following tracks, the light snow not enough to cover them yet, but they had no way of knowing if these were from their skier or the two that had already made it down. Most likely, they were from all three. The trail was marked, but some of the triangle markers were covered with snow, or the branches of the trees, now heavy with snow, were covering them. Without a map and compass, it would just be guesswork.

They crossed the stream and headed slowly up the hill. They were both tired and they stopped to catch their breath. Chris pulled off her wool cap and dusted the snow off, then put it back on and pulled it over her ears. She watched their frosty breath and wondered how cold it was. She had a small thermometer tied to her pack and she turned around, her back to Bobby.

"What's the temp?" she asked.

"Shit, it's already down to fifteen, McKenna."

Their eyes met, both worried. They started on up the trail again, their thighs aching. When they reached the top, they were able to see to the west and they stared out over the mountains. Dark, dark clouds, swollen with snow, hung heavily over the trees and as they watched, the wind increased, swirling around them, flinging icy snowflakes onto their faces.

Chris shook her head, her eyes never leaving his. She was putting their own lives in danger by staying out here, but out here they were. Even if they started back now, they would never make it down the mountain before the heart of the storm hit. They would have to find shelter somewhere, but she would worry about that later. Right now, they had to find the skier and hope that hypothermia had not taken him already.

"Let's hurry, Bobby. You check to the left, I'll take the right."

He nodded and they set out, both keeping their eyes on the side of the trail, looking for any sign of their skier. Another half-hour and the tracks they were following would be covered. Then, it would be only sheer luck if they found him.

They moved quickly over the snow, their skis sliding easily over the fresh powder. The trail was level here as it headed into the forest again. Chris's radio crackled seconds before Roger's voice called for her. They stopped and she quickly unhooked her radio and answered.

"We've got everything closed down here, McKenna. What's your ten-twenty?" he asked.

"We're probably three miles into the Nevada Trail. Maybe more." She looked at Bobby with raised eyebrows. It was hard to tell how far they were. Their usual landmarks were now buried in snow.

"I don't like it, McKenna. It's getting nasty down here."

"Yeah, the same here."

"Fifteen more minutes, then I want you turning back. How the hell are you going to get down?"

"I haven't thought about it," she lied.

"Fifteen, McKenna."

"Ten-four." She snapped the radio back on and started out again without looking at her watch. She didn't know what good it would do to head back in fifteen minutes. The storm would still catch them. She closed her eyes against the onslaught of wind and snow and headed out again.

A short while later, Bobby's voice stopped her.

"McKenna, look here. Could be skis," he said, pointing.

Two uneven tracks led off the trail, now all but covered up by the snow. She looked into the woods and saw a clearing.

"Could be. He might have seen that clearing and went to take a look, get his bearings. Let's follow it," she said. "It's all we've got."

They hurried off, leaving the relative safety of the trail behind, to follow the fading tracks. Roger's voice broke the silence and she ignored it, instead concentrating on the path ahead of them.

"Goddamn it, McKenna!" he bellowed through the radio.

She impatiently snatched it off. "We've got a trail, for God's sake, Roger!"

"Listen to me, McKenna. They've got whiteout conditions only fifteen miles from here. You've got to find shelter *now!*"

She looked at Bobby, just now noticing how thick the snow was falling. She looked at their trail, disappearing quickly. "Just a little longer, Roger."

"No! Goddamn it, McKenna, you damn fool. Let it go!"

"Ten-four."

"I mean it!"

"Ten-four." She switched off the radio and met Bobby's eyes. "What do you think?"

He shrugged. "We're this far. Where the hell are we going to find shelter anyway?"

"Yeah. Let's go."

They continued into the forest, hurrying now as the wind whistled around them, blowing snow into their faces. It was another ten minutes before they saw the blue jacket, barely visible through the snow.

He was lying face down and Chris was sure he would be dead. It doesn't take long for hypothermia to kill and they had no idea how long he had been here. Long enough to nearly cover him in snow, though. They turned him over quickly and Chris bent to his chest, clearly surprised to find his heart beating.

"Alive," she said and they both threw off their packs. Bobby quickly assembled the aluminum rack they would use to carry him and Chris took out the blanket from her pack and two chemical hand warmers, which she placed inside his jacket. They dusted off as much snow as they could, then lifted him onto the rack and covered him with the blanket.

"Hook the ropes, Bobby. I'll radio Roger."

Chapter Thirty-nine

Jessie paced nervously in the ranger station, finally stopping to meet Roger's eyes.

"You know she didn't turn around, don't you?" she asked Roger.

"Yes, the damn fool," he said. He had known all along that there wouldn't be enough time for them to get up the mountain and back down before the storm hit. Chris had known it, too.

Jessie had heard the updated forecast on the radio and had tried to call Chris. When she couldn't find her, she had even called Annie to see if she'd heard from her. She finally drove into town, relieved to find Chris's Jeep at the ranger station. Only Chris wasn't there. Roger told her that Chris and Bobby were out on the mountain looking for a skier.

Roger paced, too. He would wait a few minutes, then contact her again. God, she could be so stubborn sometimes. He looked around the room, seeing the worried look on Matt's face and the near frantic look in Jessie Stone's eyes. Only Hatcher remained impassive. When he met Jessie's eyes, he gave her a reassuring smile, then turned away. He didn't want her to see the worry in his own eyes. Blizzard conditions, whiteout, temperatures near zero. How would they survive the night?

"Roger, come in," McKenna's voice called urgently and he quickly snatched up the radio.

"Here."

"We found him. Unconscious but alive. Hypothermia for sure, maybe a concussion. He's got a pretty nice gash on his forehead. Probably hit a rock when he fell."

"Where are you?" he asked, not bothering with the radio code.

"We're still in the forest, about a half-mile off the trail," she said.

"Shit." He shook his head and met Matt's eyes. "Now what?"

"I don't know, Roger. We're going back to the trail and see how it is. We need to get down a little lower, the wind is hell up . . ." The radio crackled static over her voice.

"You're breaking up, McKenna. Ten-nine," he said, asking her to repeat her previous transmission.

"I'll check back after . . ."

"I'm not picking you up, McKenna. Ten-nine," he said again.

"Later. I'm out, Roger."

The static ended and silence hung between them in the room. Roger looked at the others and shrugged.

"I guess we wait."

"Man, I'm glad it's not me out there," Robert said.

"You know what, Hatcher? We're all glad it's not you out there. Because if it were up to you, you'd be sitting at a nice fire right now not giving a damn about anyone."

Matt stared at Roger then turned to Robert.

"Why don't you get out of here, man? We can handle it."

"Hey, I didn't mean anything," he said.

"Go home, Hatcher," Roger said. "The roads are getting bad. I'd hate for you to be stuck here with us."

"Fine with me."

After he left, Matt turned to Roger.

"Just once, I'd like to deck the guy. No wonder McKenna can't stand him."

"Yeah, he's a piece of work."

Jessie watched the exchange in silence, just barely able to hold her own tongue.

"Can they make it, Roger?"

"I don't know, Jessie. They'll be carrying an extra man," he said, letting his voice trail off. He didn't know how they could make the night. They were probably damn near exhausted as it was. Put up a tent and tie it down? Maybe, but neither of them carried a tent big enough for three. He shook his head. It was damn foolish to have sent them up there to begin with. The desperate feelings he felt last spring settled over him, and he prayed the outcome would not be the same.

"I want to stay here," Jessie said.

"No. There's nothing you can do here. Go to Annie's while the roads are still passable. Sit by the fire. I promise I'll call the minute I hear something. Promise."

"She means a lot to me, Roger. An awful lot," Jessie confessed.

"She means a lot to me, too. But there's nothing we can do now. They're on their own."

Chapter Forty

They put on their snowshoes and strapped their skis to their packs. It took them nearly forty minutes to pull him to the trail. They had to stop to maneuver him around trees and rocks, then nearly missed the trail. It was snowing so hard, they could barely see in front of them and they very nearly crossed over the trail and into the forest on the other side. Their tracks were almost completely covered and if they hadn't stopped to rest, they might have missed it.

"What are we going to do, McKenna?" Bobby asked urgently.

"Let's get down to Little Bear Creek. I have an idea," she said. She remembered the camping trip with Jessie when she had told her about caves. She said they were upstream, about a mile. A mile in this weather would seem like forever, but right now, it was all she could think of. She didn't want to consider that Jessie was a child the last time she had been here. What's a mile to a kid?

They made good time on the trail, pulling him easily in the snow.

Before they headed downhill towards the stream, Chris checked on Kenny. He was still unconscious and his skin felt cold. Very cold. She took off her pack and pulled out her sleeping bag and laid that on top of him, too. They had to get him warm or he would surely die.

"Ready?" she asked.

"Yeah, let's go."

They headed down the hill, faces turned into the fierce wind, and it took all of their strength to hold the injured skier behind them. If they weren't careful, he would go sliding down the hill without them, right into the stream. They both walked sideways, letting their snowshoes dig into the side of the hill for support. The steep hill leveled out before the stream, and they were able to relax the last fifty feet. At Little Bear Creek, which was now covered with snow, Chris turned upstream and she knew immediately that it wasn't going to be easy. Boulders littered the sides, some covered entirely with snow, and time and again they stepped, only to sink up to their waists as their feet missed a rock.

"Bobby, we've got to go a mile," she yelled against the wind. "Help me gauge the distance, okay?"

"I'll try," he yelled back.

She cringed as a gust of wind hit, nearly knocking them over. They could only see a few feet ahead as snow swirled in their faces. The blizzard had hit. She braced against the wind with every step and kept her eyes glued to the stream so that they wouldn't get lost. She thought briefly of all the stories she had heard about people lost in blizzards, wandering around in circles for hours before succumbing to the cold and surrendering to death. She wasn't about to let that happen to them. If nothing else, they would head into the trees and try to put up a tent and lie three-deep to try to stay warm. Stay warm? She couldn't remember the last time she'd been warm. She felt nearly frozen, head to toe.

She stared ahead, her eyes focused on the stream. She felt her nose running and ran a cold gloved hand under it and realized that it was numb. The wind pounded around them swirling the snow, and she lowered her head and continued on, trying to ignore the coldness that surrounded them.

She finally stopped to rest and turned to Bobby.

"How far?" she yelled.

He pushed his parka up his arm and looked at his watch. "Not a mile yet, I don't think," he said. "Where the hell are we going, anyway?"

"I'm not sure," she said, knowing he'd not heard her. God, it felt like they'd traveled at least five miles. She turned back into the wind and walked on, spitting out an obscenity as she sank again to her waist. She got back up and continued on, Bobby beside her as they pulled the unconscious Kenny Walker between them.

Fifteen minutes later, she again stopped. "Bobby, it's got to have been a mile."

"What are we looking for?"

"A cave," she yelled.

"Cave? What cave?"

"There's supposed to be a cave around here."

"Are you sure? I've never heard of a cave."

"No, I'm not sure," she said and looked around, trying desperately to see through the thickening snow. What had Jessie said? They would come to a flat area with outcroppings of granite. Right or left? She thought left, but she wasn't sure. She peered into the snow, but it was no good. She couldn't see two feet in front of them. They were never going to find the caves like this.

"Bobby, I'm going to go out looking," she said.

"No way. You'll get lost. You can't see shit," he yelled.

"I'll tie a rope to you," she said and took off her pack. She pulled out the rest of the rope and tied the end around her waist. The other end she gave to Bobby. "It's the only way."

"Be careful," he called as she walked away.

She stumbled blindly into the snow, her snowshoes now caked with wet packed snow. She knew instantly that they were in the right area. Flat, no rocks or trees that she could tell. She walked on, arms outstretched so that she wouldn't run into anything. Suddenly before her, were piles of rocks. Granite. She was close. She walked farther on, only feet from the rocks. She looked up, but couldn't tell how high they were. For all she knew, these were simply boulders, only five or six feet high, not the massive outcroppings that would form caves. It didn't feel right. She stopped and turned back, walking the opposite way along the rocks, her hands out guiding her. The wind whipped against the rock wall, bouncing back into her face, stinging her eyes as she squinted against its force.

Just as she was about to go back, her rope having run out, she saw the black hole against all the white surrounding her. She opened her eyes wide, hoping she was really seeing it and not just imagining it. There, a large hole opened up in the rocks. Her rope was tight, and she couldn't reach it to know for sure, but even if it wasn't Jessie's cave, it would give them shelter. She turned, her frozen hands gripping the rope, and made her way back to Bobby.

"I've found something," she yelled when Bobby was within sight. "It'll have to do."

She untied the rope around her waist and shoved it back in her pack, then slung it over her shoulders. "Come on."

She couldn't remember ever having been so cold. Her fingers were numb inside her gloves, and her feet felt like stumps as they walked against the wind, their heads bent as they followed her tracks.

"There," she said and pointed to the black hole facing them.

"I see it," Bobby yelled and they quickened their pace, pulling the skier between them.

They stopped at the entryway, both fishing their flashlights from their packs. They flashed the light around the room, then walked in and burst out laughing in relief. There, in the center of the small room, was a fire ring and against one wall was a pile of old, dried wood.

"Jesus, I can't believe it," Bobby said and his voice echoed against the walls.

"Neither can I. Come on, let's get a fire going."

They tossed their packs on the floor and quickly broke up the dried wood. Chris took some toilet paper from her pack and made small balls and laid it in the center of the ring. Bobby piled on small sticks and some dried bark and she set a match to it and soon the flame licked hungrily at the dry wood. Bobby laid on more, gradually building a warm campfire.

Chris took her sleeping bag and the blanket off of Kenny and pulled him closer to the fire. She nearly screamed when he spoke to her.

"Where am I?" he whispered.

"Jesus Christ!"

She found her flashlight and shone it in his face. He closed his eyes against the bright light, and she switched it off.

"We're Search and Rescue," she explained.

"Where's Michael?"

"He's fine. But right now, we've got to get you warm." She turned to Bobby. "Help me get him near the fire."

They pulled him as near as they dared, then she and Bobby stripped off their gloves and held their hands over the flames, ignoring the stinging as they warmed.

"I've never been this cold before, McKenna."

"I'm pretty much a popsicle myself." She looked to their injured skier. "Hey, what's your name?"

"Kenny. Kenny Walker," he said.

"What day is it?"

"It's Saturday . . . no, Sunday."

"What month?"

"I'm sure there's a reason for this?" he asked.

"What month?" she asked again.

"November and don't ask me the date. I always forget the damn date over the weekend," he said and offered her a smile.

"Good. Well, I pronounce you free of a concussion," she said, then turned to look at his face. He closed his eyes against the flashlight. "But you're probably going to need some stitches here." She touched the tender area around the gash and he winced.

"I must have fallen," he said. "I don't really remember. I got lost coming back. I was supposed to meet Michael back where the trail split."

"Don't worry about it now. We're going to be okay."

"I thought I was going to die," he said.

"You're damn lucky you didn't. It was just pure luck we spotted your tracks off the trail before we turned back," Bobby told him.

"He's right. I've seen hypothermia kill in a lot less time," Chris told him. She got out her first aid kit and began cleaning his wound. "Let me put a butterfly on this, then we need to get something warm in you." She felt his cheeks with both hands. "You're still too cold."

"Yeah. I'm starting to shiver," he said.

"That's a good sign. Your body's working again, trying to warm you." She turned to Bobby. "Put some water on to heat. I've got some tea bags in there somewhere."

She cleaned the gash on his head and put two butterfly bandages on to close it as best she could. Bobby filled one of their pots with water and set it on the small gas burner that he always packed and Chris filled another pot and set it near the fire. They would have tea first, then a hot meal. It was only then, as they busied themselves, that she thought to radio in.

"I better check in with Roger. He's probably out of his mind."

She opened her parka and reached for the radio, only to find the holster empty.

"Shit. Bobby, tell me you've got the radio," she said.

"No," he said, shaking his head.

"Shit," she said again. She let the beam of the flashlight zigzag across the floor, hoping it had fallen out in the cave, but she knew it had not. "I must have lost it along the creek. Lord knows I fell down enough."

She silently cursed herself. The last time she had talked to Roger, they were in a hurry to get going and she had failed to secure it in the holster. She had simply shoved it in without thinking. Well, it wouldn't do any good to worry about it now. There was nothing they could do. Hopefully, Roger wouldn't think the worst.

Chapter Forty-one

Jessie knew she was insane to be out in this weather, but she didn't want to spend the night alone. She crept through the deserted town, trying desperately to see through the snow. She had driven in enough snowstorms to know to look through the snow to the road or you would become hypnotized by the flakes as they surround your car, but she had never driven in a blizzard.

She passed the lodge at the edge of town, the parking lot full. Most of the guests were staying over another night since the roads heading back to the city were already closed. She slowed to a crawl as she approached the forest road that would take her to Annie's. Her four-wheel drive held as she made the corner, but the road was completely covered in snow and she tried to stay in the middle for fear of skidding off the side and getting stuck. She nearly took out Annie's mailbox as she turned into the driveway, her rear fender missing it by inches, and she pumped the brakes, coming to a standstill next to the house. She released the death grip she had on the steering wheel, and let out a relieved breath. She grabbed the overnight bag from the backseat, slammed the door and ran up the steps. Annie had the door open before she could knock and she hurried past her into the warm house.

"Jessie, thank God," Annie said. "You shouldn't have been driving in that. The radio says the roads are a mess."

"Well, they're not lying," she said as she took off her parka.

Annie took it from her and hung it on the coat rack by the door. "Sit by the fire. I'll bring you a glass of wine."

Jessie nodded and stood with her back to the fire, her hands held out behind her. She squeezed her eyes shut. She was so worried about Chris. Was she still battling the blizzard on the trails or had she found shelter? She didn't want to think about the possibility of no shelter. It would be below zero by morning, not to mention the wind chill.

"I'm glad you're here, Jessie, but I was worried about you driving in this. Why didn't you just go over to Chris's? I'm sure she wouldn't have minded you staying with her."

"Chris is out on the mountain, Annie," Jessie said.

"What? In this? Oh, no," she said. "Did someone get hurt?"

"Two skiers got separated at the Nevada Trail. One of them made it back. Chris and Bobby went out to look for the other one," she stated, her voice flat.

"Surely, the storm . . . they knew it would hit," Annie said. "They can't possibly try to ski in this."

Jessie heard the worry in her voice, but she had no words of comfort.

"Roger lost radio contact. It was too much static. He said he would call as soon as he knew something," she said quietly, feeling her voice catch.

"Oh, no." Annie sank down on the sofa. "Jessie, we mustn't think the worst. Chris is trained, she knows the mountain. She'll know what to do," Annie said firmly, but in a tone edged with worry.

Jessie met her eyes. "Do you think so?"

"Yes." She offered a small smile. "In case you haven't noticed, Chris can be very stubborn. She won't let this storm get the best of her."

"I hope you're right, Annie." She looked at her watch. An hour and a half since she'd left Roger. "I'm going to call in, though. Just in case he has some news."

Jessie walked to the phone and Annie watched her, surprised at her obvious worry for Chris, a woman she had only known a short time.

"It's Jessie. Anything new?" she asked.

Annie could tell by the drop of Jessie's shoulders that there was no news.

"What do you mean?" A pause. "There's static on the line, Roger. Let me give you my cell number. You promise you'll call the second you know something?"

Annie listened as Jessie rattled off her number, then waited as Roger spoke.

"I know, Roger, but I'm nearly out of my mind here. I don't know what she's told you . . . good, then you understand my feelings."

Annie watched Jessie hang up the phone, then down her glass of wine in one swallow.

"What is it?" she asked.

"There's no radio feedback at all. She's not even trying to acknowledge their transmission," she said quietly. She was on the verge of tears and she walked rapidly into the kitchen and refilled her wineglass. Oh, her sweet Chris, please let her be okay.

"Jessie, that doesn't mean anything's happened to them," Annie said from behind her. "The radio could have frozen up, the storm could block the transmission, anything."

"I know," she said softly. God, she didn't want to cry in from of Annie. How would she explain tears to Annie?

"I didn't realize Chris meant so much to you," she said.

Jessie turned around and met her questioning eyes. "We've become close," she said simply. She felt a tear slide down her cheek, and she finally gave in to them. "I've just found her. I can't possibly lose her now," she cried.

Annie wrapped her arms around the crying Jessie, soothing her, not having any idea of what Jessie was talking about.

"Shhh, it'll be okay. Come, let's sit by the fire. Then you can tell me what's got you so upset."

Jessie followed numbly behind Annie and sat at the edge of the sofa. She stared into the fire, wiping the remaining tears away. Oh, she longed for Chris to be here, to comfort her.

"Jessie?"

She turned her eyes to Annie, wondering what her reaction would be? Would she be upset? Startled? Disappointed?

"Chris is very important to me, Annie," she said quietly. "We're . . ." What? Lovers? Of course. But they were more than just that.

"You've become good friends, Jessie. I had hoped you would," Annie said.

"We're more than friends, Annie. Chris and I . . . are lovers," she confessed. At Annie's shocked expression, she continued quickly. "I know you don't understand, and this is probably a complete shock to you, but Chris and I . . . well, we have this connection between us. It was there from the beginning. And I've never needed anyone like I need her. I've never had anyone in my life, Annie, but I need Chris in my life." She felt tears form again and pushed them away. "And I can't lose her now."

Annie nodded, for once at a complete loss for words. To say that Jessie's words had shocked her would be an understatement. She knew there was a familiarity between them, but still, she didn't think there had been enough time for them to explore this type of a relationship.

"Please say something."

"I know that Chris is a lesbian. She told me awhile ago. It just never occurred to me that you were, I guess. Or is this just because of Chris?" she asked hesitantly.

Jessie shook her head. "It's not just Chris, Annie. I've never had a lover before, I've just had sex partners. But always women."

Annie took a deep breath. "Because of Jack?"

Jessie shrugged. "Maybe. I don't know. I just have no attraction to men. But Chris broke down all my barriers, made me feel something, made me want something. She's given me hope that I might have love in my life."

"You're in love with her?" Annie asked quietly, not really understanding.

"I don't know what it feels like to be in love, Annie. I only know I hurt inside thinking she might not come back to me," she whispered.

Annie reached over and took her daughter's hand and held it gently.

"I don't know why I'm surprised. Chris has a way about her, she's such a charmer. And I've not been completely blind to the looks that pass between you two sometimes." She squeezed Jessie's hand. "I'm not too old to appreciate a good romance. So tell me, it was the other night when you had dinner here?"

Jessie blushed and Annie laughed.

"Roger couldn't find Chris the next morning. That's because she was with you?"

"Yes."

Annie smiled at Jessie's obvious embarrassment. She couldn't wait to get Chris alone. Oh, the teasing would be merciless.

Chapter Forty-two

They sipped hot tea while they waited for the water to boil for their dinners. Kenny was sitting with them by the fire, his eyes staring at the snow swirling around the opening to the cave. He knew he was lucky to be alive.

"Why isn't there more smoke in here?" he asked.

"It's not a real cave. It was formed by fallen rock, an outcropping. It's just rising up and slipping through the cracks," Chris said.

"It feels warm in here."

"The rocks absorb heat." She reached for her pack and read the temperature from the thermometer tied on the back. "A balmy thirty-three degrees, if you can believe that. It's probably in the single digits outside."

They were quiet as they watched the snow and listened to the wind howl. Soon, it would be too dark to see outside, but they were warm, they had food, and the fire kept them company.

"I think the water's ready," Bobby said. He took the pot from the small stove and set it on the ground. Chris held the flashlight for him and he opened two of the freeze-dried packages and dumped them in the water. Chris put another pot on to boil and Bobby covered his and set it aside. He glanced at his watch. Eight minutes to supper!

"This is ours," he told Kenny. "She's got some meatless pasta concoction."

It was completely dark outside by the time they finished eating, although it was barely after five. The dark clouds surrounded the mountain and the wind and snow continued pelting the rocks, but they stayed warm. Bobby gave up his sleeping bag to Kenny, who was already asleep. He would make do with his parka and the wool blanket.

"Do you think he'll be okay?" Bobby asked.

"Yeah. Take him a few days to get his strength back. I'm surprised he was able to sit up as long as he did."

"Well, I know it's early, but I'm damn near exhausted," he said and he settled under his parka.

"I know. I feel like I could sleep twelve hours." She stood up and slipped her coat back on. "I've got to pee," she said.

"Don't go far," Bobby warned.

"Don't worry. I'll only go far enough to hang my butt out," she said and laughed.

Later, as the others lay sleeping, Chris added another small log to the fire and sat staring out into the night. The wind had subsided a little, but snow was still falling. She figured everyone was plenty worried about them. Especially Jessie. She cursed herself for not calling her before they left, but there had been no time. And for her to lose the radio. That was a stupid thing to do.

She finally crawled into her sleeping bag, letting thoughts of Jessie warm her. Was she with Annie tonight? Or had she stayed at her cabin, waiting? Frozen pizza. Chris smiled. She'd give anything to be sitting in front of the fire eating pizza right now. And then, later, snuggled under the covers. She closed her eyes and listened to the fire crackle, remembering Jessie's hands on her, eager hands that had nearly ripped the shirt from her body in their haste to touch. Soft hands that cradled her breasts, guiding them to a waiting mouth. Warmth settled over Chris as she thought of that mouth and all it would do to her.

She rolled over, trying to quell the ache inside her. What if she was never to see Jessie again? Never feel her touch? They could very well have frozen to death out there. She didn't want to think about how close they had been. If not for this cave . . .

Sleep finally claimed her and she slept soundly until dawn, when the morning chill invaded the small cave. She opened her eyes and Bobby was already trying to get the fire going again.

"Morning, McKenna," he said, his frosty breath swirling around him.

She looked at Kenny, who was still asleep, then sat up and grabbed the thermometer. Ten. When the fire died, it hadn't taken long for the cold to creep inside.

"You must have been cold without a sleeping bag," she told him.

"I slept like a log until about an hour ago. I was shivering and it woke me."

He had a small fire going in no time, adding what was left of the bark and small sticks. Then, he took out his small stove and put on water to boil for tea.

"I need to pee but it's too damn cold," he said. "You?"

"Yeah, but I can wait," she said. She lay back down and pulled her sleeping bag more firmly around her. "The snow has stopped."

"Yeah. It's clearing," he said. He stood up and held his hands over the fire for a minute. "Okay, I'm going out. Wish me luck."

She smiled and nodded, finally making herself get out of the warm sleeping bag. She went to the fire and squatted beside it, warming her hands. Kenny stirred in his bag and sat up.

"I thought I was dreaming, but I'm really here," he said, his voice hoarse from sleep.

"Oh, yeah, you're really here and we've got at least eight miles to go to get out of here. Hopefully they'll send someone to look for us," she said, looking towards the entrance. "And hopefully they'll be on snowmobiles, but don't you dare tell Bobby I said that. I normally hate snowmobiles."

An hour later, after hot tea and breakfast, they packed up. They gave Kenny a pair of snowshoes and Chris and Bobby would take turns on skis, breaking a trail. Bobby estimated that at least three feet of snow had fallen, and it would be slow going. Chris again hoped someone would be coming. She didn't think Kenny had the strength to make it eight miles.

"Ready?" she asked and they left the cave behind and ventured out into the cold.

Chapter Forty-three

Jessie woke with a start, dismayed that the sun was already up. She hadn't planned on sleeping so long. She sat up quickly, then held her head. Too much wine last night. She pulled on sweatpants and hurried downstairs, smelling the sweet aroma of Irish crème coffee.

Annie stood at the counter, cup in hand, when Jessie walked in. She could tell by the look in Annie's eyes that she'd heard something.

"What is it?"

"I used your little phone there to call Roger. Phone lines are down. They've still not made any radio contact with them," Annie said. "He's sent Matt and Greg out on snowmobiles, although he's not sure how far they can make it. There's a lot of snow, Jessie."

Jessie looked out the window and for a moment, she forgot her worries over Chris. The scene outside was Christmas perfect. Pristine, still, the snow sparkling in the sunlight and all the trees hanging low, barely a green bough could be seen. Then she looked again, closer. The picnic table under the large cedar was nowhere to be found and Annie's bird feeder now stood barely two feet from the snow.

She turned back to Annie. "How much?"

"It's hard to say, what with the wind making drifts. Roger said there's a ten-foot drift in front of the ranger station. He thinks at least four feet in the mountains, maybe more."

"Jesus," Jessie murmured. "Well, I've got to do something. I can't just sit here without knowing."

"There's nothing you can do, child," Annie said firmly. "They'll be all day just trying to clear the roads. Now, have some coffee and I'll make you some breakfast." Jessie looked at her with dismay and Annie added, "It'll keep us busy, if nothing else."

Jessie sat down at the table and took the coffee from Annie. She tried not to think that she might not ever see Chris again. She squeezed her eyes shut, trying to keep her tears away.

Annie saw her shoulders shaking and dried her hands and went to her. She stood behind her and wrapped her arms around her shoulders, trying to find the words to comfort her.

"Jessie, do you believe Chris loves you?" she asked softly.

Jessie opened her eyes, turning the question over in her mind. Did Chris love her? She'd never said. She said she cared for her, but was that the same thing? Then she thought of the way Chris looked at her, the way she touched her, the gentle way she made love to her.

"Yes, I think maybe she does love me," she whispered.

"I think she does, too. And if she loves you, she would do anything she could to come back to you. You must believe that. I know Chris is okay. I feel it in my heart," Annie said. And she did.

Chapter Forty-four

They heard the roar of snowmobiles in the distance and they stopped, looking at each other and smiling.

"Never thought I'd love the sound of those damn things," Chris told Bobby.

He laughed. "And I never thought I'd hear you say it."

They had been on the trail three hours, but had only made it a couple of miles, at best. They had missed the Nevada Trail and had continued following the stream, or what they thought was the stream, for nearly a half-hour before turning back. The view of Sierra Peak was too visible for them to be on the right trail. From Nevada Trail, only the top of the peak would show. Chris dug her compass out from her pack and tried to get their bearings. They backtracked and she and Bobby went in opposite directions, looking for markers on the trees. They finally found one and climbed the long hill to the junction of the South Rim Trail, only to find that they didn't know where the junction was. They could find no more markers. All the trees were heavy with snow, their branches hanging low to the ground. Nothing looked familiar to them, so they simply walked up to the trees, sinking well past their waists. They used their ski poles to knock off snow until they found a marker. Once they were in the right direction, they took out the compass and map, trying to gauge where the trail was. Every several hundred feet, Bobby would go to the trees again to look for markers, just to make sure they were on the right track.

They continued on, listening for the approach of the snowmobiles. It was another hour before they spotted them and they hugged each other and cheered as Greg and Matt stopped just a few feet in front of them.

"Well, I'll be," Matt said. "Look at you! You're not frozen at all," he said and laughed. "Glad you're okay," he said seriously.

"Are we glad to see you," Chris said. "Snowmobiles and all."

"Did I hear you right, McKenna?" Greg asked, a huge grin on his face. "Thought you hated these damn things?"

"Yeah. And I can't wait to get on that damn thing."

Bobby took Kenny on one snowmobile and Chris, after kissing both Greg and Matt full on the mouth, took the other, leaving them behind to ski down. They radioed Roger with the good news, then followed the tracks of the snowmobiles down the mountain.

Considering how long it had taken them on the skis, it seemed that in no time at all they were at the trailhead. They followed the road into town, most of the buildings unrecognizable under the heavy blanket of snow.

"Look at that drift, McKenna," Bobby yelled, pointing to the pile of snow that covered the windows of the ranger station.

Within minutes, they were standing in the warmth of the ranger station, telling their story.

"I've never heard of a cave being out there, McKenna," Roger said.

"Well, Jack knew about them," she said. "He took Jessie there when she was young."

"You're damn lucky, kid," he said, then hugged her for the third time. "How could you have lost the radio?"

"Oh, I don't know. There was a blizzard blowing, I was exhausted, my hands were frozen. Hell, how do you think?" she asked and laughed with him. It was easy to laugh now. They were safe.

He took her aside and put his arm around her. "I was worried sick, McKenna," he said seriously. "And you need to call Jessie. She's at Annie's. I called them and told them we'd found you, but she was pretty shook up about it."

Chris nodded.

"Oh, and you'll have to use your cell. The phone lines are down."

"My phone is buried in my Jeep, Roger. At least, I think that lump out there is my Jeep."

"Mine's on my desk."

She closed the door behind her, relaxing for a minute before picking up the phone. She searched her memory for Jessie's number, then found it scribbled on a note on Roger's desk. The phone was answered on the first ring.

"Thank God, it's you. Are you okay? Do you still have all your fingers and toes?" Annie asked.

"All accounted for, although I'm still not completely thawed."

"A shot of brandy and a nice fire will do wonders. Now, let me get Jessie. She's been, well, she's been nearly out of her mind, thinking she'd lost you. Here."

Chris didn't have time for Annie's words to register. Another voice was calling to her.

"Chris . . . sweetheart," Jessie whispered. "You're okay, right?"

"I'm okay."

"You know, McKenna, you missed our dinner date. One frozen pizza down the drain," she said lightly.

"Funny you should say that. Last night, while I was trying to sleep, I was thinking that I'd give anything to be sitting by a fire with you, eating that damn pizza."

"I was so afraid for you, Chris. Annie's had to put up with my fits of crying," she said. "I think she's ready for me to be gone."

"You were crying?" Chris asked. "Why were you crying?"

"I was afraid I'd never see you again. I was afraid you weren't going to come back to me, and there were still so many things I wanted to tell you. And I was afraid that I wouldn't get the chance."

Chris smiled, wondering if Annie was standing there listening. This conversation wasn't exactly between friends.

"We found your cave, by the way. It's the only thing that saved us."

"Chris, I . . ." She hesitated. The words she wanted to say weren't made for the telephone. Besides, she thought that Annie was enjoying the conversation far too much. "When can I see you?"

"I hope tonight, Jessie. I really want . . . need to be with you tonight," she said softly.

"I'll come to your cabin as soon as the roads are clear enough. And McKenna?"

"Yes?"

"There's really no need for you to dress," she whispered.

She sat there with a silly grin on her face when Roger stuck his head inside.

"Everything okay?"

"Everything's great, Roger."

He sat down in one of his visitor's chairs and studied her. She knew she must look a sight and she ran a hand through her disheveled hair.

"Jessie was over here yesterday. She saw your Jeep, thought you were here," he said. "She heard the last few radio transmissions and it shook her up pretty bad when we thought we'd lost you." He rubbed the heavy stubble on his chin, evidence that he had not gone home last night.

"It was stupid of me not to secure the radio, Roger, but it was pure hell out there," she said truthfully. "I don't mind saying that I was plenty scared," she admitted.

"I don't doubt it. We were all scared for you. You did a hell of a job, saving that man's life. He's damn lucky it was you out there and not Hatcher or someone else. They would have been more concerned about their own hide and the hell with a lost skier."

"Oh, I don't know. Bobby never once suggested that we give up. In fact, I asked him several times if he wanted to head back and he didn't."

"That's because you've taken Bobby under your wing and he idolizes you," he said.

"He does not, he just cares about things, you know. He's perfect for SAR." She leaned back in her chair and relaxed. "Roger, I want to put him on salary. Part-time, if nothing else. He does far too much to be a volunteer," she said.

"I know. I've already put in a request. With Hatcher out of here in a few months, we'll have room in the budget."

He stood up and smiled at her, then raised an eyebrow.

"I'm assuming you have plans tonight?"

"My plans include a hot fire, something alcoholic to drink, I'm thinking brandy. And of course, a very warm, very soft female body to kiss away my aches and pains."

Roger blushed scarlet and hurried to the door.

"Jesus, McKenna, I don't need details!"

Chapter Forty-five

Jessie drove carefully down the partially cleared road. It seemed like forever before the snowplows made it up Annie's way. She really had no idea how deep the snow was until she was out in it. Snow was piled high on each side of the road and there were no visible fences that she could see. She made her way past Mary Ruth's cabin and wondered how she had fared. Her car was still buried. On the drive to Chris's cabin, it was just one long snow tunnel and she parked behind Chris's Jeep, which was still heavy with snow.

It was nearly dark when she got there and a few stars were already blinking in the clear cold sky. She pulled her parka tightly around her and hurried to the door, pausing only a moment before knocking. Chris called to her and she walked into the warm room, the fireplace glowing hotly. Chris lay on the sofa, a pillow tucked under her head and Dillon curled on her stomach. Their eyes met and held, a slow smile forming on Chris's face.

"Hey."

Jessie nodded, feeling her throat threatening to close. She was nervous. As nervous as she'd ever been in her life. What if she was wrong about Chris? What if Chris laughed it off, blaming it on the snowstorm? She shrugged out of her parka and let it fall to the floor.

"Chris . . . I . . . there's something I want to tell you. Need to tell you," she started. She stood firmly rooted by the door, her legs refusing to carry her closer to Chris. "You may not want to hear it."

Chris sat up but still clutched Dillon in her lap. She had no idea what was coming, but Jessie looked ready to bolt through the door.

"Okay. What is it?" she asked hesitantly.

"It's me . . . it's us," she said. At Chris's frightened look, she hurried on. "I don't know what you want, but . . . I . . . oh, hell, McKenna, I wanted to warn you that . . . I think I'm in love with you. At least, I think that's what this is. And I wanted to give you a chance to get out or tell me I'm out of my mind before I say something really stupid or . . ."

"I love you, too," Chris said softly, interrupting her somewhat chaotic speech.

"What?"

"Come here."

"What did you say?" Jessie whispered.

A gentle smile broke across Chris's face and she stood, slowly walking the short distance to the door.

"You want me to say it again?"

Jessie nodded mutely.

"I'm in love with you. You consume my thoughts, day and night. And when I look into your eyes, I see my life there. I see everything that matters to me, and it has nothing to do with this place or this job, or Annie or the damn snowstorm. It's just you and me and the love I feel inside for you."

Jessie knew she was crying. She could feel the tears on her face, but she couldn't look away from the clear, blue eyes so close to her own. Blue eyes that burned with love . . . for her.

"That was the most beautiful thing anyone's ever said to me," she whispered. She was able to move then. Move into the arms that opened for her. She buried her head against Chris's neck and let her tears fall. Never in her life did she think she deserved this. Never once did she think she would ever find this.

Chris felt her soul open up and take Jessie inside. It filled her with such joy that she ached from it. She gently lifted Jessie's head and kissed the tears away, finally finding her lips and placing soft kisses there.

"Let me make love to you," she whispered. "Let me show you how much I love you."

The bedroom was dark, and Chris paused to draw the covers back before undressing the silent Jessie who stood numbly before her. She quickly shed her own clothes and lay back, pulling Jessie with her. As soon as she felt Jessie's weight settle on top of her, she was lost. The gentle, slow lovemaking she'd planned vanished as Jessie's hungry mouth found hers. Tongues battled and Chris rolled them over, pinning Jessie to the bed. But she wanted to go slow. They had all the time in the world. She straddled Jessie's hips, pressing intimately against her as her mouth found Jessie's breast. Her lips closed over an erect nipple and she moaned with pleasure, loving the way Jessie's hands held her firmly to her breast. She suckled her breast, teasing the tip with her tongue, feeling it swell in her mouth.

Jessie closed her eyes, giving in to the gentle touch of her lover. She heard the contented sigh from Chris, felt her move ever so slowly to her other breast. She opened her eyes, meeting blue ones that closed as her mouth settled over her. Again Jessie thought, what did she do to deserve this?

She felt Chris's lips move across her stomach, felt the cool air on her still wet nipples. Her hips arched and she pressed up, feeling Chris's wetness against her thigh. Her hand moved between them, finding the wetness with her fingers. Chris sat up, then settled back down, guiding Jessie's fingers inside her. Jessie heard Chris's breath hiss as her fingers were engulfed in wetness.

"Oh, yes . . . that feels so good," Chris murmured. Her hips rose again and came back down on Jessie's hand, impaling herself. She nudged Jessie's thighs apart, her own fingers sliding through hot silk, slipping inside Jessie in one quick thrust.

Jessie drew a sharp breath and pressed her hips up, drawing Chris inside her. Their rhythm became one as hands and hips danced together, moving in and out of each other in perfect harmony. She opened her eyes to find Chris watching her. Chris's own eyes were glazed over, her mouth slightly opened as she struggled to draw breath.

Jessie was mesmerized. With her free hand, she found Chris's breast and squeezed the nipple between her fingers. She watched Chris's eyes close, watched her head tip back. The pressure of her hips increased and Jessie struggled to maintain the rhythm. Her fingers met each thrust of Chris's hips and her own legs opened wide, allowing Chris deep within her. She felt the first tremors of Chris's body, felt muscles squeeze her fingers tight and she finally gave in to her own release. She let it come, let it nearly overwhelm her with its force.

She couldn't have held back the scream if she'd tried. It mingled in the air with Chris's as her hips went down on Jessie for one last stroke. She closed her legs tight, holding Chris's fingers inside her as Chris finally stilled, her hips settling back down on Jessie's hand. Her wetness ran down Jessie's arm and Jessie groaned. She licked her lips, wishing her mouth were there instead.

They stayed like that for a moment, Chris still sitting upright, Jessie lying back, their eyes locked together.

"I love you," Chris whispered.

"I love you."

She finally moved, letting Jessie's fingers slip away from her. She withdrew her own, then brought them to her mouth, licking Jessie's wetness from her fingers.

Jessie thought it was the most intimate thing she'd ever seen. She reached up and drew Chris's mouth to her own, tasting herself on Chris's lips.

Chris lay down beside Jessie and pulled the covers over them. She gathered Jessie in her arms and gently kissed her damp forehead.

"Are you okay?"

Jessie nodded.

"That was . . . beautiful."

"Yes. It was perfect."

Chris leaned down and placed a soft kiss on Jessie's lips.

"I told Annie about us," Jessie said suddenly.

"What? You did? Was she okay?"

"Yes. I think she was . . . surprised. Although I think she probably suspected there was more to our relationship than we let on."

"Jessie, please tell me you're not leaving. You're not going back to New York."

"No. I want to stay here with you. I want to try to have a life together, if that's what you want. That is what you want, isn't it?"

"Yes. I want you here with me always."

Epilogue

Annie paused to catch her breath, leaning against a large cedar. It had been over seventeen years now since she'd hiked up Ridge Trail and it was steeper than she remembered. She looked out over the canyon, thinking how much had changed in the last year.

Jessie had built a new home in the early summer, not far from Annie's. She had given Jessie half of the acres that her own house sat on and Jessie and Chris had hiked all over, looking for the perfect spot in which to live. They found it on the down slope of the mountains, butted up against Sierra Peak. A green, lush valley spread out in front of the cabin, and they watched herds of elk and deer in the evenings. Annie joined them often for dinner, traveling down the bumpy dirt road in the old Jeep that Chris had found for her.

She took a swallow of water from her canteen and moved on, leaving the shade of the cedar and continuing up the trail. She had not told the girls that she was coming up here and she had not signed in at the trailhead. Should Chris happen along and find her name there, she would be up the trail in an instant to check on her. She glanced at her watch and frowned. It was taking her longer than she had planned and she was supposed to be at Jessie's at five to help with dinner. They were having a cookout and Roger and Ellen were joining them, along with Matt and that nice girl from the café. Oh, and Bobby. He was quickly becoming her favorite, with his boyish good looks. They were all good friends and none of them seemed the least bit shocked when Jessie and Chris moved in together. Well, times had certainly changed.

Annie was lost in her thoughts when she stopped suddenly. She had thought that she might not remember, but here it was, the ledge with the gap in it. She jumped it easily and took a deep breath, seeing the sheer cliff underneath her, the deep drop into the canyon below. She felt her life had come full circle. That was why she had come up here. Or so she told herself. Maybe she had come up here for the same reason Jessie had last August. To talk to Jack. To shake his ghost.

Why she had ever come up here with him at all, she'd never know. Perhaps she thought him to be sincere, even though all her instincts told her he wasn't. After Jessie had gone off to school, he had come to her. He said they needed to talk, that she should accompany him on the trails. She had been dumbfounded. Never before had she been allowed on the trails with him. But she had agreed. They needed to talk about their marriage and about Jessie. They didn't speak on the hike up and she had to race to keep up with his long, purposeful strides. At this very ridge, he had jumped the gap and stood near the edge, looking over.

"Come take a look," he had said.

And she had, jumping the gap as easily as he had. She was wary of him though. Something wasn't right, she knew. The way he looked at her with those piercing black eyes. The way his lips were pressed together in grim determination.

He had turned to her, a sneer on his lips. "You thought I wouldn't find out about your old man in San Francisco, didn't you? How could you? How could you betray me and Jessie that way?"

She remembered standing tall, unafraid. For too long, she had cowered to him. "The same way you've betrayed me for twenty years," she told him.

"Men are different," he spat at her. "I'm different. You're nothing but a slut. You're not fit to live in the same house with us."

She instinctively took a step back. His eyes were so very black. He looked crazed and she was suddenly so very afraid.

"You're not really fit to live at all, Annie. You know that, don't you?"

He had turned to her and she knew immediately what he planned. She backed up a step, her hands outstretched. She remembered his wicked smile when his long arm had reached out to her and his hand had captured her small wrist.

"Jack, no," she had pleaded with him. "You don't know what you're doing."

"I know perfectly well what I'm doing. I'm getting you out of our lives for good. You don't deserve us. You've never been a wife to me, never a mother to my Jessie. I should have done this years ago."

He pulled her to him with such great force, her feet left the safety of the ledge, and she was suspended in air, thinking briefly that it would all be over quickly and it wouldn't hurt too much. One push by him and she would be over the side and into the canyon.

Thinking back now, she knew it was his smile and laughter that had done it. He had already thought he'd won again and she was tired of losing to him. She curled her hands into claws and angrily struck his face, her nails cutting into his skin, drawing blood. He dropped her forcefully and she landed on her back, just feet from the edge of the cliff. He frantically wiped at the blood on his face and she quickly stood, and without thinking, kicked him in the groin, her hiking boot hitting him squarely between the legs. So hard, he fell to his knees, air whistling from between his teeth. He had looked at her then, eyes so angry she knew he meant to kill her with his bare hands. How he was able to stand, she never knew. But he did, very slowly.

"Bitch!" he screamed at her. "How dare you? You'll be sorry now, Annie."

She looked out over the canyon, seeing it all so clearly now. Seventeen years ago, it had all been a blur. How had she jumped out of the way? She never knew. But now she saw it all as if it were happening again.

His face was red with rage and their eyes met, locked together in fight. He had lunged at her, so quickly she didn't have time to think. She simply dropped to her stomach, intending to protect herself, but he sailed over her, stumbling at the edge of the cliff, one foot hanging over, suspended. He had screamed once, a high, girlish scream, and seemed to catch his balance. Annie had turned to look at him and he had reached out to her as he teetered on the edge.

"No! Please . . ."

She reached for him without thinking, but it was too late. Their eyes met for an instant. Shock and disbelief flashed across his face as he tumbled backwards over the cliff and into the canyon below.

How long she sat there, she didn't know. Still didn't. She had walked home. No one saw her. She was in shock, she knew that much. She had bathed and washed her clothes and simply waited for Roger to come tell her the bad news. And he had.

Sitting on the edge now, she breathed a sigh of relief. Over the years, she had often wondered if maybe it would have been better for her to have gone over the edge instead of Jack. Her life had been so empty for so long.

Then Roger had moved back and had drawn her out a little. Then, of course Chris. She was the one who made Annie feel alive again, made her look forward to life again. Finally, her sweet Jessie had come home. All those lonely years were worth it. Now, she had everything.

She stood up and looked out over the canyon and smiled.

"Goodbye, Jack," she said softly, her words carried away by the wind. She turned and headed back down the trail, a smile firmly on her face. She needed to hurry. The girls would be waiting.

ABOUT THE AUTHOR

Gerri lives in East Texas, deep in the pines, with her partner of thirteen years. They share their log cabin and adjoining five acres with two labs, Max and Zach and three cats. A huge vegetable garden that overflows in the summer is her pride and joy. Besides giving in to her overactive green thumb, Gerri loves to "hike the woods" with the dogs, a pair of binoculars (bird watching) and a couple of cameras.

Publications from
BELLA BOOKS, INC.
The best in contemporary lesbian fiction

P.O. Box 10543, Tallahassee, FL 32302
Phone: 800-729-4992
www.bellabooks.com

HIGHER GROUND by Saxon Bennett. 280 pp. A delightfully complex reflection of the successful, high society lives of a small group of women.   ISBN 1-931513-69-4 $12.95

LAST CALL A Detective Franco Mystery by Baxter Clare. 240 pp. Frank overlooks all else to try to solve a cold case of two murdered children...   ISBN 1-931513-70-8 $12.95

ONCE UPON A DYKE: NEW EXPLOITS OF FAIRY-TALE LESBIANS by Karin Kallmaker, Julia Watts, Barbara Johnson & Therese Szymanski. 320 pp. You've never read fairy tales like these before! From Bella After Dark.   ISBN 1-931513-71-6 $14.95

FINEST KIND OF LOVE by Diana Tremain Braund. 224 pp. Can Molly and Carolyn stop clashing long enough to see beyond their differences?   ISBN 1-931513-68-6 $12.95

DREAM LOVER by Lyn Denison. 188 pp. A soft, sensuous, romantic fantasy.
ISBN 1-931513-96-1 $12.95

NEVER SAY NEVER by Linda Hill. 224 pp. A classic love story... where rules aren't the only things broken.   ISBN 1-931513-67-8 $12.95

PAINTED MOON by Karin Kallmaker. 214 pp. Stranded together in a snowbound cabin, Jackie and Leah lives will never be the same.   ISBN 1-931513-53-8 $12.95

WIZARD OF ISIS by Jean Stewart. 240 pp. Fifth in the exciting Isis series.
ISBN 1-931513-71-4 $12.95

WOMAN IN THE MIRROR by Jackie Calhoun. 216 pp. Josey learns to love again, while her niece is learning to love women for the first time.   ISBN 1-931513-78-3 $12.95

SUBSTITUTE FOR LOVE by Karin Kallmaker. 200 pp. When Holly and Reyna meet the combination adds up to pure passion. But what about tomorrow?   ISBN 1-931513-62-7 $12.95

GULF BREEZE by Gerri Hill. 288 pp. Could Carly really be the woman Pat has always been searching for?   ISBN 1-931513-97-X $12.95

THE TOMSTOWN INCIDENT by Penny Hayes. 184 pp. Caught between two worlds, Eloise must make a decision that will change her life forever.   ISBN 1-931513-56-2 $12.95

MAKING UP FOR LOST TIME by Karin Kallmaker. 240 pp. Discover delicious recipes for romance by the undisputed mistress.   ISBN 1-931513-61-9 $12.95

THE WAY LIFE SHOULD BE by Diana Tremain Braund. 173 pp. With which woman will Jennifer find the true meaning of love?   ISBN 1-931513-66-X $12.95

BACK TO BASICS: A BUTCH/FEMME ANTHOLOGY edited by Therese Szymanski— from Bella After Dark. 324 pp.   ISBN 1-931513-35-X $14.95

SURVIVAL OF LOVE by Frankie J. Jones. 236 pp. What will Jody do when she falls in love with her best friend's daughter?   ISBN 1-931513-55-4 $12.95

LESSONS IN MURDER by Claire McNab. 184 pp. 1st Detective Inspector Carol Ashton Mystery   ISBN 1-931513-65-1 $12.95

DEATH BY DEATH by Claire McNab. 167 pp. 5th Denise Cleever Thriller.
ISBN 1-931513-34-1 $12.95

CAUGHT IN THE NET by Jessica Thomas. 188 pp. A wickedly observant story of mystery, danger, and love in Provincetown.   ISBN 1-931513-54-6 $12.95

DREAMS FOUND by Lyn Denison. Australian Riley embarks on a journey to meet her birth mother . . . and gains not just a family, but the love of her life.   ISBN 1-931513-58-9 $12.95

A MOMENT'S INDISCRETION by Peggy J. Herring. 154 pp. Jackie is torn between her better judgment and the overwhelming attraction she feels for Valerie.
                                                    ISBN 1-931513-59-7 $12.95

IN EVERY PORT by Karin Kallmaker. 224 pp. Jessica has a woman in every port. Will meeting Cat will change all that?   ISBN 1-931513-36-8 $12.95

TOUCHWOOD by Karin Kallmaker. 240 pp. Rayann loves Louisa. Louisa loves Rayann. Can the decades between their ages keep them apart?   ISBN 1-931513-37-6 $12.95

WATERMARK by Karin Kallmaker. 248 pp. Teresa wants a future with a woman whose heart has been frozen by loss. Sequel to *Touchwood*.   ISBN 1-931513-38-4 $12.95

EMBRACE IN MOTION by Karin Kallmaker. 240 pp. Has Sarah found lust or love?
                                                    ISBN 1-931513-39-2 $12.95

ONE DEGREE OF SEPARATION by Karin Kallmaker. 232 pp. Sizzling small town romance between Marian, the town librarian, and the new girl from the big city.
                                                    ISBN 1-931513-30-9 $12.95

CRY HAVOC A Detective Franco Mystery by Baxter Clare. 240 pp. A dead hustler with a headless rooster in his lap sends Lt. L.A. Franco headfirst against Mother Love.
                                                    ISBN 1-931513931-7 $12.95

DISTANT THUNDER by Peggy J. Herring. 294 pp. Bankrobbing drifter Cordy awakens strange new feelings in Leo in this romantic tale set in the Old West.
                                                    ISBN 1-931513-28-7 $12.95

COP OUT by Claire McNab. 216 pp. 4th Detective Inspector Carol Ashton Mystery.
                                                    ISBN 1-931513-29-5 $12.95

BLOOD LINK by Claire McNab. 159 pp. 15th Detective Inspector Carol Ashton Mystery. Is Carol unwittingly playing into a deadly plan?   ISBN 1-931513-27-9 $12.95

TALK OF THE TOWN by Saxon Bennett. 239 pp. With enough beer, barbecue and B.S., anything is possible!   ISBN 1-931513-18-X $12.95

MAYBE NEXT TIME by Karin Kallmaker. 256 pp. Sabrina has everything she ever wanted—except Jorie.   ISBN 1-931513-26-0 $12.95

WHEN GOOD GIRLS GO BAD: A Motor City Thriller by Therese Szymanski. 230 pp. Brett, Randi, and Allie join forces to stop a serial killer.   ISBN 1-931513-11-2 $12.95

A DAY TOO LONG: A Helen Black Mystery by Pat Welch. 328 pp. This time Helen's fate is in her own hands.   ISBN 1-931513-22-8 $12.95

THE RED LINE OF YARMALD by Diana Rivers. 256 pp. The Hadra's only hope lies in a magical red line . . . climactic sequel to *Clouds of War*.   ISBN 1-931513-23-6 $12.95

OUTSIDE THE FLOCK by Jackie Calhoun. 224 pp. Jo embraces her new love and life.
                                                    ISBN 1-931513-13-9 $12.95

LEGACY OF LOVE by Marianne K. Martin. 224 pp. Read the whole Sage Bristo story.
                                                    ISBN 1-931513-15-5 $12.95

STREET RULES: A Detective Franco Mystery by Baxter Clare. 304 pp. Gritty, fast-paced mystery with compelling Detective L.A. Franco   ISBN 1-931513-14-7 $12.95

RECOGNITION FACTOR: 4th Denise Cleever Thriller by Claire McNab. 176 pp. Denise Cleever tracks a notorious terrorist to America.   ISBN 1-931513-24-4 $12.95

NORA AND LIZ by Nancy Garden. 296 pp. Lesbian romance by the author of *Annie on My Mind*.   ISBN 1931513-20-1 $12.95

MIDAS TOUCH by Frankie J. Jones. 208 pp. Sandra had everything but love.   ISBN 1-931513-21-X $12.95

BEYOND ALL REASON by Peggy J. Herring. 240 pp. A romance hotter than Texas.   ISBN 1-9513-25-2 $12.95

ACCIDENTAL MURDER: 14th Detective Inspector Carol Ashton Mystery by Claire McNab. 208 pp. Carol Ashton tracks an elusive killer.   ISBN 1-931513-16-3 $12.95

SEEDS OF FIRE: Tunnel of Light Trilogy, Book 2 by Karin Kallmaker writing as Laura Adams. 274 pp. In Autumn's dreams no one is who they seem.   ISBN 1-931513-19-8 $12.95

DRIFTING AT THE BOTTOM OF THE WORLD by Auden Bailey. 288 pp. Beautifully written first novel set in Antarctica.   ISBN 1-931513-17-1 $12.95

CLOUDS OF WAR by Diana Rivers. 288 pp. Women unite to defend Zelindar!   ISBN 1-931513-12-0 $12.95

DEATHS OF JOCASTA: 2nd Micky Knight Mystery by J.M. Redmann. 408 pp. Sexy and intriguing Lambda Literary Award-nominated mystery.   ISBN 1-931513-10-4 $12.95

LOVE IN THE BALANCE by Marianne K. Martin. 256 pp. The classic lesbian love story, back in print!   ISBN 1-931513-08-2 $12.95

THE COMFORT OF STRANGERS by Peggy J. Herring. 272 pp. Lela's work was her passion . . . until now.   ISBN 1-931513-09-0 $12.95

CHICKEN by Paula Martinac. 208 pp. Lynn finds that the only thing harder than being in a lesbian relationship is ending one.   ISBN 1-931513-07-4 $11.95

TAMARACK CREEK by Jackie Calhoun. 208 pp. An intriguing story of love and danger.   ISBN 1-931513-06-6 $11.95

DEATH BY THE RIVERSIDE: 1st Micky Knight Mystery by J.M. Redmann. 320 pp. Finally back in print, the book that launched the Lambda Literary Award–winning Micky Knight mystery series.   ISBN 1-931513-05-8 $11.95

EIGHTH DAY: A Cassidy James Mystery by Kate Calloway. 272 pp. In the eighth installment of the Cassidy James mystery series, Cassidy goes undercover at a camp for troubled teens.   ISBN 1-931513-04-X $11.95

MIRRORS by Marianne K. Martin. 208 pp. Jean Carson and Shayna Bradley fight for a future together.   ISBN 1-931513-02-3 $11.95

THE ULTIMATE EXIT STRATEGY: A Virginia Kelly Mystery by Nikki Baker. 240 pp. The long-awaited return of the wickedly observant Virginia Kelly.   ISBN 1-931513-03-1 $11.95

FOREVER AND THE NIGHT by Laura DeHart Young. 224 pp. Desire and passion ignite the frozen Arctic in this exciting sequel to the classic romantic adventure *Love on the Line.*
ISBN 0-931513-00-7 $11.95

WINGED ISIS by Jean Stewart. 240 pp. The long-awaited sequel to *Warriors of Isis* and the fourth in the exciting Isis series.
ISBN 1-931513-01-5 $11.95

ROOM FOR LOVE by Frankie J. Jones. 192 pp. Jo and Beth must overcome the past in order to have a future together.
ISBN 0-9677753-9-6 $11.95

THE QUESTION OF SABOTAGE by Bonnie J. Morris. 144 pp. A charming, sexy tale of romance, intrigue, and coming of age.
ISBN 0-9677753-8-8 $11.95

SLEIGHT OF HAND by Karin Kallmaker writing as Laura Adams. 256 pp. A journey of passion, heartbreak, and triumph that reunites two women for a final chance at their destiny.
ISBN 0-9677753-7-X $11.95

MOVING TARGETS: A Helen Black Mystery by Pat Welch. 240 pp. Helen must decide if getting to the bottom of a mystery is worth hitting bottom.
ISBN 0-9677753-6-1 $11.95

CALM BEFORE THE STORM by Peggy J. Herring. 208 pp. Colonel Robicheaux retires from the military and comes out of the closet.
ISBN 0-9677753-1-0 $11.95

OFF SEASON by Jackie Calhoun. 208 pp. Pam threatens Jenny and Rita's fledgling relationship.
ISBN 0-9677753-0-2 $11.95

WHEN EVIL CHANGES FACE: A Motor City Thriller by Therese Szymanski. 240 pp. Brett Higgins is back in another heart-pounding thriller.
ISBN 0-9677753-3-7 $11.95

BOLD COAST LOVE by Diana Tremain Braund. 208 pp. Jackie Claymont fights for her reputation and the right to love the woman she chooses.
ISBN 0-9677753-2-9 $11.95

THE WILD ONE by Lyn Denison. 176 pp. Rachel never expected that Quinn's wild yearnings would change her life forever.
ISBN 0-9677753-4-5 $11.95

SWEET FIRE by Saxon Bennett. 224 pp. Welcome to Heroy—the town with more lesbians per capita than any other place on the planet!
ISBN 0-9677753-5-3 $11.95

Visit

Bella Books

at

BellaBooks.com

or call our toll-free number

1-800-729-4992